Sex & Violets

by

M. Spencer

Copyright Mark Spencer 2016

Mark Spencer has asserted his right under the Copyright, Designs and Patents Act, 1988

to be identified as the author of this work.

This book is sold subject to the condition that it shall not by way of trade or otherwise, be lent,

resold, hired out, or otherwise circulated without the publisher's prior consent in any

form of binding or cover other than that in which it is published and without a similar condition

including this condition being imposed on the subsequent purchaser.

ISBN: 978 1530626335

Cover design and copyright Mark Blamire

Second Edition

Facebook: Mark Spencer-Writer

Twitter: Mark Spencer_Writer

Dedication

For my Dad, who was everything a father should be. I only wish I'd let you read this when I'd had the chance.

Contents

1:	Reunion	1
2:	Inception	7
3:	Childhood	21
4:	Death	38
5:	Love	58
6:	Sex	75
7:	Union	94
8:	Violence	116
9:	Anniversary	134
10:	Falling	144
11:	Dreaming	160
12:	Dissection	167
13:	Celebration	176
14:	Shame	198
15:	Fear	213
16:	Loss	226
17:	Confrontation	252
18:	Revelation	257
19:	Conclusion	262

"These violent delights have violent ends"

- Romeo and Juliet (Act II, Sc. 6)

Chapter 1: Reunion

Thursday. A day like every other, unremarkable in nearly every way. The watery sun hung low in the pale autumn sky. Damp, russet leaves swirled sadly in the lonely corners of the empty park. The casual wind moaned, sensual in its prying it whispered softly through the trees. Ink wash clouds drifted uneasily, uncertainty in every wisp. Light traffic swished through the freshly rain-washed suburbs, oblivious to the fact that Adam Clare's wife had returned.

It had been a surprise, of course. No message. Yet there she was, on his doorstep, as gorgeous as ever. Adam Clare did not know what to do; did not know what to say. Words caught in his throat like fish-hooks. He muttered an incomprehensible greeting and stood aside for her. As she, finally, swept past him he noticed a slight uncertainty in her step. This was her home, her husband yet, somehow, she no longer belonged.

"Hello Adam."

Those four tiny phonemes, spoken as only Elle knew how, with such softness and sincerity, took his coldness away from him, stripping him of his defences; leaving him naked in the snow. His intentions of bitterness crumbled and left behind only the pain and his desperation. The despair he had felt when she had first walked out moved sluggishly in his guts. It had been an eternity since that day; it felt like it was only yesterday. He had known that there was something wrong that morning; with hindsight he would have said so. His stomach had felt peculiar all day. The look that she had given him over breakfast had told him everything, though he wasn't listening. A hint of anger, a flash of sorrow. A touch of fear. Her eyes always gave her away.

The house had seemed so very still that evening. It had even smelled a little musty, as if no-one had breathed there for lifetimes. Dust-mites hung languidly in the air, drifting in their spotlighted sun dance. It had never seemed this cold before, not even when he had found his Granddad. He swept through the house, searching room after room, his panic rising as his hope diminished. The bland white envelope on the kitchen table stopped him in his tracks. It glared at him impassively. A starkly frightened *Adam* was scrawled across its face. He thought that the pain would never end, the tears would not stop. The tightness in his chest enveloped the gaping void. He retched with the effort of breathing. Deep sobs tore through him. His eyes burned dry.

It had been dark when he had felt able to finally move away from the kitchen table. His stomach ached with a dull emptiness that was not just hunger. He poured himself a glass of water and, leaving the house open to the darkness, he had gone to bed. Alone.

"Hello, Elle."

He followed her into the lounge, his bewilderment evident on his face. She scanned the room, deftly picking out all of the changes he had made since she had left. So few: the wedding photo remained, her curtains still hung. She smiled slightly to herself, a smile that had no trace of smugness or congratulation, only pity. She sat in one of the armchairs; casually, but intentionally, avoiding the spot on the sofa where she had used to sit. Adam's face dropped slightly. He sat at the end of the sofa closest to her.

"Tea?" he asked.

"No."

The tension was unbearable. Adam looked nervously at Elle, desperately trying to make eye contact, trying to think of something that might make her laugh. He loved her laugh: the way her teeth glistened and the way she moistened her lips; the way she tilted her head back, exposing her throat; the way she shook her hair from her face; the way her eyes sparkled like life itself. It had been so long since he had heard her laugh, heard the gentle chuckle as her laugh faded away – just like she had. He longed to hear her laugh again, he ached to be able to make her.

"No. Thank you," she said.

"Something else?"

She shook her head.

"Well, I'm going to have something," he said. Quickly, and with some relief, he took a bottle down from the bookcase.

"Whiskey?" asked Elle.

"Yes?" Indignation rose quickly in him.

"Nothing. You never used to, is all."

Adam knocked back his drink and refilled the glass. His eyes settled on Elle. He frowned. He marched across the lounge, placed his glass confidently on the coffee table and approached the fireplace. He picked up the poker from the hearth and attacked the glowing embers.

"Bloody thing," he muttered.

Adam had loved coal fires ever since he had begun to spend time at his granddad's house when he was a child. He had loved his granddad more than he had loved anybody else; he had loved the funny faces he used to pull; loved the way he smiled his granddad smile, laughed his granddad laugh. He had loved the way he always used to slip 'Little Ads' a nice shiny new 'ten bob bit' when his Daddy wasn't looking – Granddad always looked really naughty when he did that, and he'd always hold his finger to his lip to stop Adam saying anything. A kiss from his favourite grandson was all the thanks he ever needed; a smile and a wink. Adam's favourite thing though was sitting in front of the open fire, trying to see pictures in the small violet flames. He never did see anything but he never gave up trying. He would sit there for hours staring into the flames, listening to his granddad's voice, until there was nothing but a red glow in the hearth and a tired glow in his head. He used to breathe in the smell of cigars on his granddad's clothes as he was carried up to bed. So deeply that even now he felt his heart give a little leap every time he smelled that smell. It was always somebody else's granddad. He paused.

Still holding the poker, he turned. He looked at Elle. "Why are you here?"

She looked away. She fumbled nervously with her fingers. He looked closer. She had instinctively gone to fiddle with her wedding ring. It was no longer there; the eternal circle, the gilded cage. "Til Death us do part." The indentation still lingered in her flesh like a ghost of a marriage, almost as if it was still there in spirit. Her lip, which had lost none of its youthful fullness, trembled.

"Why are you here?" he repeated.

She looked him in the eye. "Can't you guess?"

"Tell me." He put the poker down. He sat and reached for his drink. Calmly, he said it again. "Tell me."

Elle pursed her lips, drew a deep breath, and said "I want a divorce."

"Mummy, what's a divorce?"

"What?"

"A divorce, Mummy, what is it?"

"Where did you hear that?"

"I don't know what it is, Mummy."

"Adam, where did you hear that word?"

"You asked Daddy if you could have one and I thought I might like one too 'cause they might be something nice and I asked Michael and he said it's what you get when you don't love somebody no more and then you can go away and I love you Mummy and I don't want you to go away. Don't you love us no more?"

"Oh Adam, honey, of course I still love you. And Michael too. I'm not going to go away, baby. I'm always going to be here for you, and your big brother. Now come here and give me a great big hug and a big wet kiss."

"Mummy, why are you crying?"

"Because I love you, sweetheart."

"No," said Adam quietly.

"What?" Elle frowned.

"I said 'No'!"

"Well, excuse me, but I don't think you have a fat lot of choice in the matter *Adam*. 'Irreconcilable differences.' I thought it would be better coming straight from me rather than randomly dropping through your letterbox." Elle could feel the colour rising in her face as she stood.

"Sit down," he said. As he looked up at her Elle felt all of her anger fade away. He looked so lost and sad.

She sat. "I'm sorry," she said. "I could have been gentler than that."

Adam looked into his glass. He swirled the golden liquid around. The water of life. He downed it and reached for the bottle once again. He looked at the label ruefully, smiled at a private thought, and returned it to the table.

"I love you Elle. Please don't do this to me again."

"Oh Adam," she groaned, "you're not in love with me, you're in love with being in love. It's nonsense. How can you say you love me after the way you treated me?"

"I never treated you badly. I always gave you everything you wanted," he said.

"Bullshit!"

"Everything!"

"Everything except a life I could call my own."

"I love you Elle," he said.

"It's too late Adam, it's all too late."

Chapter 2: Inception

"You're too late."

"Eh?"

"You're too late. The meeting finished about fifteen minutes ago."

"Bugger!"

Adam Clare hung his head in disappointment. The girl looked him up and down appraisingly. He hardly noticed her at all.

"You didn't miss much," she said helpfully.

He raised his eyebrows. "Did they give the times for transport?"

"Yea, 9.30 from here. It was pretty dull, to be fair."

Adam shrugged and turned away.

"I'm Elle," she said as she took a step towards him.

Adam half turned back to her.

"It's short for Eleanor but only my folks call me that. I hate it. It's so…middle-class, don't you think?"

Adam shrugged.

"Do you fancy a coffee?" she asked.

"Not really."

"Oh."

"I wouldn't mind a pint though!" He smiled.

The student Union bar was practically empty. The few people there sat hunched over their drinks trying to make them last as long as possible. The juke-box squatted in the corner, conspicuous in its silence. Adam and Elle sat at an empty table. As awkward as he felt, Adam was beginning to enjoy himself.

The girl was quite pretty really: sparkling eyes, infectious laugh, full moist lips, long legs. She was similar to Kath in many ways. It felt like it had been a long time since he had had to do this; get to know someone from scratch. He felt unsure of himself. He wasn't even sure that he *wanted* to get to know her better. He was just going with it, letting life wash him along.

"…dreams!"

The word interrupted his thoughts like a parent interrupting a kiss.

"I'm doing dreams," Elle repeated. "In art. It's my theme. What's your Major?"

"Dreams? Your Major is dreams?"

"No. That's my chosen theme. In Art."

"Oh right!" said Adam, realisation dawning.

"Are you okay?"

"Yeah, yeah. It reminded me of a dream I had, that's all."

"Really? What was it?"

"I don't really remember. I remember feeling scared. I mean *scared*!"

"Oh!" She sounded disappointed. A chance for artistic inspiration flitted past her like a moth. "So, what is your Major?" she asked again.

"I haven't got one," he said.

"What do you mean?"

Adam smiled. "I did my finals in June. It's my Graduation soon, I only came in to find out about the demo."

"Are you working then?"

Adam snorted with derision. "You've got to be joking! I'm taking a few months off. Get my head together, y'know!"

"God! You are *so* lucky! I'm just starting my second year. It's difficult. Unbelievable!"

"It gets worse!"

"Oh, thanks for that! That's really encouraging!"

They smiled.

Adam was really enjoying himself now. Things seemed to be going along quite nicely now. She was making him smile. She seemed happy. There was a lot of eye contact. They were sitting close. He was not uncomfortable with her. The watery September sun shone in her hair. Small diamonds of spittle lingered on her lips. As she laughed she tilted her head back, exposing the soft thin skin of her throat.

"What?" she said.

"Nothing," said Adam, slightly embarrassed to be caught in his thoughts.

"Have I got something on my face?"

"No, no. It's nothing. I was just looking at you, that's all."

"I see. What were you thinking?"

"Nothing. Really. I always look at people when I'm talking to them, it's only polite!"

Elle frowned at him.

He was enjoying the fact that she seemed to be having trouble figuring him out and the sense of control it gave him. He was trying to stop himself from having fun but revelling in the way that he could let himself go and then, with disturbing suddenness, withdraw from the conversation. There was a long pause.

Elle leaned over slowly and kissed him full on the lips. It was nothing special, just a kiss. She tasted of coffee and her lips were trembling. Adam felt guilty, like he had betrayed someone. He stood.

"I've got to go."

"What is it? What's wrong?"

"Nothing. I've got to meet someone."

"Will I see you again?"

He hesitated. "Probably. I'll be in touch." He walked away.

"Let me give you my number," she called after him. Too late.

Adam hurried off the University campus and headed straight home. A thousand thoughts tumbled through his head. He felt happy and angry; ecstatic and mournful. He was confused. How could he like a girl so much when he had only just met her? How could he still be in love with Kath?

"What a mess," he muttered.

He did his jacket up against a day that was exactly how he felt: warm to look at. Appearances can be deceptive. He hunched his shoulders against the wind. A flurry of leaves were blown from the bough of an oak, a golden flock of Autumn. Adam snatched one from the air. He turned the broad, crinkled leaf over in his hand. It was dead. He smiled at its complex beauty and threw it away.

"I wonder if Tom's in?" he thought.

Elle sat in the Uni bar for a while. She stared into the cold, thick-skinned coffee that she was nursing. She thought of Adam, the attractive man that she had just spent two hours talking at. He was so distant. Yet when he did speak he was so direct and incisive that it was difficult to not like him. She stirred a pencil in her coffee to collect the skin, flicked it into the saucer, and drank the foul liquid in one quick gulp. She shuddered.

"Oi!"

Elle looked up.

"Jesus, Elle!" said Trudi as she slumped down. "Where the hell have you been?" Trudi tucked her hair around her glasses and glared at Elle. "You were supposed to meet me after the march thing. In the main hall. Me. Trudi. Remember?"

"Oh my God, I'm so sorry! I completely forgot!"

"Really? No!" Trudi quaffed her pint. "Well? Go on then," she urged.

Elle's enthusiasm shone through as she told Trudi all about it. When she had finished, Trudi sat back with a sigh.

"I might have known that there was a guy involved. There always is."

They laughed. Elle and Trudi had been best friends since they were three years old. They knew each other as well as they knew themselves. They shared everything. At nine years old they had even shared a boyfriend – John, a small mousey boy who did not want to know either of them – and they were proud of it. They had even been going to marry the poor boy and had often practised the wedding. At fifteen, Elle and John had shared their virginity, something that they had both instantly regretted. They had loved each other but only as friends and, with that one special thing between them, had gradually never spoken again.

Trudi and Elle's closeness stemmed, subconsciously on Trudi's part, from a desire for the twin that she had lost at birth and, consciously on Elle's part, from a desire for a sister although a brother would have done.

"So? When are you going to see him again?"

Elle sighed. "He didn't say"

"I don't know what to say," Adam said. Tears streamed down his face.

"There's nothing to say. I still love you, Adam, but I'm not happy any more. I need it to end while it's still good."

"Please don't leave me, Kath."

"I have to. Don't make me hate you, Adam. Don't make it difficult."

Adam had been sitting alone at the head of the stairs; Mikey was downstairs. He didn't understand why everybody was still here;

Granddad had gone home ages ago – he had looked very cross when he'd left but he had still kissed Adam on the forehead and given him a big hug. "Why are all these people still here, Auntie?"

"They're all here to pay their respects, sweetheart. Everybody loved your mummy very much."

"Why are they all happy now? They were crying earlier but everyone seems to have forgotten they were sad."

"They've not forgotten, Adam, they're remembering all of the good times they spent with your mummy; all of the times she made them laugh. Do you understand?"

"I think so," said Adam.

"They're still very sad but they're saving their sadness for later when they're at home." His auntie reached over and began to brush his hair. "I do wish your grandfather would stop ruffling your hair so, it makes you look very untidy."

"My granddad loves me very much."

"Yes he does. More than is fair on poor Michael, I think."

Adam looked at her, puzzled.

"Never-you-mind me and my silliness," she said. "What's all this stuck around your mouth?" She licked her thumb and rubbed hard at the corner of his mouth.

"Does Granddad love me more than Daddy loves me?"

"Oh, darling, I couldn't say. What a silly little question."

"I sometimes think that Daddy doesn't love me at all."

"Now that is being silly," she said. "Of course he loves you, darling. He just doesn't know how to show you, is all. He can talk to Michael because he's a little bit older than you; he doesn't know how to talk to little boys like you." She shifted heavily on the stair. "This isn't very good for my hip," she said.

Adam frowned.

"I'm very old," she said. "All of my bones are wearing out. It'll happen to you, one day, make no mistake; if you're lucky. Although I'm not sure *lucky* is the right word. Nobody wants to get old."

"I want to get old," said Adam. "Then Daddy will talk to me too."

"Let's hope so, Adam," she said. She struggled to her feet, hauling herself upright with the banister. "Now, why don't you help your dear old auntie down these terribly dangerous stairs and to the sherry bottle?"

Adam grabbed her hand and led her safely downstairs.

Adam stared defiantly at the brickwork. His jaw clenched; his teeth ground together. His hands were balled into fists at his side; he had never felt so angry. His heart hammered in his chest; he shook with pure, clear, rage. The Head-Master's door snapped open. A boy stepped out, turned, and faced the wall on the other side of the door-frame to Adam.

"Mr. Clare, if you'd care to step inside," said Mr. Farthing.

Adam stepped in to the Head-Master's office. It was a large room, almost as large as some of the classrooms. A heavy, dark wood desk, expansive, expensive, dominated the room. Wood grain glistened wetly, seeping age, thick with history. Mr. Farthing sat behind the desk; he was not diminished by it. Adam stood before him as his headmaster flicked through a file.

"Tell me what happened," said Mr. Farthing, without lifting his eyes.

"Nothing, sir, it was just a misunderstanding," said Adam.

Mr. Farthing glanced up. "Don't lie to me, boy, I already know what happened; Pierce told me. Tell me your version of events."

Adam swallowed dryly; he could feel the tips of his ears burning; his chest felt full of air bubbles. "Honestly, sir, it was nothing."

Mr. Farthing placed the file on his desk and stared at Adam. His gaze was cold, unblinking. Adam felt like his layers were being stripped away, one-by-one; that Mr. Farthing could see every bad thing he had ever done; like his eyes were boring into Adam's very soul. Adam tried to hold the stare but had to quickly look away.

"I wouldn't call a riot in the corridor 'nothing', Mr. Clare. I wouldn't call running down the corridors 'nothing'; I wouldn't call leaving school premises and missing lessons 'nothing.' Now tell me what happened." Mr. Farthing slapped the surface of his desk with the flat of his hand.

"Some of the other boys held me down, sir. They kept hitting me with rulers. I fell over. I grabbed my bag and ran away, sir. That's all, sir."

Mr. Farthing steepled his fingers as he relaxed back in to his chair. "Who were these *other boys*?"

"I don't know, sir, they grabbed me from behind."

"And Pierce? What was his part in all of this?"

"I really don't know, sir. I couldn't even say if he was there or not. Everything's jumbled-up and confused." Adam hung his head. "I'm sorry, sir. I'm sure they just meant it as a joke."

"Fun? You stupid boy."

"Excuse me, sir?"

"Do you think that by covering for these obnoxious little bullies that they're going to stop? That, somehow, your pathetic playground sense of honour will endear you to them; that they'll suddenly leave you alone?" He marched to the door and snatched it open. "Get out, now."

Adam walked out of the office and took up his position facing the wall.

"You will both stand here, in absolute silence, and think on what's been happening here. You will consider your roles in the events of yesterday and when I think you're ready to talk about this, honestly and maturely, we'll try again, understood?"

The boys nodded and Mr. Farthing shut his office door.

"Cheers, come-pants," sniggered Pierce.

Adam clenched his teeth and remained silent.

"What?" shouted Tom.

"It's Adam! Let me in!"

Tom wrapped a towel around himself and ran down the stairs.

Tom was just six months older than Adam and nearly twice his size. While Adam was average in every way – height, weight, build – Tom was the tall, muscular type. Ruggedly handsome, he had had a long string of short-term relationships during his University years. Now, though, he was looking for the girl he was going to spend the rest of his life with. Maybe.

"What do you want? I was in the sodding bath!"

"Don't be such a tosser," Adam laughed as Tom stood dripping at the front door.

"Stick the kettle on, you tit," Tom said. He ran back to the bathroom.

"Where are your mum and dad?" Adam shouted up to him.

"Buggered if I know!"

They had been best of friends for nearly two years now. When they had first met they hated each other with a vengeance. Through mutual friends they had loathed one another and, through those same friends, eventually grew to tolerate and, finally, to like each other. They often discussed their days of hatred, mourning the wasted drinking time.

"What do you want then?" asked Tom, joining Adam in the kitchen.

"Not really sure," said Adam.

Tom guessed immediately what was on his mind. "Did you find out about the march?"

"Yeah! Exactly when I thought it was. Transport is arranged. I missed the meeting, naturally, but there was this girl there when I arrived. She told me everything."

"Anyone I know?"

"No. She said her name was Elle."

"L?"

"Short for Eleanor. She hates it!"

Tom smiled to himself. It was about time Adam left the remains of his relationship with Kath behind.

"What's she like?"

Adam frowned. He rubbed his temple.

"I don't know really. Nice. I think. We got on really well. I could have talked to her for hours."

"Why didn't you?"

Adam sighed. "It didn't seem right. I was talking to her and, out of nowhere, Kath would pop into my head, y'know? It felt like I was being unfaithful or something. It was weird."

Tom shook his head. "Look. She's gone. Forget her. She's not coming back. You have to move on or it will drive you insane. There's nothing wrong in remembering the good times, or remembering her with fondness, with love even, but you have to let her go. For your own good, if no one else's."

"It's so difficult."

"Did you get this Elle's number?"

Adam looked pathetic and shook his head.

"You pillock! You're just going to have to hang around the bar until she turns up again aren't you?"

Adam nodded.

Darkness falling; night rising. Shifting shadows; chittering insect sound. It moves. It shuffles wetly. It slides and scurries and slides in the dark, dank corners. Watching. Waiting. Flash of light. Pin-prick laser, burning retina. Searing nerves. Electric pulse of panic; bowel loosening horror; bladder empties; fear overwhelms.

Petals waft in gentle breeze. Penetration. Falling. Falling in to the pit. Never-ending plummet. Cricket in the park; soft summer breeze. Melancholy mood-swing. Rumble in the darkness. The beast moves within. It grows. It growls; a snicker in its throat; bone catching sound, snagged breath, breaking, tearing, snatching at the air.

It breathes. It waits.

Adam shook his head. "I can't."

"Why not?" breathed Elle.

"It just doesn't seem right." He felt his cheeks flush.

"Why not?" She kissed him softly. Her lips brushed his like a summer breeze.

He stepped back.

Shadows scuttled across the walls. The moonlit room shifted sensually, a chiaroscuro of silver and black. The night held its breath in anticipation. Moisture gathered in the darkness.

Elle stepped closer to him. He was trapped.

"I want you," she whispered. She pressed herself against him. She ran the tip of her tongue across his throat, the glistening wet trail a sliver of silver. She bit his earlobe hard enough to hurt, just a little. She ran her hands over his body. She pulled up his shirt and dragged her nails gently across his back. "I want you."

He bent his head forward and allowed her to kiss him. He resisted the force of her mouth against his. He savoured the wetness around his mouth as she pulled away. He relished the pressure in his trousers. "You haven't known me for very long," he said. He kissed her shoulder.

"Long enough." She pulled her shirt over her head and threw it to one side. The blue grey light caressed her body. Her skin looked like marble – cold and unapproachable. Smooth. Her breasts, small and perfect, gleamed with tautness. Her nipples were dark and erect. "I want you," she whispered. She pulled his shirt up and pressed her nakedness against his.

"I want you too," he said. They kissed with an angry passion that neither of them had ever experienced before. They tore the rest of their clothes off, urgent in their hunger for each other. There was a moment's pause as Elle, in longing moistness, looked down on his naked, erect member. She lowered herself on to him, pushing gently against his resistance, then gasped as she allowed him to enter her fully. Their breath came in short rasps. Elle lay on him, felt him deep inside her, her legs trembling as he moved in pleasure.

His hands explored her body, up her back and over her shoulders. He cupped her breasts. She squirmed. Her fingers trailed across her stomach and brushed against her pubic mound. He pushed himself deep into her. She gasped. Then she began, slowly at first, to grind upon him. Their breathing increased as their passion rose. She could feel her insides tightening as wave upon wave of muscular tension moved through her. A sweat sheen gleamed across their bodies as he released himself into her. Elle cried aloud as she felt his contracting muscle. She moaned as she leaned forward. She rested her head against his shoulder, her face on the pillow. He held her tight to him, pulled her pelvis hard against his, as the sweat began to dry on their flesh.

"I want you too," he whispered as he fell into another troubled sleep.

Chapter 3: Childhood

"I want you to do as you're told," shouted Mrs. Clare

"Why?"

"Because I do!"

"Why, Mummy?"

Mrs. Clare sighed. "Just be quiet, Adam."

"Why?" Adam's chubby little face beamed with mischief.

"Because if you don't I'll tell Santa and he'll put you in his Book of Naughty Little Boys and then you won't get any presents at Christmas."

Adam's bottom lip protruded and his face fell.

"Right," said Mrs. Clare. "Now, go and tell Michael…" She paused, her lips pursed in thought. "Good boys do what they're told, don't they, Adam?"

Adam nodded vigorously.

"Well, I'm *telling* you that I want you to go and tell Michael that I want him to go to the shop for me. So it's okay for you to speak now."

"Yes, Mummy."

"Off you go then," she said, stroking his cheek.

Adam ran out of the house. Mrs. Clare smiled after him.

"You spoil that lad," said Adam's father walking in from the hall where he had been stood listening to her.

"No. No, I don't," she said quietly.

"You bloody well do. You treat both of 'em like girls – if either of my boys turns out to be a bleeding shirt-lifter I'll know who to blame, won't I?"

"Don't be so daft."

"Who do you think you're calling daft, woman? You stupid cow, what do you know about anything? All you do is whine and molly-coddle *my* sons. Stupid fucking woman."

Mrs. Clare hung her head. She knew where this was going; the same place it always went. And there was nothing she could do to stop it. The outcome was inevitable. Joseph had been like this with her for longer than she cared to remember. It seemed to be the only way he could communicate with her. If she was a better wife he wouldn't have to resort to this.

She said nothing.

"Don't just stand there, woman, say *something*."

"There's nothing I *can* say Joe."

"Nothing to say? Nothing to fucking say? Think you're *better* than me do you? With your airs and graces. Stuck up bitch!" He slapped her across the face

Her head snapped left. Her cheek burned. Tears sprang to her eyes. "I'm sorry," she said.

"It's too fucking late for sorry!" He grabbed her by the throat and pulled her face close to his. His breath stung her face as he snarled, "It's too fucking late." He shoved her across the room. A sharp pain seared through her back as she fell to the floor.

"Bitch!" He slammed the front door behind him as he left.

Adam and Michael ran, shouting and giggling, in from the garden. Mrs. Clare gathered herself together and wiped the tears away. She could still feel the pressure of his fingers at her throat. Her cheek throbbed.

"What's wrong, Mum?" asked Michael.

"Nothing. I slipped and fell is all."

"I fell over too and scrazed my knee," said Adam proudly.

"I know, love, Mummy's already kissed it better."

"I know! And it *is* better, look!"

"Oh yes, Adam, that's lovely," she said. The lump in her throat made it hard to talk. Her face burned with familiarity.

"Adam said you wanted me to go to the shop?"

"I did, but it doesn't matter now. Take Adam and you can both buy some sweets anyway."

She watched her two boys as they ran down the street. Michael watched Adam, ensuring he didn't run too fast or too far. They were such beautiful children. She looked at her hands, her wedding ring glistened through her tears.

The air was heady with excitement. Wheels rumbled heavily on tracks, carriages spun frantically, screams reverberated through the night air. Kaleidoscopic lights strobed and flashed as Clarissa was jostled and shuffled around, disorientating her even more. Electricity sparked in the air as bumper-cars rammed each other and their passengers squealed in delight.

She felt herself being swept away. Rifle fire cracked to her left, the sharp retort of metal on metal as the pellets found their targets. The smell of candy floss and toffee apples and soft wet grass hung thickly, cloyingly, in the air.

She held her arms up in front of herself protectively as she tried to fight her way through the crowd. She kept her eyes fixed firmly on the ground in front of her, determined not to slip or fall. She was terrified and lost. Her friends had insisted that she come tonight, even though she had made it clear that she did not want to. They had teased and cajoled her until she had agreed, reluctantly suppressing her fear of being snatched away by gypsy-folk, never to be seen again. She hated the way they leered at her - the way they talked to her and undressed her with their lascivious eyes.

It had taken her hours to get ready. Her make-up had to be just so and she had lost count of the number of pins she had used in her hair to get it to sit perfectly. Her parents were not at all happy about the way she was dressing herself up.

A hand grabbed her firmly by the shoulder and turned her around. "You're looking lost, little girl. You need to be more careful; the fairground men will see it as a sign of weakness and pounce."

She looked up into the large, smiling eyes of a complete stranger. Handsome: a strong jaw, firm features and a masculine brow. He looked so virile. She averted her eyes, blushing at her own thoughts. "Sorry," she said, "I've lost my friends."

"As long as that's all you've lost tonight." He winked at her mischievously.

Her heart skipped, shocked and breathless at his innuendo. "I've got to find them, they'll be worried about me."

"I'm not surprised; a poor, timid little sparrow like you, out here all on your own. Why, any old wolf could swoop down and take advantage of you. Gobble you all up, if you're not careful. What you need is a big strong fellow like me to protect you."

Clarissa smiled up at him. "Are you not an old wolf then?"

"Not me," he said. "I'm your knight in shining armour, I am!" He slipped his arm casually around her shoulder and guided her gently out of the milling crowd. "I'm going to buy you some candy-floss and I'll look after you until we find your friends."

"Thank you but I don't like candy-floss."

"A toffee apple then."

Her lips twitched into a small, nervous smile and she nodded. She didn't really like toffee-apples either, they made her teeth hurt, but he was being so kind and helpful that she couldn't bring herself to refuse him twice. She watched him as he leaned into the van and insisted on the two largest toffee-apples he could see. He was so forceful, so determined to get his own way, that she couldn't help but admire his strength of will. She took the apple from him. "Thank you," she said.

He reached around the back of her head with his free hand and pulled at the pins in her hair. It cascaded loose, falling around her shoulders and face. "You should wear your hair loose," he said. "It makes you look wild and untamed, like a wolf. I prefer it that way."

Irritation tugged at the corners of her emotions, he had undone all her work in a matter of seconds. He was right though – she felt liberated. She removed the remaining pins she could find and shook her hair free.

He took a bite from his toffee-apple. "Come on," he said, "Let's have a go on the dodgems."

Clarissa stood her ground.

"What?" he asked. "You're not going all shy on me now, are you?"

"I can't go anywhere with you," she said. "I don't even know your name."

"Joseph. But you can call me Joe." He took her by the elbow and guided her through the crowd.

"My name's Clarissa," she said as they climbed into the nearest car.

He watched the bumper-cars around them, his gaze steely like he wasn't really with her. She licked at the toffee as the car jerked into life. Sparks exploded above like fireworks as they shot off. She squealed excitedly and hung on for dear life. They rammed into the other cars; she laughed wildly and freely as he tried to dominate the floor. He spun the steering frantically, dynamically, his foot always pressed full to the floor. She could barely control her laughter, her sides hurt and tears smeared her make-up. Then it was over.

Her legs trembled as he helped her out. Her toffee-apple was lost but she didn't care. As she stepped on to the wet grass her friends seemed to swarm around her from nowhere, surrounding her, smothering her, scolding her and sweeping her away. She looked back over her shoulder.

Joseph leaned casually against a booth and winked her way. "I'll see you again soon, Clarissa," he called after her.

She waved coyly and nodded as he disappeared into the thronging mass of people.

"Mikey?"

"What?"

"Did Mummy really fall over?"

Michael shrugged.

"Mummy's always crying, isn't she, Mikey?"

"Yes."

"Is she very sad?"

"Maybe."

"I always cry when I'm sad. And sometimes when I fall over and hurt my knee I try not to cry but it really hurts and I can't help it."

"Come on, Adam, can't you walk a bit faster?"

"Maybe Mummy fell over and hurt her knee and that's why she was crying."

"Maybe."

"I don't like it when Mummy is sad."

"Me neither," said Michael. He pulled his little brother along as fast as he could. He didn't like leaving his mum when she was upset. Adam was just a baby but he understood what was going on.

"Can we get Mummy some sweeties?"

"I don't think that would help."

"Why not? Sweeties always help me not to cry when I'm sad."

"We haven't got enough money."

"We could give Mummy some of our sweeties."

"Okay."

They raced home.

"We brought you a sweetie, Mummy," said Adam holding his gift aloft. His sticky face looked a little disappointed to see his last sweet going elsewhere.

"Thank you, love," she said. "Now, run upstairs and get ready for bed. Both of you. And I'll be checking that you've brushed your teeth!"

"Mummy, Adam's trying to eat a worm!" cried Mikey, laughing.

The worm writhed and slithered in Adam's pudgy little fingers. Dirt clung to his hands along with mucus and saliva. He sat proudly in the little scoop of earth he had made and giggled happily as he clamped the thing between his gums.

"Oh no, you don't," said Clarissa, snatching it from his mouth.

Mikey giggled. "Adam's eating worms again, Granddad," he said, pointing.

"Plenty of protein in worms," said Granddad. "It'll do him the world of good."

"Dad, don't be so disgusting," said Clarissa. She tossed the worm across the garden and pulled a handkerchief from her pocket. She spat on the delicate material and wiped Adam's mouth and face clean. "Filthy boy," she said.

Adam looked surprised.

"There you go, petal," she said, settling on the grass next to him. "No more worms until dinner-time, okay?" She winked at Michael who laughed and went back to playing with his yellow digger in the flower border. She smiled over at her father; he nodded to her reassuringly. "I don't know what to do, Dad," she said finally.

"I know, sweetheart. And I can't tell you what to do, you know? It's your life and I can't, I won't, make your decisions for you. Your life would be a very different thing if I had."

"I know, Dad. You don't have to tell me that. My life hasn't been my own since I fell pregnant with Michael."

"You didn't have to marry him. We'd have looked after you, me and your mother."

"Oh, Dad, I couldn't *not* have married him. I couldn't have brought a child into the world without a father. What would people have said?"

"Who gives a damn what people would have said? People know nothing and need to mind their own business."

"*I* give a damn. I know I shouldn't but I *do*. I couldn't have coped with their whispering and snide comments when they thought I was out of ear-shot; the smiles on their faces and the cold, judgemental looks in their eyes. I would do anything to make sure my boys' lives are as normal as possible."

"Even at the expense of your own happiness?"

"Yes, Dad, even that. I'd give my life for them. You know that, you must have felt the same?"

"Of course I did and that's what I'm trying to do now – protect you. From him. Does he hurt you?"

Clarissa averted her eyes, wafting a fly away from Adam's face. "Not in any way that matters," she said. "And he's never touched the boys."

"If he ever hurts you, Clarissa..."

"No, Dad. I don't want you to get involved. I just need you to be here for me to talk to. I need you to be here for my boys to talk to when they're old enough. They need someone to look up to, someone they can admire and love. They need a man who isn't Joe. That's all I want from you, Dad: I want you to be here for my boys."

"You don't have to ask. I'll always be here for them both, for as long as they want me."

"Thank you." Clarissa struggled to her feet and hugged her father. She could feel the loneliness burning through him. He was the rock in her life, the one who anchored her emotionally. He provided her with sanctuary, with safety, with love and devotion – just like a father should. Just like all fathers should.

A train rumbled heavily along the foot of the garden. Adam squealed happily.

"So, what happens now?" he asked.

Clarissa dabbed at her eye. "Oh, you know, we'll go back home and make the best of a bad job." She laughed. "That's actually not fair," she said. "I still love him very much. He has always done his best to provide for me and the boys but things have become so much harder since he lost his job. He dwells on things now. He seems to be stewing in bitterness like he resents me or his life or what his life has become. I don't know what I can do to help him."

"He can only help himself, sweetheart. He needs to sort himself out."

"I wish things were...different," she said.

"We always wish things were different."

Joseph Clare stormed out of the house. He had loved Clarissa more than he had ever loved anything in his life. True, had she not fallen pregnant with Michael he never would have married her but he understood his responsibility. She had never truly appreciated the sacrifice he had made for her. The stupid cow had probably got pregnant on purpose, that was the only way she could be sure of keeping him.

He hated the way she doted on the boys, especially Adam. She was turning the child into a right nancy-boy; if he wasn't crying or hanging from his Mother's skirts he was hankering after his granddad.

"All right Granddad!"

"Hello, lad, come on in."

The old man stood aside and let Adam through the door. Adam knew the house would be his one day, Granddad had told him so, but he hoped it wouldn't be for a good long while yet. He sat in his favourite spot with a sigh. They passed a pleasant afternoon together, chatting about this and that, nothing really important or earth-shattering, and that was just the way they liked it. Adam hated the way that he could see his granddad getting a little bit older every day – his skin was hanging looser on his bones these days and a slight tremble accompanied every one of his now slower movements. It was such a waste that one day all of the experiences, the thoughts, feelings and emotions that had accumulated over so many years, would in the matter of just a few seconds be wiped out. Lost forever.

Granddad grinned happily.

"Let me in, you stupid bitch!"

He hammered at the front door. The sides of his fists were red with tenderised capillaries. His chest heaved with the effort and sweat pricked at his temples.

A light snapped on.

Clarissa scuttled down the stairs, quickly wrapping herself up against the night time chill.

"Where's your key?" she hissed as she opened the door.

"Shut it!" he growled. He pushed past her.

Clarissa Clare emotionally braced herself.

The street was still. Curtains no longer twitched with curiosity. The street warmed itself in the isolation that their four walls afforded them. Adam and Michael huddled together in the darkness at the top of the stairs. They took comfort from each other's proximity as they listened to the rhythmic thudding from below. The sound of fist on flesh. The muffled cries of their Mother.

The room was full of thick, blue cigar smoke. The taste of it burned the back of Adam's oesophagus and pricked tears from his eyes. A small tatty tree, sparsely decorated, sat forlornly in the corner. He wanted to rub his eyes; wanted to rub them dry.

Adam sat alone in the house. He was trying – how he was trying – to conjure up the happiness he had once known in his youth. The joy of opening mysterious parcels from the family he loved, the smell of tree sap and smouldering pine needles, the pop of crackers and sizzle of turkey. The television talked to itself in the corner. The laughter track reverberated around his head.

Adam had always loved Christmas.

He was so lonely. Elle was gone. The months dragged by, each day an emotional barb in his too-tender flesh. The love ran too deep. He staggered into the kitchen. The pain in his chest was expanding, festering. He felt ready to implode, the sucking wound of his heart a black hole of immeasurable numbness. He picked up the small brown bottle of round white pills.

He slumped back into a chair and spread the powdery tablets out along the length of his legs. He took each pill with a slug of whiskey. He lay down. He thought of Elle. His eyes grew heavy. Dust gathered. The television laughed on.

The Christmas tree lights twinkled like a kaleidoscope of stars in the corner of the room; gaudy decorations clung to the branches, glistening happily; tinsel sparkled and glittered magically. Adam stood before the tree, his eyes wide in amazement. "It's so beautiful," he said quietly to himself. Pine-needles lay scattered around the base of the tree, rapidly browning in the hot, dry room. Ripped paper crunched underfoot and laughter bubbled quietly from the kitchen.

Michael sat reading his new book, his feet tucked-up under his bottom, in the chair in the corner; a paper crown angled jauntily on his head. The aroma of hot turkey wafted in from the kitchen. Adam could hear the murmur of his father's voice, a deep under-current accompanying his mother's stifled giggles.

"No, Joe, not now."

His father muttered something and staggered lazily in to the living-room, closely followed by his mother. She looked flustered, her hair was askew and her cheeks were burning red. Michael looked up from his book.

"Dinner's almost done, boys," she said. "Come and help me lay the table."

Joseph grabbed at her, trying to slip his arm around her waist. She stumbled forward a little and placed her sherry glass on the dining table. Joseph snuggled up behind her, his face buried in her neck. Clarissa tucked an errant strand of hair behind her ear and rolled her eyes.

Michael placed his book on the arm of his chair and laid the table. Adam watched, rooted to the spot in front of the tree. He had never seen his daddy acting like this before; he was fascinated. Adam smiled happily.

"Joseph," said Clarissa. "Stop it. Now."

Joseph stood upright behind her. She turned to face him; her hand reached up and stroked his cheek softly. "Save it for later, when the boys have gone to bed. The turkey will burn. Come on, take your seat and we'll have a nice Christmas dinner. Get some food in your belly, eh?"

Joseph glared at her briefly then slumped in to his chair at the table. Clarissa scurried back in to the kitchen.

"Daddy?"

"What?"

"Are we having a *very* merry Christmas?"

"I am; very merry!"

Michael placed the last of the cutlery on the table and scampered in to the kitchen to help his mother. Adam stood next to his daddy and pointed. "The tree is very beautiful," he said.

Joseph looked from his son to the tree and back again. "I suppose it is," he said.

"It's probably the beautifullest tree I have ever seen," said Adam.

"And you've seen quite a few, haven't you?"

Adam nodded thoughtfully.

"Mind yourselves," said Clarissa as she emerged from the kitchen, a sizzling turkey held out before her. Adam squeezed in tight next to his daddy.

"I love turkey too, Daddy. Christmas is the best, isn't it?"

Joseph patted Adam on the bottom and guided him safely away from the hot turkey-tray. "Go and sit in your chair and be still while your mother and Michael sort dinner out."

Adam watched in amazement at all of the food that was brought out and placed before him. His daddy wielded a knife as big as a sword, expertly carving the turkey but saving a massive leg for his own plate. The brightly coloured vegetables reminded him of the lights on the tree. He tucked-in eagerly and cleared his plate in record time. Clarissa smiled at Joseph and reached out a hand to him across the table. Joseph didn't seem to notice.

Michael hardly said a word, desperate to get back to his book. Joseph teased him all the time, laughing at Michael's reactions. The ceiling decorations shuffled like leaves in a light summer breeze, balancing on the knife-edge of autumn.

Later, lying in bed, exhausted by the day's excitement, Adam could hear his parents downstairs. Their voices were stifled by distance, muffled by his encroaching sleep. He could hear Michael breathing heavily in the darkness. He took comfort in the sound of that breathing as he listened to the rhythmic pounding of flesh on flesh.

"I mean it! Really!"

"But marriage?"

"Yes! I love you *so* much, Elle. Marry me. You don't have to decide now, take as much time as you like. I'll be here for you, whatever you decide. Don't be scared to let me down. I'll understand. Just promise me that you'll think about it."

Elle leaned across the table. Her blouse dragged into her meal, a small crimson stain bled into the material. She kissed Adam on the forehead. "I love you too," she mouthed.

"I love you, Adam."

"I love you too."

"And I want to stay with you forever."

"And I want to stay with *you* forever."

"You're mine and I'm never going to let you go."

"Good, because I don't want you to ever let me go. You make me so happy, Kath."

Adam snuggled down into bed with her, his head resting on her breasts. They lay together in the mid-afternoon sunlight. They talked about their long future together, their marriage, children, grand-children. Nothing would ever go wrong.

The crack of leather on willow reverberated through Adam's head as he sat up in bed. The sheets were drenched in sweat once more. He trembled as he wiped a cold hand across his face. The shredded remnants of the dream faded into obscurity.

Adam retreated quickly and put the kettle on. The whiskey had been a mistake, he realised that as soon as he had seen the disapproval on Elle's face. The disappointment. The steam from the kettle wafted across his face like the ghost of passion – hot and wet.

Elle did not feel secure here anymore. She watched Adam nervously. She stood and peered outside, reassuring herself that the world was outside.

"What?" said Adam.

"Just looking outside," said Elle.

Adam placed the two cups on the table. Elle returned to her seat. He was so glad that she had decided to stay and talk a little longer. A heart-to-heart might be all it took. He glanced out of the window. A shadowy figure sat in an unfamiliar car. White knuckles clenched the steering wheel.

"How did you get here?"

She glared at him. "A friend gave me a lift."

"A friend?"

"Yes."

"Who?"

She glanced away.

"*Who?*"

"Just a friend, Adam. It doesn't matter who it is. I asked someone to come with me, they agreed. It's none of your business."

Adam sucked air through his teeth. "What are you afraid of?"

"You, Adam. I'm afraid of you."

Chapter 4: Death

"Why's he so afraid of you, Joseph?"

Adam had been silent all morning. His grandfather had woken him and Michael up early. They both dressed in silence. He understood little of what was going on; why were there so many people in the house? Why did they all look like they were trying too hard to be happy?

"Why are you making him come to this? It's not right to make a child his age do this," Adam's Auntie hissed. Joe glared at her.

People, both the familiar and unusual, milled around. Michael and Adam sat quietly together in a corner. Occasionally Adam had his hair ruffled by a relative stranger, closely followed by his Auntie brandishing her comb. Their father prowled. The air buzzed.

Adam and Michael slipped quietly away and sat glumly at the head of the stairs. They rarely spoke to each other here. They knew how the other was feeling.

"What did Mummy die of?"

"I think it was a heart attack," said Michael.

Adam rested his chin on his knees.

"Do you think these people will be here long?"

"I hope not."

"Did Mummy *have* to die?"

"Granddad said that we all have to die sometime."

"How old's he then?"

"About eighty-eight, I think," Michael guessed.

"How old was Mummy then?"

"Thirty-two I think."

"Shouldn't Granddad be dead then?"

"Don't be daft! It doesn't work like that!"

Adam pursed his lips.

"Come on, you two," called their granddad from the foot of the stairs. "The cars are here."

The boys sat silently in the large black car flanking their father. They watched the streets crawl by. Strangers peered curiously into their bereaved little world. An old lady crossed herself, her eyes downcast. Adam wondered why. His granddad patted Adam's arm reassuringly.

The novelty of the day compelled him to silently question everything. The church was huge, hollow and oppressive. Sound echoed eerily in the space, becoming confused and distorted, the usual becoming strange and uncomfortable. Adam desperately wanted to go to the toilet.

He was fascinated by the whole thing. His grief was swamped by the strangeness, the spookiness, of his surroundings. This place frightened him. His stomach fluttered as he sat through the service. He watched tears of condensation run across the bodies of martyrs frozen in stained glass. Clear pools gathered at the feet of the dead-eyed. A sparrow in the rafters plumped its drab feathers against the chill. It watched Adam with small beady eyes then flew quietly out of an open window.

"No, no! My weirdest Christmas was when I was a kid. My mum had died earlier that year, just before my birthday. It was *so* strange. My whole life this person had been there for me, at every single special occasion and this year she just wasn't. It was *really* odd. I don't remember feeling upset at all. I cried, obviously - she was my mum - but it was like my favourite piece of furniture was missing or something. That sounds horrible, I know. I really missed her. Dad really didn't give a shit, of course. He acted like she had never existed to begin with. He just carried on as normal. Strange that he could act like that. I never understood him, never will."

"Didn't you ever ask him why?" asked Kath.

"My father was an ignorant bastard at the best of times. He wouldn't have known how to hold a civilised conversation."

Kath frowned.

"Look. He never cared about Mum as far as I could tell. All of my earliest memories are of Mum crying. The rest of it is pretty vague, more sensations than memories. I just remember feeling sad most of the time. There was this warm, soft person. Light seemed to come from inside her. She would lean over me, talk to me, but I couldn't hear what she was saying. There was warmth on my face, wetness, but I didn't know what it was. She would reach out to touch me and then she'd be gone. I know for a fact that the bastard used to hit her. I'll never forgive him for that.

Kath slipped her arm gently around his shoulder. She kissed him on the cheek. He brushed a strand of violet hair out of her eyes.

"I love your hair," he said.

"I know."

"My mum would have loved it too. She'd have made fun out of you for it, I'm sure! She'd have said that you looked like somebody's grandmother. I wish I could have known her better."

"She sounds nice."

"Everyone's mum is nice!"

"Mummy?"

"Yes, dear?"

"Would you mind if I brought somebody home next weekend?"

"Who?"

"Somebody I've met at Uni," said Elle. Her face flushed crimson.

Her father looked up from his newspaper.

"Eleanor!" said Mrs. Chamberlain. "He's not another one of those hopeless hippy types you keep bringing home is he?"

"Jesus, Mummy!"

"Don't blaspheme!" said Mr Chamberlain.

Elle shot a withering look his way. "No," she said. "His name's Adam. He's an English graduate. He's taking a year out and then he's going to start work. He has his own house and he's not the hopeless hippy type and I resent the implication that I only bring people home to piss you off."

"It certainly seems that way sometimes, dear, that's all I'm saying," said Mrs Chamberlain.

"What do you mean he's 'taking a year out'?" asked Mr Chamberlain.

"That he's taking a year out to get his head together before he starts working."

"'Get his head together'? He *is* one of those damned hopeless hippy types!"

"You're not even prepared to give him a chance are you? You're both so judgemental, why can't you just accept people the way they are? Don't you want me to be happy? Adam makes me happy and that's why I want him to meet you both." She paused. "Won't you *please* just give him a *chance*?" She stormed from the room.

"I think we upset her," said Mr Chamberlain.

"As usual," said Mrs Chamberlain.

Elle sat cross-legged on her bedroom floor. She flicked nonchalantly through her albums wondering if she had anything to match her mood. Why didn't they understand? All she wanted was to be loved for who she was. All of her boyfriends - with that one awkward exception - had taken advantage of her; had used her to clear their debts, to make someone jealous or as a substitute for someone else. Adam was different. He really loved her. She longed to be with him all of the time. She loved waking up next to him, loved watching him sleep, listening to him breathe. She loved to snuggle up to his warm sleeping body; loved making love to him while their breath still smelled of the night before.

"I love him so much," she thought. She put a record on and lay back on her bed. Her mind drifted away to the night before as her hands began their first tentative exploration of her body.

Elle sat on the sofa, her foot tucked-up under her bottom, reading. She seemed engrossed in her novel but her ears were constantly pricked for the sound of Adam's arrival. She had cleaned the house from top to bottom today, then bathed and pampered herself.

She rubbed her thumb absent-mindedly up and down the soft skin of her forearm; the bruise there was sepia yellow, faded by time. She tilted her head to one side as she heard the garden gate swing open. She smelled good, she felt good. Her hair was luxurious, her skin prickled . The smell emanating from the kitchen made her feel hungrier than she already was.

Adam should have been home an hour ago. His work hours had been erratic the last few months though; he had been working longer and later. They needed the money, although she wasn't sure what they needed it for exactly. She put the book down and straightened herself out. She positioned herself seductively on the sofa; she wanted to give the impression of languid sensuality.

His key slid in to the lock and the front door opened. Elle shifted her weight slightly; she tossed her hair and licked her lips; she draped one arm along the back of the sofa. She heard Adam shuffling in the hall. "Adam?"

He walked in to the living-room. "Sorry I'm late," he said. "Work." He pecked her on the forehead and continued in to the kitchen.

Elle looked after him, maintaining her position.

"Smells good," he said. "I've already eaten though; I had to have something at work. Sorry. I should have phoned."

Elle's face fell. She had prepared this meal specially; it was his favourite, he could never resist. This meal always signalled something special for them both; the first meal she had ever cooked him; it was so tied-up in their history that it never failed to arouse a reaction.

Adam walked back through the living-room. "I really need a shower," he said. "I absolutely reek of work. He pecked her on the forehead again as he swept past. "I might just go straight to bed after I've showered," he said, climbing the stairs. "I'm absolutely exhausted. The bathroom door closed and she heard the shower burst in to life.

Elle sat dumbfounded on the sofa. Eventually she cleared the table of its setting and drifted in to the kitchen. She turned the oven off and sat watching their meal slowly congeal. She scraped it all in to the bin, turned the lights off and padded softly upstairs.

Adam had finished in the bathroom. She could hear him snoring softly from the bed. She stared at herself in the condensation smeared mirror and, bit by bit, removed her make-up. There was no hurry. There was no point. Her skin glowed healthy and pink and clean. She brushed her teeth mechanically, turned the light off and slipped in to bed beside Adam. She lay in the darkness, next to her sleeping husband, and a tear slid silently on to her pillow.

The darkness swirled around Adam, through him. Its black tendrils searched out the deepest secret parts of his mind. It twisted and burned him. It exposed things he had never known about himself in the secret hieroglyphs of the subconscious. Stars glittered like ice. The wind moaned in violent ecstasy. The crack of leather on willow. A vase falls. Violets spill in shattered perfection. Tears of stagnant water splash in sorrow. Breasts heave in synchronicity with pelvic thrust of lust. Sweat trickles down nakedness. Breath moans of soft pleasure. Cockroach crunch underfoot. Red eye glows confused, shot with blood hunger.

"Adam! Adam! For fuck's sake, will you wake up!" said Elle. She shook him violently. Dream sweat ran across his brow, his hair was plastered to his face. His eyes twitched spastically under his lids.

His eyes snapped open. He shot bolt upright in bed. Fear scampered through him like spiders. He pushed Elle away. He gasped for air.

"What the fuck?" His face sagged as his emotions collapsed in on themselves. He threw himself at Elle, wrapping his arms around her tightly and crushed his head to her breasts.

"Hold me." Deep, wracking sobs forced their way from him.

"It's okay, it's okay," she said. "It was just a dream, baby, just a dream."

"Shit me!" he sobbed. "I don't even know what just happened but I'm terrified."

"Fancy having a nightmare on our honeymoon," she said. "I thought you *wanted* to marry me."

He held on to her tightly. "I love you," he whispered.

A now familiar stillness had settled like snow on the house since his granddad had died. It was peaceful, quiet, dead. Adam breathed deeply: his granddad's smell was already beginning to fade, to drift away like cigar smoke on a gentle summer breeze.

"You daft old bugger," said Adam.

He had already been through the wardrobes and drawers. All of the old boy's clothes were bagged up and ready to go off to the charity shop; now it was just a case of making the place his own. It was time to decide what he was going to keep and what he was going to replace, time to choose how much of his grandfather he was going to cling on to.

Adam's nose was thick with displaced dust; decades old layers of grey stirred-up by his meddling. Rolled-up carpets revealed charmingly hideous linoleum and that, cracked and broken into shards, in turn revealing fresh red floor tiles; vibrancy hidden beneath years of comfort.

He ran the palm of his hand sadly across the chimney-breast, a final goodbye to a place that was solely his grandfather's. He had to find a balance; a way to say goodbye, to let go and make the house his own but, at the same time, to hold on to what he could, to retain the best of the old man.

The front bedroom was stripped now, bare boards glared at him accusingly, the wardrobe in the corner all that was left of the original furnishing. Dust motes swirled thickly as Adam looked out on to the main road, cradling his granddad's ancient cricket bat. Adam loved this bat, loved the heft of it and the still-strong smell of linseed oil. He loved the way that the wood seemed to glitter with memories, a repository of a past mostly unknown to him – shadows of trying to lift the damn thing when he was still too young to play, of Granddad's closeness when he was teaching Adam how to hold the bat properly. He smiled fondly at the memory of the loud crack of leather on willow as he hit his only ever six. And all of it had been for his granddad's benefit. Adam hated cricket.

"What the bloody hell does he want?" said Adam to himself. He scampered down the stairs, bat in hand, and flung the front-door open just as Michael knocked.

"Adam!" said Michael.

"Yes?"

Michael sighed. He held his hands up in a conciliatory manner. "Look" he said, "I'm really sorry about last week. It should never have happened."

"You're damn right it should never have happened."

"He promised me he would behave," said Michael.

"It wasn't about him, was it? There was a reason I left, you know that. Bringing him to my grandfather's funeral was never going to end well, was it? What the fuck were you thinking, Michael?"

"I was thinking it might have been a good time to build some broken bridges. Loss brings people together, Adam. I thought it might be the time."

"You were wrong. You'll always be wrong as far as he's concerned."

"You have nobody now, Adam. You need to talk to him, sort out your differences."

"I don't need anybody, Michael, him, least of all. Our differences are too great."

"Your similarities are too great, you mean. You're just like him, you know that? That's why the two of you don't get on."

Adam brandished the cricket-bat at his brother. "What the fuck is that supposed to mean?"

"Nothing, nothing, I'm sorry. Look, I didn't come here to argue with you, Adam. I came here to apologise. I didn't mean for things to go the way they did, I was trying to do what I thought was right. And I've come to offer you a hand, to give you help clearing granddad's house out, if you want it."

"I don't need any help, Mikey. I can cope just fine on my own. I don't want to see you; I don't want to see him. I'm better off without either of you." He lowered the bat.

Michael stepped back from the doorstep. "Fair enough," he said. "But if you need a hand with anything, just give me a shout."

Adam shut the door softly. The latch clicked into place with a finality he had never noticed before. He went back upstairs and tucked the cricket-bat safely away.

"Now I know you're taking the piss," said Tom.

Adam looked at him stony-faced.

"You're serious? Jesus, Adam, I'm sorry, mate! Congratulations!"

"Thank you. And, in spite of what you just said, I would like you to be my best man."

"Superb!" said Tom. "I'd love to. Date set or anything?"

Adam laughed. "We haven't even told Elle's parents yet. I'm dreading it."

"Adam." Tom hesitated, searching for the right words. "You've known me long enough to know I'm a dick so please don't take this the wrong way but are you sure? I mean *marriage*! That's a biggie!"

"I'm sure." Adam clapped his best friend on the back and they hugged.

"Are you sure?"

"Yes."

"Promise?"

"Promise."

Kath smiled at Adam. When he promised something she knew he really meant it. She could always see the truth in his cold, blue eyes. If he said he wouldn't laugh then he wouldn't laugh. She whipped her hat off. Cascades of violet hair fell like rain.

"It's purple," he said.

"It's violet. Do you like it?"

He opened his mouth, then closed it. He frowned. "Purple?"

"Violet! I like it. I thought you would too."

He felt the softness of her hair, ran the strands of it through his fingers. He examined it hair by hair, marvelled at the minutiae of it, of every subtle nuance. Light sparked off it; every wave and curl wound around itself.

"It's beautiful," he said.

"I used to have a girlfriend called Kath," said Adam. "She was beautiful too." He nestled his chin in to his hands, his elbows propping him up at the table. The canteen was quiet this afternoon. The staff were gossiping quietly behind the counter; the aroma of hot coffee mingled unwillingly with the smell of greasy bacon and barely warm pizza. A low murmur of conversation, a burble of voices, accompanied the reluctant shuffling of furniture.

Catherine smiled. "Is that a fact?"

Adam nodded.

Catherine flushed slightly, a rouge-blush of heat brushing her cheeks. "Flatterer," she said.

"It's true." He smiled at her across the Formica wilderness that lay between them. He lifted his head and reached a hand out towards her; he could feel the grains of sugar rolling, grinding, beneath his palm. His fingertips touched hers.

"Not here, Adam." She snatched her hand away and looked around worriedly. "What if somebody sees?"

"What are they going to do; tell on us?" He laughed.

"They'll talk; they already do. What if Elle finds out?"

Adam withdrew his hand and relaxed back in to his seat. He gazed in to his coffee. The mention of Elle made him feel uncomfortable. "There's nothing for her to find out, is there? And even if there was, she never would," he said. "She doesn't love me. I don't think she ever has. I don't think she'd care if she found out about us, I really don't."

"Of course she'd care. I'd care if I was your wife."

Adam sighed. "But you're not, are you? She's... I don't know... I don't want to say 'she doesn't understand me' but I really don't think she does. She hardly ever wants to go out or do anything. I'm pretty sure she stays in all day apart from when she goes out shopping. She cooks, she cleans. She's lifeless."

"I'm sure she does what she thinks is best, Adam."

He shook his head. He knew this conversation couldn't go anywhere, knew it shouldn't have even got this far, but here he was. Catherine was alluring – the glint of light in her eye; the way her breasts heaved when she laughed; the cheeky coyness of her smile. Adam sipped his coffee and watched her over the rim of his mug. "I can't remember the last time she made love to me," he said.

Catherine's eyes flickered. Adam knew what had flashed through her thoughts – the two of them, together – the same thought that had just flashed through his. He yearned to be inside her. He knew it was wrong; knew he shouldn't be thinking these things but it felt right, a delicious contradiction. It would feel so good to be with her, deep inside her, to be with someone who wanted him as much as he wanted them. He cleared his throat. "Maybe we should meet-up after work for a coffee one day?" he said.

She hesitated. The indecision flickered across her brow until, finally, she nodded. "Maybe we should," she said. "One day."

Adam placed his mug on the table. "Maybe more than one day?"

Catherine's eyes met his; they sparkled mischievously. She tucked her hair back behind her ear; her other hand lingered at her throat. Her neck tinged pink. "I'm not sure you'd be able to cope with more than one day," she said quietly.

"I think you'd be surprised at what I can handle," he said. He winked.

"Oh, Jesus!" She laughed out loud. "I can't believe you just did that, cheesy wink-man! What a way to kill the mood."

He blushed. "Come on," he said, awkward and embarrassed, "we need to get back to it."

"Hey, don't be so serious, I'm just having a bit of fun with you." She glanced around the canteen and, once she was sure no-one was looking their way, she brushed her fingertips lightly across his arm. "It's my turn to follow you up to the first floor; I want to see that nice tight backside of yours right at eye-level." She growled throatily and winked.

"She's beautiful, isn't she?" asked Joseph Clare.

The boys said nothing.

"She looked like this when I first met her – peaceful, quiet, beautiful. She's sleeping now. I thought it would do you both good to see her like this. To see that death is nothing to be afraid of."

Michael and Adam looked at their mother lying in bed, cold already seeping into her. Her lips tinted blue. She wasn't asleep. There was an emptiness about the room, a void where there had once been warmth. Their father talked into the void. He talked about a world they did not know, a woman they had never known. They watched him, this big, angry man, as a small gentle tear crept unnoticed from an eye and drifted slowly away.

"She's gone to a better place now," he said. "Kiss her goodbye, both of you."

They each leaned onto the bed and kissed her gently. The waxiness of her skin held remnants of warmth; her perfume, a mere whisper of violets. This was not their Mummy.

"Now go and tell your grandfather what's happened. I'll be waiting here."

"Mikey?"

"Yes, Adam?"

"Why did Daddy make us kiss Mummy?"

"We were kissing her goodbye."

"But why?"

"Because she's not coming back."

"Oh. But that wasn't really Mummy anyway, was it?"

"Not really, no."

"It felt funny on my lips, Mikey."

"Mine too."

They walked in silence for a while. Michael held his little brother's hand tightly; the lump in his throat was making it difficult to breathe. His tears flowed freely and he did not care who saw them. Grown-ups watched him as they passed; Michael could see their worried expressions but he didn't care. He really didn't care. 'Let them look,' he thought. He pulled Adam along, faster than he could properly walk. Adam stumbled but Michael just pulled him to his feet and walked on. The pavement swam before his eyes; the whole world swam before his eyes. His mummy was gone; Adam's too. Everything had changed. Their daddy would have to look after them now and, when he was older, Michael would look after Daddy and Adam.

"I've hurt my knee again, Michael," said Adam.

"I know. You'll just have to cope with it for now, okay?"

"But it really stings."

"You have to be big and strong now, Adam, just like Daddy."

"Mummy would kiss it better."

"Yes she would but Mummy's gone now, Adam." Grief balled in Michael's chest.

"Will she be coming back soon?"

"She won't be coming back at all," said Michael. "There's just you and me and Daddy. We have to look after each other now. Daddy will look after me, I will look after you."

"Who will I look after?" Adam's bottom lip protruded slightly.

"You can look after your mouse."

Adam smiled. "I love Woffley, she's the best mouse in the world."

"I know, Adam."

"If I pick her up by the tail she climbs up it like a rope. Did you know that, Mikey?"

"I do know that. You showed me, remember?"

"It's very funny. I think she's four, no, five years old now."

"I don't think she's that old, Adam."

"I think she must be. I've had her for ages. She must be the oldest mouse there ever was."

"I think she must be."

They turned the corner into their granddad's street.

Adam gasped. "Who's going to look after Granddad? Can I look after him too?"

Michael nodded; he couldn't understand how everything could be so ordinary; it was like the rest of the world hadn't noticed or cared about what had happened. His world had just come crashing down around him and everybody else was still going about walking their dogs or doing the gardening or fetching a newspaper. Nobody cared. The street was quiet.

He opened the gate to Granddad's house. A blackbird burst from the hedge, its staccato warning ringing in Michael's ears. The sparrows carried on their quarrelling, their lives carrying on as normal, just like everybody else's.

Michael knocked on the front door, as hard as he could. His knuckles reddened at the impact and he gripped Adam's hand tighter.

"I need a wee," said Adam.

"In a minute."

Granddad opened the door. Happiness swept across his face at the sight of the boys and then he noticed the tears.

"Oh no," he said quietly. He crouched down in front of Adam and Michael. "It's my Clarissa, isn't it? Your mother?"

Michael nodded. Granddad wrapped his arms around the boys and pulled them close.

"*What?*"

"I said I'm afraid of *you*, Adam," said Elle.

"I've never given you anything to be afraid of! Everything that has ever happened, you brought about."

"Yes, Adam, it was always me, wasn't it? Well forget it, you don't have that hold over me anymore. You can tell me it was all *my* fault as much as you like now because I don't care. I *know* it's you. It was *always* you. It will always *be* you. *You're* the one with the problems."

"Bollocks!"

"Is that the best you can do? Jesus! I always thought you were so clever. Quick with the put downs. So very eloquent. I was *so* impressed you know? I could never think of anything to say, you always made me feel small. You're the one who's small. You're *nothing*."

Adam looked at her, at the anger that was exposed on her face; the hatred and bile that was spilling out of her; all of the repressed loathing and festered emotion. She had loved him once; loved him enough to marry him. She had loved him for longer and deeper than she cared to admit. If she didn't care, why was she here now?

"Didn't you ever love me?"

"Of course I did!" she replied.

"What changed then?"

"You did." She paused, glanced away. Her lip trembled as a tear swelled at her lid. "No," she corrected. "I changed. Everything changed, everything but you. I'm leaving now."

"No, you're not." He barred her way. "We've still got too much to talk about."

"You've got too much to talk about you mean."

They filed out of the church in silence. The wind whipped at them. The cold cleaved them to the bone. Adam held his granddad's hand tightly. The wetness on his granddad's face surprised him. He wished he could cry for himself; who was going to love him now? Who was going to look after him? He didn't want to cry. The lump in his throat hurt too much. He would save his tears for later. He followed his granddad. He listened to conversations far above his head and shivered inside. He clenched his teeth.

It was much later in the day when he released that reassuring hand. Granddad was the only person who could now offer him these things. He felt like he was in a bubble. Mummy was never coming home.

Chapter 5: Love

Adam felt like he was coming home. The small detached house hunched at the end of the path, its drabness bearing the weight of the summer's day. The windows peered at him; the curtains like half-closed lids of a weary old man. The sedentary air stirred at the sound of a diesel locomotive as it thundered along behind the row of houses that lined the road. The sound gradually receded until the calm meniscus mirror of the pond-like day was restored.

Before he even reached the front door it opened. Adam's grandfather peered around the door frame, a look of feigned horror on his face.

"All right, Granddad!"

"Hello son, come on in."

Adam stepped in to the familiar old house and breathed in. One day this smell – the ethereal mixture of old cigar, old whiskey and old man – would be gone. They both knew it. Adam flung himself down into his favourite old chair.

"Drink?"

"Please, Granddad."

"Anything in particular?"

"What have you got?"

The old man pursed his lips, a habit Adam had subconsciously picked up. "The usual," he said.

"Tea please, then."

Adam's granddad clipped him affectionately around the back of the head as he returned from the kitchen. The afternoon, as usual, passed peacefully enough. They chatted about University, Granddad moaned about his bones and his bowels, but there was an unusual undercurrent. Something was on Adam's mind. There was a brief lull in the conversation.

"So what is it? What's wrong, Adam?"

Adam looked at his lap. The remnants of his tea swam before his eyes. He tried to swallow. He bit his lip. He frowned, glanced at his granddad and then back to his tea. A fat droplet fell heavily from his eye. Then it was too late, he couldn't stop the tears. He trembled as he strained to contain the emotions. Adam's granddad held him closely.

"Come on now, let it out son. Let it all out."

Eventually Adam's tears receded. He wiped angrily at his eyes. "Jesus! I'm such a twat! Sorry, Gramps."

"You've nothing to be sorry for, lad. Feels a little better now, doesn't it?"

Adam nodded.

"Good. There's nothing like a good cry for getting all of the pain out; it clears the emotions. Now tell me what's happened."

"It's Kathy," said Adam. "She won't be coming round anymore; I won't touch her violet hair, or kiss her or hold her ever again." Tears began to swell in his eyes again. "She's left me."

Granddad scratched his unshaven chin thoughtfully. He took a cigar from its wrapper and lit it. As he puffed, clouds of thick smoke billowed from it like memories.

"I never did tell you about my first love, did I?" He grinned around his cigar. "It was while I was on leave during the war. I was back home for two weeks. You'll never know what it was like, I hope you never will. We were all so full of just being *alive*. Anyway, one night, early on, I met a girl. Beautiful, she was. A lovely young lass; not what they call 'Hollywood beautiful' or anything as superficial as that. She had such a pretty little face, especially when she smiled or laughed – that's true of every woman though, isn't it? She sparkled. But it was the tiny flaws in her that made her irresistible. Her front teeth were a little crooked, she had fat ankles, do you know what I mean? All of these little things, these tiny imperfections, were what made her special. Her name was Vera."

Adam tutted.

"No, hang on. It's not what you're thinking. There was nothing 'casual' about relationships in those days. Everybody knew that each day could be their last and, more often than not, lived it like it was. So we fell in love. Simple as that. And the night before I was due to fly back I asked her to marry me and she said yes. I was floating on air, I was so happy. I had a girl back home waiting for me which was all that most of the chaps wanted – to know that there was someone special waiting just for them. One month, one bloody month after I got back to the front, I had a letter calling the whole thing off. She said she'd been 'swept up by the romance of it all'. Broke my heart it did. I killed two men because of that letter." He paused. "Don't look at me like that. I'm not proud of it but what can I say? We were at war, if I hadn't killed them they'd have killed me. That hadn't changed. I just had personal reasons that day.

"Anyway, the point I'm making is this: I thought I'd never get over her. I loved her as much as I thought it was possible to love any woman. Eventually the war was won, of course, and we all went home. And *that* was when I met your Grandmother. You never know what the future has in store for you, Adam. I thought my heart was broken forever and then I found the one true love of my life. It's never as bad as you think it is, son." He slapped Adam reassuringly on the knee.

Adam shook his head. "I know you're trying to help, Granddad, but I feel like shit."

"Yes, well, I could have told you that too. Like everything else though, that will fade and die."

Elle tucked the loose strand of hair behind her ear. She had tried to keep it under control, had tucked it all in tightly under an old headscarf but, over the course of the afternoon, it had worked its way free of its restraints. She wiped her brow with the back of her hand and scratched the tip of her nose carefully. She stepped back and admired her work so far: tatters of damp paper hung limply from the freshly stripped wall; it lay scattered on the floor sheet, curled like origami swarf and lily petals; bits of it clung to Elle.

She wielded the scraper deftly; it skipped and skimmed across the wall, a dancer on ice – elegant and precise in its movements – until the wall was bare. The smell of the paste was thick in her nostrils; she loved the cold sweetness of it, would bathe in its viscosity if she could. Memories of her father's laughter and her own squealing as she ran through the hanging remnants of wallpaper in her childhood flashed before her. She smiled wistfully as she began to hang the new paper.

She had been waiting to do this for months; since they had come back from honeymoon, in fact. It was time to make the house their own, freshen it up. There were still thick tobacco stains throughout the house and there was still a smell about the place that could only be described as stale. She wrinkled her nose.

Adam had loved his granddad very much, that much was clear to her, even though she had never had the chance to meet him. He had told her stories about the old man, about him trying to teach Adam to play cricket, and with each story a gentleness came over her husband; a wistful sorrow that she had never seen in anybody before. It was a look that broke her heart; that made her fall even deeper in love with him; a look that made her love for him hurt her somewhere deep inside.

By the time she heard his key slide in to the lock she had almost completely re-wallpapered the living-room. She posed elegantly half-way up the stepladder: a presentation for him, to enhance their home.

His cheery greeting choked off as he entered the room. His face fell. His shoulders dropped. His eyes flicked around the room, jumping from the walls to the sheets, across the furniture and the mess, to the unused rolls of paper propped up in the corner, until they finally settled on Elle. His mouth hung slackly.

Elle scampered down the ladder. She knew immediately what she had done, knew how thoughtless she had been. She rushed over to him and flung her arms around his neck. "I'm sorry, Adam, I'm so sorry. I didn't think."

"What have you done?"

"I thought it would be a lovely surprise for you. I'm so sorry. I should have told you what I wanted to do; I should have discussed it with you. I wanted it to be a surprise; I wanted to show you how much I love you, how much I want to make a life and a home with you."

Adam looked at her. "It's so...different," he said.

"I know. I never even thought about how much it might mean to you to keep things the same as they were."

"No, you misunderstand me," he said. He held her at arms' length. "It's wonderful," he said. "I love it and I love you for doing it and Granddad would have loved it too." He drew her to him and held her tight.

"You twat!" shouted Tom through the window.

He had knocked on the front door several times before making his way to the window. He knew Adam was in; where else would he go on Christmas Day? He could hear the television cackling; the lights were on. He frowned. He peered through the gap in the curtains. He could see Adam slumped on the sofa. "Arsehole is fast asleep!" he muttered to himself. He banged on the glass.

"Come on!" Next to Adam lay the discarded husks of empty bottles – whiskey and pills. Tom's voice caught in his chest. He yelled at Adam through the window. He ran and tried the doors – locked. Without hesitation he scooped up the largest stone he could find and put it through the window. He clambered frantically into the house.

Clarissa Clare smiled. It was a perfect day. The first day she had brought her child home. The doors and windows were open and a gentle summertime cacophony swelled through the house. Fat bees droned; birds hid in the heavy shadows, sheltered from the oppressive heat. The house was cool.

Joseph Clare sat in the corner. He watched her every move, the way she leaned over the child, the way she stroked its cheeks and smiled down at it. He watched the way she fussed over it. Watched the gentle way she did everything.

"Well?" he said.

"Well what?" She didn't take her eyes off her child.

"What's its name?"

"*His* name, Joseph."

"What are you going to call him?"

"I've always liked 'Adam'."

"Why?"

"From the Bible silly!" She turned to look at her husband.

Joseph Clare lowered his gaze. Clarissa turned back to their new son; a little brother for young Michael. He was so excited about getting a little brother that he hadn't even considered the possibility that it might be a sister.

Joseph Clare stood quietly and looked out of the window. "It's hot," he said, wiping his forehead on his shirtsleeve.

"Very."

Adam gurgled softly in his cot.

Joseph looked down at his second son. His face remained dispassionate as Adam burbled up at him, waving his chubby little limbs around.

"Hello, Adam," he said. He reached down, one finger outstretched. The child grasped the enormous digit and dribbled. The corners of Joseph Clare's mouth twitched upwards slightly. "Very pleased to meet you," he said.

He kissed his wife on the temple and left them alone.

"That was your Daddy," she said.

Adam's eyes glinted in the glow of her love.

Adam bent his head over his colouring. The tip of his tongue protruded as he desperately tried to stay within the lines. He had tried his very hardest to draw the very best picture he could of his family.

"Who's this, Adam?" His teacher pointed at a figure floating above the ground.

"That's my Mummy," said Adam. "She's watching me and Michael burying Woffley over here." He pointed at a small mound of brown at the feet of the three figures in the fore-ground.

"Was Woffley your pet?"

"She is the best mouse I ever had." He drew a little cross next to the grave. "She was beautiful but not as beautiful as my mummy. She died too."

Adam's teacher rested her hand on the nape of his neck.

"It's okay though," said Adam, "she turned into a pigeon and flew away. Daddy is always at home now."

"Is this your daddy, here?" she asked, pointing at the third figure in the fore-ground.

"No, that's my granddad. He looks after me now. He always makes sure I'm okay; he loves me a lot. He loves Mikey too but I'm his favourite."

"Is your daddy not in this picture then?"

"Of course he is," said Adam. He barely paused in his colouring to point at the house he had drawn in the background. "He's in the house, watching the telly."

Adam's teacher sat down next to him. She put her arm around him and looked hard at him. "Things must be very difficult for you, at home, Adam. If you need to talk to someone, you can always tell me things. You can tell me anything you like, you know that? I'm sure you must miss your mummy very much and that's okay. You don't have to hide it; you can tell me all about it any time you like, okay?"

Adam nodded. She kissed him on the temple and gave him a little squeeze before moving on. He coloured harder; the picture swam before his eyes. He blinked the tears away. He had gone over the lines. His picture was ruined.

"I don't *want* to get married in a bloody church, that's why!"

"Why not?"

"Because I don't!"

"*Why?*"

"Because I don't! It's as *simple* as that!"

"Why are you being so fucking *selfish?*" Elle said.

"I'm not the one trying to force my beliefs on you."

"*What?*"

"You're trying to force me to go against everything I believe in. You're trying to emotionally blackmail me to stand in the house of a God I don't believe in, in his '*Divine* sight' and pledge my undying love for you. *I* don't need to stand in a building designated a 'holy' house by an organised religion that's responsible for *more* deaths than Hitler to tell you that I love you."

"Don't you want to marry me? Don't you want to make me happy? Are you deliberately trying to put me off you? Why are you doing this, Adam?"

"I'm not doing anything."

"Then why won't you put aside these beliefs? Just for one day. You're not the only one involved in this you know? Marry me in a church, it means so much to me."

"But I don't believe in it."

"I do, Adam, I do!"

Adam clenched his fists at his side. He pursed his lips, annoyed. He muttered something to himself and looked Elle right in the eye.

"I'm not getting married in a church," he said.

"I am," she retorted.

They glared at each other, neither willing to back down. Adam let out a howl and he threw his mug across the room. It shattered against the wall, hot brown liquid splayed across the paper, a Rorschach test of anger.

"Shit! Adam, what the fuck are you doing?"

Adam stared at her. A shadow of confusion crossed his face. "Sorry," he said and walked calmly from the room.

"Come on, Elle, this will be the last time, I promise."

"I've heard that one before, haven't I? said Elle.

"True, but this time, I really mean it. Look, it's two hundred and fifty quid, that's all. You can afford that easily. You know I'm broke and your family's loaded."

Elle sighed. She loved Dan so much but he was just like all the others. He was only attentive when he wanted something and he had only chased her after he had seen her parents' house. She had paid off his car loan first, just the last few hundred pounds; it was nothing but it had been a sign of things to come. That first payment had been as much for her sake as his; after all, he did use his car to drive her around – to take her shopping, to her University interview, to pick her up on a Saturday night after she'd drunk herself into a stupor with Trudi. It was only fair that she paid for half the petrol money too.

Next came the gambling debts. The admissions of loss and the "I'll win it all back, I promise. Don't worry about it." She hadn't considered it a problem at first; how much money could one lose on a fruit machine?

"You only want me for my money, don't you?" she said.

"Don't be ridiculous," he said. "I love you more than you'll ever know." He reached out and stroked her cheek. He cupped the back of her head and pulled her towards him for a kiss. Elle turned away.

"Don't," she said. "I'm not being ridiculous, it's true. Why won't you just be honest with me? Everything you do is a calculation of how much you have to do in order to screw me for money."

"I'll screw you for free, baby," he said, groping her breast.

Elle knocked his hand away. "I want you to leave," she said. Her voice caught in her throat but she knew she was doing the right thing. She was sick of this; the way she always fell for this 'type'. They were so easy to spot but there was something about them that she couldn't resist – something edgy, something dangerous. They all had that glint in their eye, that was the thing that did it for her – the suggestion of mischief, the hint of darkness.

"You what? You want me to leave? His voice was raised in disbelief.

"Yes. It's for the best." Elle spoke quietly, resigned to the loss she was already feeling, prepared for Dan's righteous anger.

"You bitch!" he said. "You know how broke I am. How am I going to pay for the work on the car now?"

"And that sums you up precisely," said Elle. "I break-up with you and your first concern is your debts." She scrabbled in her handbag for her purse. "Here," she said, throwing a wad of notes at him. "It's all I have."

He scooped them up and counted them quickly. He glared at her. "This doesn't even cover half of it," he said.

"It's all I have," she repeated.

"Have you found someone else? Is that what this is all about?"

She shook her head. "This is purely about us," she said, "and the mistakes I keep making. We should never have got together in the first place. I made a mistake. I'm sorry."

He shoved the money into his pocket. "I swear, if this is about someone else, I'll find out and I'll beat the crap out of him. Got it?"

"Why don't you ever listen to me? I've only ever been honest with you and that's not changing now."

"Yeah, well, if I find out it is, I'll beat the crap out of him, understood? I'll be watching you, Elle, and he'll get what's coming to him."

"Goodbye, Dan. Look after yourself; I guess that's what you're best at, after all."

He slammed the door behind him.

Adam was bored. He lounged back on the bench, his arms stretched out on either side. He blinked slowly, his lids verging on the languid. His granddad leaned forward, perched expectantly on the edge of the seat. Light wisps of cloud drifted lazily across the blue, almost making the effort to create shadows. Leather cracked on willow.

"Good shot, sir!" said Granddad, clapping.

Polite applause rippled around the small grounds as the men in white ran to improve their innings. It was the perfect cliché.

"There's nothing quite like it, is there?"

"What's that, Granddad?"

"A Sunday spent watching the cricket! A warm summer evening and a lovely light breeze. It's almost magical. No other sport has this feeling, son, not one of them."

Adam knew what he meant. There was a wistfulness to this, a sense of a lost time, a bygone era, but it was a feeling for old men. A feeling for men whose time had passed, whose best days were long behind them. A sensation for men who had lost too much to carry on moving forward; who were content now to gaze into the distance; men who were content to look over their lives and smile gently in remembrance of all those things they had done or hadn't done or should or shouldn't have done. No time for regrets but plenty of time to appreciate the mistakes.

"I don't suppose you remember your Grandmother do you?"

"Not really," said Adam.

"I didn't think so, you were only a baby when she died. She couldn't wait to see you grow up, and she dreaded it at the same time. She was scared about the kind of world you were going to grow up in. You know what she'd have said about Kath?"

Adam shook his head.

"Of course you don't. But she would have told you the same as I've just told you, young man. Do you know why? Because it's the truth, that's why. Your Dad would have said the opposite, less eloquently mind, but essentially – 'No woman's worth it.' I'll never understand what my Clarissa ever saw in him. He always missed the point, that man. They're *all* worth it Adam and there's always a special one who's worth more than all of the others. Problem is, you never know which one it is. Not until it's too late, anyway. I loved your Grandmother more than anything; she was as perfect for me as I think I was for her. I've never felt the need for anyone to fill the gap she left in my life. Do you see what I'm getting at here?"

Adam nodded thoughtfully.

"Good. You're young. You've got your whole life ahead of you. There's no point pining away for something that you can't have. Forget her. Remember the good bits and move on. Deep down inside, only you know what's right for you but don't live your life with regrets in your heart. Do what is right for you and don't let anyone stop you from doing what you want. I ignored much the same advice and look at me now. I'm a sad old man and I'll still be a sad old man on the day I die. Romantic, really, isn't it?" He smiled wistfully.

"I suppose," said Adam.

"Thank you for coming along with me, son. I know you don't like the game much so I really appreciate you keeping me company. You've got better things to do, I'm sure."

Adam was going to protest, to tell his granddad that he loved the game, the complexities of the rules and the gentle progress of the scores and the subtleties of the bowling and batting but he couldn't lie. "You know I absolutely have nothing better to do, not since Kath left."

The old man glanced over at his grandson. He reached out and patted Adam on the knee. "Cricket's like life, son," he said.

Adam rolled his eyes.

"No, no, you listen to me. Life keeps throwing all the balls at you and all you've got to protect yourself is a flat bit of wood. You can deflect the balls, you can ignore them if they're going to miss or you can knock them out as hard as you can but there's always just a fraction of an inch between getting away with it and having your wicket wiped-out. Then you've got the bloody fielders to complicate things – you think you've saved yourself and then one of those buggers jumps-in and catches you and you're out anyway!"

"So your advice is what exactly?"

"When life throws a ball at you, you need to do whatever it takes to protect your wicket. It doesn't matter if you sweep it or slice it or deflect it, block it, or hit it with an open bat. You have to protect that wicket with everything you have and if you're out, at least you gave it your very best."

Adam laughed gently and patted the old man's hand. "You're the best, old man," he said, "I don't know how I'd cope without you."

"You wouldn't, and less of the 'old', if you please." He turned his attention back to the pitch at the sound of another ball well hit. He clapped appreciatively, engrossed in the game once more.

Lightening flash of fear. Crack of pain. Wood on bone. Skin of marble and flesh on flesh. Escalation of moan on moan. Predator prowl through dampness. Eye glare of hate; snarl of guilt. Growl of animal thunder. The storm-head gather. Head throb of pressure; anger builds as jaws close in sexual hunger. Passion. Needle stab in larynx, breath rasps, limbs ache. Slow as death. Friction burn on soft so soft skin. Scorched insect, cockroach crunch; teeth grind. Hurricane wind plummets earthward. Leaves fall as Autumn approaches. Ice cold breath. Heat of pain. Ache of love. Sigh. Spittle glistens in wet strands of liquid silver. Night. Darkness swirls, oil on water. Rainbow dream.

"So?" said Elle.

"What?"

"What's so important that you have to force me to stay and listen to it?"

"I don't know."

"You don't know?"

"I mean I don't know where to start. How to start," he said.

"How about, and I know this may be a little obscure, but how about the beginning?"

He sniggered.

"What now?"

"You," said Adam. "You picked that up off me. Your sarcasm, I mean. You hate me so much that you've even started talking like me."

Elle shook her head slowly. "Just get on with it."

"What's the rush?"

"I have someone waiting for me, remember?"

"Yes. I remember."

"Please, just get on with what you've got to say so I can leave."

He sighed.

Chapter 6: Sex

They sighed heavily in unison. Their breath caressed each others' bodies. Sweat trickled across their partially naked forms. She moaned as her breasts pressed flat against Adam's chest. He bit her neck, the pleasure teetering on the edge of pain. She sucked his ear-lobe hungrily. She ran her tongue round the flesh of his ear, pulled at it with her teeth. She tilted her head back as his ravenous mouth worked across her throat, his bites growing more gentle. He sank his teeth into her trapezius; she cried aloud in ecstatic pain. Her nails dragged up his back and sides. Red lines glowed on his white flesh; the red sensation burned deep within him.

Her hands ran down his body. She grasped his flesh and pulled him against her. She pushed herself against his hardness and writhed. He groaned deep inside. He kneaded her breasts. He ran the tip of his tongue from her ear to her chest. He took one of her breasts in his mouth, his tongue lovingly encircling her erect nipple. She breathed inaudible words as she kissed the top of his head.

His mouth lingered. His breath was hot on her skin.

"Oh God," she sighed.

He began to work his way downward. He kissed her navel; she barely suppressed a giggle. He ran his tongue along her pant-line. He kissed the shadow smudge of soot formed by her protruding hip. She gasped. He ran his tongue back along the edge of her pubis, his finger tips hooking into the top of her pants. He tugged on them slowly and they glided willingly down the length of her legs and fell to the floor. She kicked them away.

Adam looked up at her towering nakedness; the round fullness of her breasts; the texture of her skin; the beautiful swelling of her pubic mound. She smiled down at him. Her face glowed with pleasure, her cheeks flushed. He nuzzled into the wetness between her thighs. He inhaled deeply. Her knees threatened to buckle. His tongue darted, teased, tempted. He breathed in her musk as she clasped his face to her.

"I can't," she sighed. "I can't, I'll fall. She moved across the room and sat on the edge of an armchair. She leaned back languidly and parted her knees. "Now," she said.

Adam crawled slowly towards her, undressing as he did so. She nodded.

"Not yet," he said.

He pushed his face between her thighs once more and plunged his tongue into her. He opened his mouth wide and made love to her with his lips and tongue. She clamped her eyes tight shut. Her body was growing weak with building tension. She could feel his tongue inside her, feel him manipulating her, feel his lips pressing hungrily against hers. She could feel the fiery crimson of herself and a yearning deep within. She was helpless in the face of her body's physical response.

He thought she was going to crush his head between her thighs as her body went into convulsions. He pushed his palm down on her pubis; he could feel the muscles deep inside her pulsating as waves of energy passed through her. He sat back on his haunches. Her body glistened. Her chest heaved. He wiped her wetness from his face.

He shuffled forwards, pressed himself against her. They moaned. He bent forward to kiss her. She almost devoured him in her eagerness. He pushed himself into her. She welcomed him with a groan of animal instinct. He pushed deeper and deeper into her, the heat inside her growing. She arched her back, raised her hips, to encourage him farther. He pulled away. Almost withdrew completely. He teased her with just the tip of himself, tiny thrusting movements making her groan in exasperation. He thrust deep into her again, sliding slowly all the way in. She writhed as he penetrated her fully and moaned as he withdrew.

He teased her again: tiny quick thrusts; long slow deep penetration. She could hardly breathe.

His eyes scrunched closed. He bared his teeth. A cry escaped him as he came. He collapsed against her. They embraced, pulling each other close.

They lay quietly together for eternity. Their bodies cooled, their skin dried, their hearts slowed.

"Let's go to bed," said Kath. She kissed Adam on the forehead.

"Can't," he said.

"Why not?" Her forehead creased.

"My knees," he said. "My poor broken knees."

She thrust her pelvis against him, pushing him away. "Get off me, man!"

"I'm not on your man," he said. He withdrew. Sperm oozed from her.

"Doesn't that feel horrible?"

"Yes," she said.

"You love my stickiness inside you; all warm and thick. It's *so* sexy."

"*Shut up*," she said.

She kissed him and led him upstairs.

The clenched fist struck Adam across the right temple. His head snapped back against the wall. His eyes floated in confusion. His mind refused to register. He was stunned. He tried to see who had hit him; tried to defend himself. Fist after fist struck him about the head and chest. The pounding rain and cold sharpened the pain.

It had been a long time since he had been this drunk.

"Move on," his granddad had said. "Forget her."

So that's what he was doing: drinking himself into oblivion and pissing her out of his system.

He had sat in a quiet corner of the Union Bar all evening, drinking as much as he could manage and talking to only those very few people who approached him – the two guys looking for some draw; the plain girl who had tried to chat him up; the pretty one who had given him a cigarette; and Tom. Tom, who had only come over to try and talk him out of his solitude.

"If you're going to get shit-faced, come and get shit-faced with us."

Adam shook his head. "I'm okay."

Later Adam staggered through the haze of the early morning. Shadowy figures stepped out of the mist. One of them stepped towards him. Adam squinted.

"Tom?" he slurred.

"Who the fuck is Tom?" a voiced snarled.

"Who gives a fuck?" said another.

The first shadow grabbed Adam by the throat and shoved him against a wall. His head cracked loudly on the brickwork.

"Jesus! I dunno who you are but I don't want any trouble, okay? I just want to go home."

"You're already in trouble," breathed the shadow holding him.

"What am I supposed to have done? For fuck's sake, whatever it is I'm sorry, okay?"

The shadow sniggered softly through gritted teeth.

Adam rubbed a hand across his eyes. "Please," he said. "Leave me alone."

"Pathetic, isn't it," said the shadow. A ghost of recognition passed across Adam's face. A blow caught him straight in the face. Blood filled his mouth as warm numbness spread through his nose and behind his eyes. Blood oozed like saliva from his mouth. The shadow released Adam. He turned to his friends as Adam slid drunkenly to the floor. They drifted away like wisps of smoke. "You stay away from Elle, understand?" whispered a voice from the darkness.

Rain-water seeped insipidly through his clothes, the cold gnawed at his drunkenness. He wiped his wet hair back from his forehead and peered down the empty road. The playground stood like charcoal skeletons in the artificial light; a discarded shell of laughter and happiness. This was real, the sun only hid the shadows.

Violets blossom; orgasm howl of penetration. Insect wings fold, staccato legs chittering, bone on flesh, pollen pollution. Grasping, wrenching, tearing fear. Willing resistance; welcoming rebuttal. No. No; *why eee ess*. Playing hard to get, leading and teasing, prompting and provoking arousal and refusal. Darkness enfolds, envelops, welcomes. A growl in the twilight. Loins glisten hungrily in the night. Hot-house fever; moist, earthen smell. Sweat beads in anticipation; tears of wantonness on Earth Mother thighs. Grasping, clenching, muscles move and shift, maggots beneath skin, hatching, eating from within. Chitinous jaws cut to the surface, fold back skin like wet paper. The hive erupts; black flood of beetle bodies flow and flow; insect legs scurrying across eyes, in to ears, biting, scratching, burrowing back in.

Adam sat halfway up the stairs, listening to and watching the ebb and flow of the party as it roiled beneath him. A small dog sat next to him and licked his hand. He scratched it behind the ear. He didn't know anybody here, he didn't know why he had come, but he couldn't think of a good enough reason not to when he was invited. So he sat and he watched.

He hadn't brought any beer with him because he hadn't been able to afford to bring any beer with him. He cradled the can he had been offered on arrival, swilling the warm dregs around. The volume, of both noise and people, had been steadily increasing as the night wore on and the dog was now sitting on his lap to avoid being trampled. Adam was firmly rooted to his spot and had no intention of moving, no matter how many people jostled him on their way to the bathroom. 'I am *not* going to mingle,' he thought to himself.

A hand grabbed him by the scruff of his jacket and pulled him roughly to his feet. The dog yelped and tumbled down the stairs. Adam turned furiously, knocking the hand away from his neck, to confront whoever it was who had just manhandled him.

"Shit, mate, I'm sorry," said Tom, hurrying past Adam and scooping up the dog. "I had no idea you had a dog on your lap. He held the dog in his arms, checking it over, making sure it wasn't hurt, before putting it carefully on the stairs. The dog scampered up and hid in one of the bedrooms.

Adam shook his head, disappointment written on his face.

"Hey, I said I was sorry," said Tom. "You looked so bloody miserable, sitting there on your own, that I thought I'd give you a bit of rough and tumble to liven you up a bit!" He slipped his arms around Adam and gave him a bear-hug, lifting him off his feet. Adam cried out as the air was squeezed from him. "Come on, buddy, let's get you a drink, tonight's my treat."

They lay in the darkness, entwined in each other. They breathed together, listening to each other, comfortable in their silence.

"Shit," said Kath.

"What?"

"We've left all of our clothes downstairs."

"So?"

"I don't think the others will be too happy when they come home to find your spermy clothes everywhere."

Adam sighed. "I suppose you want me to fetch them," he said.

"Hurry back." She kissed him.

When he had gone she stared out of the open window. Traffic whispered along the road. The moon struggled against the flow of clouds. Something rummaged in the bin and there was a clatter of claws on concrete. A fox barked eerily. She wondered how to tell Adam that terrific sex wasn't enough anymore; that there had to be more. She didn't feel it.

He clambered back into the bed and nuzzled up to her with a kiss. She shifted away from him.

"What?"

"You're cold," she said.

"Well warm me up then!" He snuggled closer.

She looked at him from the corner of her eye. She wished they hadn't just made love – had sex. She wished she could put this moment off.

"What is it?" he said.

He propped himself up on one elbow and looked at her.

"Tell me," he said. "What's wrong?"

"It's nothing."

"I *know* there's something wrong. Just *tell* me."

"I don't want to hurt you."

"I can take it, I'm a big boy." He smiled at her.

She lifted her eyes. He plumbed the depths of her ever varying pupils. Her iris radiated fibrils of blue and black and grey and violet. She regarded him as Eve at her second awakening might have.

"I don't want to be with you anymore," she said.

Numbness descended upon the room. A tear of sweat ran down the inside of Adam's arm.

"Why?"

"I don't know, not really, but I know I don't love you. Not anymore. Maybe not ever."

Fat tears broke from Adam's lids.

"I'm not happy anymore," she said. "I need it to end while it's still good."

"I don't understand. I don't *want* to understand. I love you, Kath." He buried his head in her bosom and wept.

"I *need* this to end before we descend into public arguments and private resentment. I don't want what we've got to go bad."

"It won't," he said.

"I think it will and, deep down, you know it's true. We're too young for this. We need to… I don't know."

"Is there somebody else?"

"No! That's not why I want to go!"

"Don't leave me," he said.

"I have to. Please don't make me hate you, Adam. Don't make it more difficult than it already is."

They lay and held each other for most of the night. They talked of the things they had done together, the things they had planned to do together. They joked about things and all the while Adam's heart was breaking. *If you love someone, let them go.* It hurt so much, like nothing he had ever felt before; like *nobody* had ever felt before.

"You shouldn't be encouraging him to come around here," said Michael.

"Adam's old enough to make up his own mind now and so are you. You could have started coming around years ago if you'd wanted to. I've always been here for both of you."

"We haven't seen you in years," said Michael. "*See you both soon*, that's what you said, and that was the last time we heard anything from you."

"There were complications."

"You were there for both of us but there were *complications*? What's that supposed to mean? Do you have any idea how much you hurt us by leaving like that? Do you?"

Granddad breathed heavily and rubbed his forehead. "It's more complicated than you know," he said. "You were both only babies really, there was nothing I could do. It was best for you if I stayed out of the way."

"You should have been there for us; been there to help Dad cope, help us cope. Our mum had just died and you thought the best thing to do was stay out of the way? How does that make sense?"

"You don't know what was happening, Michael. There are things you don't know; things that it's not my place to tell you. You just have to trust that I did what I did for the best of reasons."

"What possible reason could you have for abandoning your own grandchildren at the time when they needed you the most?" The contempt in Michael's voice was hard and sharp like flint. "I have no idea what you've been saying to Adam but I'm going to tell Dad what's been going on as soon as I get home and that'll be the end of it."

"Please, don't," said Granddad. He looked at Michael, his eyes watery. "Adam is all I have. I was hoping we could all come together again, one day, you and me and Adam. I'm sorry I hurt you so deeply, Michael, I never meant to. I really thought I was doing what was for the best; I was only doing what I was told." He met Michael's eyes, held them for a second, hoping that the thought might implant itself.

Michael turned away and scowled. "Fine. I don't really care. Just make sure Adam never says anything to Dad and stay the hell away from me."

Granddad nodded, a resigned sigh escaping from him.

Adam and Michael crept out of their room, hand in hand. They moved across the landing like the ghosts of children, insubstantial and silent. Shouts reverberated from below. Crockery smashed. Glass splintered across the floor. A shriek. The sharp retort of hand across gentle cheek. Silence descended. They breathed in unison.

"Why are Mummy and Daddy always fighting?"

"I don't know."

"This changes *nothing*!" said Clarissa Clare out of the silence below. "I still want a divorce."

A slap.

"Listen. We are *not* getting divorced. *You* are going to stay *here*, with *me*, and look after *my* children. *They* need a mother. *I* need a wife. *You* are not going to embarrass me in front of my friends and family. Do you understand?"

"I was going to take them with me," she said.

"Do you understand?"

Clarissa Clare hung her head.

"Do you?" He stepped closer to her, his chest forcing her to take a step or two back.

"Yes." Her voice was small, timid.

"What?"

"Yes," she said. "Yes, yes, yes!"

"Mikey. What's a divorce?"

"It's something you get when you don't love someone anymore. First you get married then you get divorced. It lets you go away."

"I don't want Mummy to go away."

"Me neither."

They wafted silently back into their room. Eventually they slipped into worried sleep.

Clarissa Clare's arm and hand cradled her gently swelling belly. There was comfort in this; a peacefulness, a contentedness, that she had never known before or ever expected. The aches and twinges and stabbings and shooting pains were unexpected but these moments when she was sat at rest, and she could feel the life inside her fluttering like a moth's wings on glass, made it all okay.

She felt a great happiness descend on her. She knew everything was going to be good; that her baby was well; she could feel that deep inside. This was going to be a strong child, powerful and loving. Their first child, and he, she was sure it was a 'he', would bring them so close together that they would never part.

Something moved inside her, pushed against her arm where it lay. She moved it, amused by the tiny insistence inside her and a little sad that she had caused discomfort to one so very helpless. She smiled to herself and struggled to her feet. She was still not used to the extra weight in front of her, this bump, the unfamiliarity of her own body-shape made everything strange. Whenever she walked down a busy street she found herself instinctively protecting it, shielding it from harm. Nothing was going to hurt her baby; nobody was going to bring him harm.

Adam awoke gradually. He felt dreadful. The first things to penetrate the thickness in his head were the remnants of morning – a quiet radio somewhere, the postie. Gentle conversation intruded through the open window from next door's back garden.

Adam's eyes were heavy. His mind was stuffy. He squinted through dry lids. Slowly he came to alertness and the gradual realisation of where he was – his house. Home - Granddad's house. It had been twelve months since he'd been able to talk to the old man. *We're a long time dead, lad.*

He eased one eye open. *Shit*! He hadn't had *that* much to drink; he hadn't even had *that* late a night. What the hell was wrong with him? He stretched and groaned and rubbed his face. He swung his legs out of bed and staggered sleepily to the window.

He opened the curtains. Sunlight washed over him like the tide. He frowned. Down past the bottom of the garden, up along the railway line and near the bridge, ribbons of fluorescence were strung like spider-webs. The cutting swarmed with hi-vis jackets as they milled back and forth, peering into gardens the length of this section of the line. Emergency vehicles squatted expectantly on the bridge.

Adam dressed quickly and rushed the length of the garden. He clambered through the small bushes and leaned over the fence.

"What's happened?" he said to the nearest uniform.

A constable picked his way over to where Adam was leaning over the fence.

"Good morning, sir," he said. "Are you the owner of this property?" He gestured towards Adam's granddad's house as he produced his notebook.

"Yes. What's happened?"

"We can't rightly say at the moment, sir; there appears to have been an incident under the bridge. Can you tell me where you were last night, please?"

"I was at a fancy-dress 'do' up at the Uni. Why?"

"Are you a student there?"

"I used to be; it was an open bar last night so non-students could go. Why? What's going on?"

"Just routine questions. Can you say if you noticed anything unusual in the night: noises, voices perhaps?"

"No, I don't think so." Adam frowned. "I went to bed quite early and I'd had a fair bit to drink so…"

"I see. And your name?"

Adam told him.

"To be honest," said the constable tucking his notebook away, "it looks pretty straightforward. Some young woman's decided to end it all, lay down on the track and waited for the first train through."

Adam shuddered. "Messy."

"I don't know why people feel the need to do this sort of thing. What's wrong with a good old-fashioned razor blade in the bath or a bottle of pills? At least nobody else gets traumatised that way. That poor bloody train driver has to live with this now. Poor bugger."

Adam laughed politely and strolled back to the house. He shivered.

Adam stood poised to enter his granddad's house. The last couple of visits, at Granddad's request, he had taken to walking straight around the back and going in through the kitchen. The old man never locked the door these days and was growing ever more fragile.

The day was still. A stickiness pervaded the air. The world was uncomfortably hot. Adam glanced around the garden nervously. The too long grass moved in the slight breeze. The door handle was cool in his hand. A large, old, ginger cat shifted his weight in the shadow of the shed and yawned.

A familiar sweet dread gripped his heart. He parted the sickly, violet lips of the door. The house exhaled in his face. A fat, uninterested fly buzzed past him heavily.

"Oh no," he whispered.

He knew what he was going to find yet felt compelled to see for himself; to see if it was true.

Plates lay unwashed in the kitchen sink. The living-room door was closed. It was bigger, heavier, than usual. His hand reached out like it was not a part of him; a disembodied extremity. The door was pushed open. It creaked.

Granddad sat upright in his chair; a cigar had burned right into the finger flesh and extinguished. His skin was tight and cold. The room was humid and stuffy. Adam took a heavy step. Granddad stared blankly forward through glazed eyes. A large bluebottle landed and probed the tear duct.

Adam brushed the fly away. He kissed the old man on the forehead.

"I love you, you silly old sod." He quietly telephoned for help.

"Mate, she is well out of your league. I don't think she's even playing the same sport."

Tom scowled at Adam. "I think you underestimate me, my friend. There isn't a woman on this planet who can resist my powers of seduction."

Adam raised his eyebrows. "You say that like you really believe it."

Tom nodded.

"Really?" asked Adam.

Tom nodded. "Watch and learn, son, watch and learn." He weaved his way through the milling crowd; paper plates and champagne flutes parted as he slipped by; conversation dipping as he passed and rising in his wake. He was honing-in on his target.

Black cocktail dress; tight, elegant. Simple and sophisticated. She looked like she had had the thing sprayed on.

She radiated sensuality. Men were drawn to her; bodies drawn in to her orbit. Tom ground to a halt behind her.

She turned, sensing his presence. She looked him up and down appraisingly. Her eyes locked on to his. He suddenly felt very small. Words died in his mouth.

"Yes?" she asked.

Tom looked at her shoes. "Can I get you a drink?" he asked.

She raised a full glass to her lips and took a delicate sip.

"I'm Tom, Thomas, my friends call me Tom."

"Hello, Thomas. My friends call me Connie. You may call me Constance."

Tom could feel his cheeks burning. He pointed awkwardly back towards Adam. He stepped away from her. She turned her back to him and joined the nearest conversation. Laughter tumbled from her like water over stones.

Tom flumped back in to his seat next to Adam who had a huge grin spread across his face. "Shut the fuck up," said Tom.

"I think that's possibly the funniest thing I've ever seen. What did she say?"

"She said I can call her Constance and that she finds me irresistible."

"That's not what it looked like from here," laughed Adam. He patted Tom on the shoulder. "Never mind, old friend, you can't win them all."

Tom stared across the crowded room. His eyes glistened. She was everything he had ever wanted.

"I *hate* this," said Adam.

"Don't be stupid," said Elle. "They're only my parents, for God's sake."

"*Only!*"

"All that's going to happen is we'll go in, I'll introduce you, you'll be polite, they will make small talk then we'll go up to my room and listen to some music before dinner. Easy!"

"Can't we just go straight to your room?"

"No."

"I'm just so nervous! I'm an adult, for fuck's sake, and I feel like I'm fourteen again. This whole 'meet my parents' thing makes me feel genuinely ill!"

"And be careful what you say. Please. Think before you open your mouth. And don't blaspheme!"

"Or what? They'll crucify me?"

"Correct."

As they entered the house Adam could hear voices from inside. His stomach gurgled uncomfortably. He swallowed. He felt a light prickling at his armpits as he broke into a sweat.

Elle shouted excitedly as she trotted in to the lounge. She clasped Adam's hand tightly and dragged him along in her wake. Two faces looked at him as they entered the room. Mr Chamberlain rose.

"Mum, Dad, this is Adam. Adam, this is my mum and dad."

"I'm David," said Mr Chamberlain, his hand outstretched, "and my wife is Laura."

"Hi," said Adam shaking his hand.

"Would you like a glass of beer?" said Mr Chamberlain.

"Fuck yes!" said Adam into the now-stony silence of the Chamberlain household.

Chapter 7: Union

Adam swayed in stony silence at the front of the hall. Grey light from an overcast sky filtered through the blinds. A burning sensation swept through his stomach; his lids felt puffed up as if they belonged to someone else. There was a slight pressure at his elbow where Tom offered support. He tugged at his tie. His saliva felt thick and unpleasant.

He glanced over his shoulder. A small group of mostly unfamiliar faces ranged out behind him. Mr and Mrs Chamberlain sat close together; he whispered something to her. Adam thought of all the people he wished could be there. He winced at the pain in his ribs and looked round angrily.

Elle scowled at him and gestured to the front. She looked beautiful. She peered at him through her veil. Her dress was narrow and understated; the colour of pearls. It flattered her perfectly. She wore a small corsage with violet ribbon on her breast.

"I do," he said.

He looked at his feet then back at Elle. Kath flashed through his mind: she was there before him, her hair tumbling across her shoulders. She smiled at him through the rain. She leaned forward to kiss him, stopped, then mouthed an apology. She retreated into darkness. Elle smiled at him as he placed the delicate golden band on her finger. He lifted her veil and kissed her.

"I love you, Mrs Clare," he said.

"I love you too, Mr Clare."

The small gathering left the innocuous registry office as one, barely waiting until they were outside before they let fly with the confetti. The kaleidoscopic swirl of paper danced madly around them like psychedelic snow; like the thoughts in Adam's head – the colours flashed in the dull light, snatching this way and that in the gusting wind.

Laughter and shouts mounted one upon the other, a cacophony of happiness some of which was obviously forced. People pushed and scuffled good humouredly to congratulate the married couple, to kiss them, to hold them.

"Well done!"

"…died in…"

"Congratulations!"

"…back at the house…"

"…beautiful"

"…and plenty of it…"

"…his father?"

"…his father…"

"No…"

The group separated out into their cars and headed straight back to the Chamberlains'. Adam's relief was palpable. The morning had gone without a hitch; no-one had passed out or been sick on the registrar. Mrs Chamberlain had just shot him a look that threatened everything. He climbed into the back of the car with Elle and grinned broadly as they pulled away.

"Okay, look, I get that you don't like him, okay? But he's my best friend. We've been mates since Uni, we've been through a lot together. Well, he's been through a lot since I've known him and I've always been there for him. You not liking him is never going to change that."

Connie snuggled in to Tom's chest. Her delicate arms held him, her fingers teasing his ribs. "I know that. I'm not asking you to stop being his friend, that would be ridiculous."

Tom kissed her softly, like she might break.

"I just don't understand him, I suppose," she said. "I don't understand what's going on inside that head of his. There's something behind his eyes that makes me uncomfortable, something that concerns me."

"There's nothing 'behind his eyes.' I don't even know what you mean by that."

"What I mean is that you've known him and Elle for a long time, since they first got together, in fact, but when was the last time you had a conversation with her?"

Tom frowned. "I don't understand what you're getting at. Elle's a very private person, always has been."

"So private, in fact, that I've never even met her, let alone had a conversation with her. As you said, you've known her since the very start of their relationship and yet she didn't even come to our wedding."

"I told you, Adam said she was ill. It happens, people get sick."

"She never seems to leave the house. She doesn't seem to have any friends. I've seen this sort of thing before, you know? He seems like a nice enough sort on the surface but there's a darkness there, Tom."

"You're worrying over nothing. Adam and Elle love each other very much; they're very private people is all. Elle has this artistic streak in her that means she submerges herself in whatever it is that she's doing. She doesn't need other people to validate her existence. They are happy, alone, together. That's all."

Connie pulled him tight to her. "I hope you're right, Tom, I really do."

"Pardon?" said Mrs Chamberlain.

"I said me and Adam, Adam and I are getting married." Elle bounced excitedly.

Mrs Chamberlain looked at her stony-faced.

Elle's excitement washed away. Her face fell. She grasped Adam's hand tightly.

Mr Chamberlain rose. He smiled with a sideways glance to his wife. "I'm extremely

happy for you both," he said.

"Oh Daddy!" Elle flung her arms around his neck.

The lounge door slammed shut as Mrs Chamberlain left the room. "I'll crack open the champagne shall I?" she shouted from the hall.

"I *hate* her sometimes," said Elle.

"Don't you mind your mother, she'll come round. As soon as she sees how happy you two are together she'll be here. This is the day she's been looking forward to most since you were born – her baby's wedding day – she wouldn't miss it for the world."

"And what if I don't want her there?" said Elle.

"Don't be daft," said Adam. "of course you'll want her to be there, she's your

mother."

Elle threw herself into a chair, exasperated.

"I hate the way she treats you, like you're pond-scum."

"I don't think you should speak about your mother while I'm present," said Mr Chamberlain. "I'll go and calm her down and see what I can do."

Mr Chamberlain left them together, a knowing smile playing across his lips.

"She's not *that* bad," said Adam as the door closed.

"She *is* though, that's the point. She's really two-faced about you. She'll be really polite while you're here and then stick the knife in when you go. She just *pisses me off*!"

"I'm not bothered so why should you be? I let it all wash over me. The less hassle the better."

"She's never forgotten you swearing, never forgiven you either. Silly cow!"

The door swung slowly open and Mr and Mrs Chamberlain stepped calmly into the room. Mr Chamberlain urged his wife forward. She reluctantly approached the couple.

She scowled at Adam. "I apologise," she said. "I am going to try and stop reacting like this. It's your life, Elle, as you're so fond of reminding me, and as long as you're happy then I'm happy too." She glanced at her husband. "I think you're making a very poor choice but I won't interfere. I hope for both your sakes that everything works out and you'll be very happy together." She bent forward and kissed Elle lightly on the cheek.

"Thank you, Mummy." Relief and resentment mingled in her voice.

Blood stench on breath; drool ooze from hot, slavering jaws. The beast shifts in the shadows. A growl rumbles in its chest, thunder on the tracks, tectonic plates shift; eyes glint with cold, dark hunger. It lopes off into the night; moonlight shimmering on steaming shanks, muscles rippling tightly; fury bound in flesh.

"It's such a waste," said Laura later that night. "My beautiful little girl getting married to that…" She sighed, unable to express her disapproval. "He's such a horrible boy."

"We've been through this already, darling. You handled things rather badly earlier. We knew this would come sooner or later."

"I know, but when she finally said the words I got so angry with her; with myself."

"Why with yourself?" David sat on the edge of the bed.

"Well, we'd already agreed to not interfere if she decided she wanted to marry him, that we'd only succeed in pushing her farther away if we tried to oppose her. 'Let her make her own mistakes.' Then I go and react like that. I felt awful." She climbed into bed and turned the light off.

"Too late now," he said. "Try not to worry about it."

"Oh, alright then," she said, as if it was that easy.

"Granddad, why do you love violets so much?" Adam knelt on the grass at the edge of the flower beds; a large plastic tray of small flowers sat beside him. He held a trowel in his right hand.

"They're such beautiful, delicate, little things," said his granddad. He sat on the garden bench. He placed his cricket bat and oiling cloth gently on the seat next to a tin of linseed oil. "Each tiny flower holds the sun at its centre. I wanted to call your mother 'Violet' but your grandmother wouldn't allow it."

Adam looked at the tiny plants; the deep blue petals shifted in the breeze, the yellow centres holding secrets and promises.

"They look so innocent and pure, don't they?" his granddad said. "But they're little temptresses; luring bees in to pollinate them. That's why your grandmother didn't like it as a name."

"Don't all flowers do that?"

His granddad laughed. "Yes," he said. He picked up his bat and continued to oil the wood. "I think you're probably still too young to understand what I mean but violets pretend to be something they're not. I love the delicate deceit of them." He laughed again. "I don't know what I'm talking about, lad, pay me no mind. They're pretty little flowers and I love them for that alone. Now, make sure you're spacing them out properly or they'll all wither and die."

"I'm old enough," said Adam. "I'm not a child anymore." He thrust his trowel into the dark soil and continued to plant his granddad's flower-border. He loved doing this – helping, digging, planting, making things grow; especially now that his granddad couldn't do it for himself.

"What happened to your knees, Granddad?"

His granddad brandished his cricket bat. "This bloody thing," he said. "I took a fast bowl right in the kneecap when I wasn't much older than you are now. Shattered it." He pointed the bat at Adam. "Always wear pads, my boy, even when you're just messing about in the park. It healed, of course, but it was never the same. Eventually it just wore-out completely; if I knelt down beside you now I wouldn't be able to get back up again and it would hurt like buggery! Stupid, isn't it? That one decision to not wear pads on that day has had an impact on both our lives."

Adam nodded as he planted another flower.

"These violet delights have violet ends," his granddad said, chuckling at his own joke. "I'll make us a cup of tea. You finish-up there and come on in."

Adam watched as his granddad limped up the garden path, cricket bat over one shoulder; a lonely, sad old man.

Elle looked flustered. Her hair was awry as she opened the door. Charcoal smeared her fingers; a light smudge swept across her brow where she had brushed her hair away. She looked nervously over her shoulder. A ring of violet bruises was pinned upon her arm; she tugged nervously at the sleeve of her t-shirt, trying to hide the marks.

"Hello, Elle," said Trudi.

"Oh, hi! Come on in; you scared the life out of me." She chuckled breathlessly. "I thought it was Adam."

Trudi frowned as she crossed the threshold. "What do you mean?"

Elle rolled her eyes skyward. "He doesn't like me sketching."

"Tell him to sod off!"

Elle laughed. "I used to find it really relaxing but now…" Her voice trailed off. "I just seem to be more uptight these days. I might give it up all together. Give all my stuff to charity."

"Don't you dare!" said Trudi. "It's all you've got left. The only reason you're so uptight these days is because of the way that bloody husband of yours treats you. Don't you *dare* give it up."

Elle bit her bottom lip. She hesitated. "I don't enjoy it the way I used to. My art used to be my life but now… Adam said '*If you don't enjoy doing something then stop doing it.*'"

"*Adam* said! Jesus Elle, use your brain. It's *because* of him that you don't enjoy it anymore."

"That's not true; he's just very perceptive."

"Persuasive you mean, I've seen the bruises."

Elle blinked slowly.

Trudi sighed heavily. "Look, *I* think it's about time you left the bastard. I know he hits you. You can't honestly expect me to believe the excuses you come up with – how many times can you walk into a door for fuck's sake? Do yourself a favour, Elle, and leave him."

"I love my husband." Elle glanced towards their wedding photo. "I love him very much. He only does what he does because he loves me; he's trying to help me." She glared at Trudi with fire in her eyes. "He was right about you, too. You're just jealous of what we've got; because nobody wants you. I hate the way you keep having your snide little digs at him, at our relationship. It's pathetic."

"Elle…"

"Shut up! I don't think it's a good idea for you to come around here anymore."

"But Elle…"

"Until you learn to accept that I'm happy with my husband you should stay away."

"I'm sorry Elle, I really am."

Elle opened the door for her in silence. Trudi held Elle's fingers tenderly between her own. She kissed Elle softly.

"If you ever need me, best friend, you know where I am."

Elle walked to where her pad lay on the table; the partially complete portrait of Trudi stared mournfully off the page. She pulled it slowly and deliberately out of its binding, crouched down in front of the fire and slid it in amongst the hot coals. She blinked twice as it roared away into ash. She washed the charcoal from her hands then surrendered to domesticity.

Elle watched Adam through the kitchen window. Water steamed in the sink, hot and soapy, ethereal wafts of moisture rising, ghostly, like hair in water. It burned; her hands reddening as she held them beneath the suds.

She could see him pottering around, bending occasionally to pull a weed, tending to what he still saw as his grandfather's flowerbeds. The hosepipe hung lazily from his left hand, his thumb planted firmly over the end, controlling the flow and spray of water. She could tell that he loved this garden, loved what it represented, what it stood for. It was Adam's own memorial to the man he had loved the most.

She refocused on what she was doing and swished the crockery in the sink, her thoughts wandering as she placed each plate carefully on the draining-board. It wasn't so long ago that they were being swept along by the romance of it all; the heady days of honeymoon and constant lust. She tingled at the thought. How quickly things became ordinary; how quickly they had settled in to a routine of regular bedtimes and early mornings and sex on a Sunday.

She flinched as Adam pressed close to her from behind. "Jesus!" she said, almost dropping a plate.

"No, it's just me," said Adam.

"I didn't hear you come in," she said.

"You were miles away," he said in to the nape of her neck.

Elle hunched her shoulders. Electricity sparked down her spine. "I was just thinking," she said.

"Yes?" he asked. He placed his hands firmly on her hips. He kissed her neck and ears; delicate bites making her gasp quietly.

"Of how ordinary things have become," she said.

He slid his arms around her; his left hand snaking over her stomach, fingers finding the opening of her blouse.

Her breath caught in her throat. She could feel him pressing into her from behind. He pulled her to him. The pressure of his hand through the fabric of her jeans was making the heat rise within her. She could feel his other hand moving over her, from her breasts to her stomach to the small of her back; kneading, caressing, pawing at her body.

She reached down, hot water dripping from her fingertips, and unzipped her jeans. His hand slid inside, probing her, parting her. She moaned his name. She could feel him fumbling, struggling, to pull her jeans down; she wriggled helpfully and let them fall to the floor.

"Can't you see I'm busy," she whispered.

He smelled of earth: musty and musky. He grabbed her by the back of the neck and forced her to bend forward. She could feel him pressing against her, hear his broken breathing. She reached down between her thighs and guided him inside her.

His right hand reached round and tightened on her throat, pulling her upright. She straightened, the front wall of her insides exploding with sensation at the sudden stimulation. She could feel him, hot and hard, inside her, the angle tight and awkward. Blood pounded in her temples. It was difficult to breathe. Heat was building inside her. His hand was tight on her, fingers digging into her windpipe. Spasmodic movement. Shallow gasps. He relaxed his grip on her.

Elle leaned her elbows on the edge of the sink, staring into the steaming water. Her hands were red, scalded by the burning water. Her pulse slowed; semen ran down her thigh.

"Yes," said Adam. "Very ordinary,"

She could hear the smile in his voice. He nuzzled in to her back, his arms wrapped lovingly around her. She took his hand in hers and bit him affectionately on the knuckles.

"Adam! No!" said Elle.

"Why not?" He lay her down on the bed.

"Because we've got a house full of people."

"Don't you worry about them." He ran his hand up her thigh, under her dress.

"You'll ruin my dress."

"No I won't." He lifted her wedding dress up around her waist. "They're all too busy enjoying themselves downstairs and they think we're up here getting changed anyway. We won't be disturbed."

She bit her bottom lip as he reached down between their bodies and pulled her underwear to one side. They made soft, slow, gentle love in the afternoon of their marriage day. Chattering voices reached up to them through the floorboards. Their stifled passion weighed them down in their love for one another.

Adam listened to the click of approaching heels. He turned to the shelves behind him and fumbled nervously with a box of stationery. The door opened; Catherine stepped in to the store-room. She pushed the door closed behind her as she leaned back against it, reached over her shoulder and clicked the lock in to place.

"Oh! Hello!" she said.

Adam swallowed nervously. He moved towards her. Her hands snaked around his head and pulled his lips to hers. She kissed him hungrily. Her breath became a deep sigh as she pushed her body against his. He could feel her thrusting her pelvis forward; he held her by the waist, pulling her tightly to him.

She tilted her head back as his mouth explored her throat and neck. He bit at a muscle and she groaned through clenched teeth. "Gently," she said breathlessly. Adam ran his hands over her body; up her back, around her ribs and to her breasts. He could feel her arousal through the cloth. He unbuttoned her top, his fingers fumbling at the buttons. She pulled his head to her bosom.

He kissed the heaving flesh, kneading her body; he forced his hands under the cotton and wire and hoisted her bra up, freeing her breasts. He cupped the weight of them, scooping each nipple in turn in to his hot mouth, teasing and nibbling and sucking them to hard points.

He slid his hand down her stomach, around her hips and pulled her forward, his fingers digging in to the ample flesh of her buttocks. His hand strayed farther down to the back of her thigh. She moaned quietly and kissed the top of his head. He moved his hand around and up the front of her leg, up and under the skirt she had carefully selected to wear that day.

He touched her lightly between the thighs, his palm cradling the hot dampness nestling there. She breathed out endlessly. He applied gentle pressure with his palm and she began to move against him. He kissed her, smothering her moans with his mouth. She could barely breathe. He felt her shudder against him, felt her knees weaken; a red rose blossomed across her chest.

He kissed her down across her stomach, butterflies twitching beneath the touch of his lips. She shook her head as he knelt before her, looking up. He nodded. He nuzzled in to the musk between her thighs.

"Oh, God!" she whispered. She pushed back against the locked door. Her hands grasped clumsily at the shelves for support. Adam pulled her underwear to one side and teased her clitoris with the tip of his tongue. She bit down hard on her knuckles to stifle a cry. His fingers probed at her, pushing gently in to her, seeking that secret spot at the front. Deeper, bit by bit; her pelvis angled forward. He felt the ridges beneath his fingertip and pushed. His tongue circled her clitoris as his finger slipped to and fro along the hard lines inside her. He could feel her tightening inside; her legs collapsing and locking rigid. Her breath came in ragged, staccato gasps.

Adam stood and kissed her, his mouth wet with her juices. "Turn around," he said.

"We can't," she said. "We'll get caught."

"Turn around," he said. He undid his trousers. She reached down and grabbed him firmly. He knocked her hand away and forced her to turn around. She bent forward and braced herself against the door as she pulled her skirt up high around her waist. He pulled her pants down roughly and forced her legs wider as he nestled in behind her. She reached down between her thighs and guided him in to her. He thrust at her; she cried out and bit her lip.

He held her tight to him by the hips, one hand cupping her breast. He thrust at her again; hot seed spurting into her. He held her upright. Catherine giggled. Someone tried to open the door. They turned to face one another; panic raced across their faces. They tucked their clothes in and straightened themselves out. The door rattled again; a key slid in to the lock. Catherine pulled the door open nonchalantly as Adam hoisted a box off a shelf.

"I'm so sorry," she said as they left. "I must have caught the lock as I pulled the door closed behind me."

"Well *fuck off* then!" said Joseph Clare.

"Is that the best you can do, you sad old tosser?"

Joseph grabbed Adam by the shoulders and threw him backwards. Adam fell to the sofa and immediately sprang back to his feet.

"*Go on* then! *Hit* me! Give me an excuse, you *prick*! Just *fucking* once, come on!"

Joseph raised his hand. Adam glared at him in defiance. Michael stepped between the two of them; his face was unreadable.

"I think you'd better go, Adam," he said.

Adam raised his brows incredulously.

"Go. Now," said Michael.

"You're taking *his* side? After *everything* we've seen him do, you're taking *his* side?"

"I'm not taking anybody's side; there are no sides. Dad is all we have left."

"I'd rather have nothing," said Adam.

He pushed past his brother and father and stormed angrily out of the house. He did not look back.

Adam sat quietly at the table. He held a well-thumbed novel in one hand, his thumb pressed firmly in to the gutter to keep his page. He picked his drink up, absent-mindedly, with the other; he did not take his eyes off the page as he sipped from the tall glass. A dribble of beer ran from the corner of his mouth. He placed the glass back on the table and wiped his mouth with the back of his free hand.

"Any good?"

Adam looked up from his book. A burly, broad, figure stood silhouetted by the light streaming through the open bar doors. Adam squinted against the glare. "What?" he asked.

"The book; is it any good?"

Adam glanced down. "Do I know you?"

"Not really; I'm Tom. We met the other day, remember? I was being a bit of a dick; do you mind if I sit here?" He sat down opposite Adam.

Adam looked around at the virtually empty Uni bar. "It doesn't look like you have much choice."

Tom took a deep drink and placed his glass on the table. "What do you mean?"

"Nothing. I remember you now; you're one of the rugby crowd."

Tom nodded. "Spot on!" he said. "So, is it any good?"

Adam waved the book dismissively in the air. "Jane Austen," he said. "The over-privileged wittering of the conceited middle-class. If she was a dog, she'd be a French Poodle. I hate it. The whole time I'm reading it, I'm thinking: 'Why should I give a shit?'"

Tom laughed. "Set text?"

"I wouldn't be reading the bloody thing if it wasn't. Everybody else seems to love it but I think that says more about them than it says about me; hiding their heads in the sands of historical irrelevancies rather than looking at something that might actually matter."

Tom raised his eye-brows. "But you know you're better off keeping your mouth shut and getting on with it rather than saying anything to challenge what *they* say?"

"There's no point, is there? If you disagree with a lecturer, or an accepted 'wisdom', especially in an assignment, you lose marks. Every time! You're better off just writing what they want to hear and collecting your marks."

"Hear, hear!" said Tom. He raised his glass in salute. Adam raised his in response; they clinked together and both boys drank.

"You *were* being a bit of a dick," said Adam.

Tom nodded.

"But, to be fair, I was being an uptight little prick."

Tom nodded.

"I was way out of my depth and felt it," said Adam.

"No worries," said Tom. He glanced over his shoulder at the sound of someone coming in to the bar. "Here we go," he said.

Adam looked up; a short, blonde, girl was being served at the bar.

"Here's today's bit of totty. Buckle-up, it's going to be a bumpy ride!" He laughed as he swaggered over to the bar. The girl slipped her arm around his waist and kissed him on the chin.

Adam shook his head and went back to his book.

The sun was shining. A gentle wind wafted softly across the warm ground. Grass danced. Adam lay on the ground, dozing. His eyes were closed against the heat; he could see his eyelids glowing red. He rolled over on to his stomach. He cracked his eyes open slowly, purple blind spots danced before him. A vast field of small violet flowers surrounded him. He wiped the sweat from his forehead.

The noise started softly, slowly encroaching on his perceptions. He frowned. He could see for miles; there was no sign of anything. The noise grew; it swelled until it was the only thing there was. It was like a heavy industrial engine, deafening, vibrating through his chest cavity. Adam clamped his hands over his ears. He tried to hide his face in the ground.

A section of grass near his elbow was scuffed up like a badly placed carpet tile; dislodged when he had rolled over. He reached out to it. He picked at the earth like it was a scab; dry flakes of dirt fell away. He dug his fingers in and pulled back the ground like an old piece of linoleum.

The machinery beneath him ground on. Huge cogs and wheels and chains rumbled on relentlessly, oblivious to his intrusion. An abyss, crammed with this machinery, fell vertiginously away. He pulled the ground back farther and climbed inside.

The machinery stopped.

He looked up. The sky was nothing but a tiny glint of light far above him; a pinprick star. Two stars. Huge glittering eyes stared down at him like he was bacteria. A voice called his name. He squinted into the darkness, only able to see the gears closest to him. The voice called again. Over there, in the machine. What was that?

He clambered through the metal tangle of industrial chaos. He shouted out. He struggled through the gears becoming covered in grease and oil. A child's body lay crushed and mangled; blood dripped eerily. The child's head hung limply, swinging like a pendulum. Adam struggled with the cog, desperate to save the child. He pulled at the teeth, his hands unable to get a grip. He took hold of the child and pulled; a piece of material tore free. Adam reached out and lifted the child's head.

He looked deep into his own dead eyes. The child winked and laughed as the engine started once more. Adam screamed as he was crushed by the indifferent machinery.

Adam screamed as he woke. The pain in his stomach was more intense than when it had burst in the gears. He groaned and sat forward. Elle stirred beside him. He clamped a hand across his mouth and ran for the bathroom.

"The honeymoon's over now, Adam," she muttered with a heavy tongue. "I can't still be giving you bad dreams."

"I've just been sick," he said. His face dripped with water.

Elle sat up.

"I've been sick," he repeated.

"I told you not to eat that local stuff." She laughed sleepily.

His hand caught her full across the cheek, the sound like the crack of a whip. "Don't laugh at me."

Elle sat upright in bed, stunned at the unfamiliar pain in her cheek. Adam leaned towards her. She flinched. He looked at her guiltily.

"I'm sorry, baby, I'm so sorry. I have no idea where that came from. I'm not feeling very well." He reached out to her tentatively and pulled her into his arms. He kissed the top of her head and apologised and apologised. His kisses transitioned slowly from apologetic to insistent.

"I'm sorry, baby," he said as they made love. "I love you so much."

"I know what you've done; you're wasting your time."

Elle frowned. She wanted to leave, to run for the car waiting for her outside.

"Your art; you've gone and got an agent or something haven't you?"

She nodded. "A waste?"

"Yeah, don't you remember why you gave it up in the first place?"

"Yes I do!"

"Because you didn't enjoy it!" he said.

"No!" she said. "I gave it up because I didn't enjoy rushing to do what I wanted to do before you got home. I gave up everything I loved because I loved you."

He laughed. "If you say so."

"And this is all you have to say? That you think I'm wasting my time?"

"I found some of your stuff."

"Stuff?"

"Brushes. Canvases. Old paintings. I burned them."

"Why?"

"I didn't know you were coming back, did I." He smiled.

"You're evil, Adam, pure evil."

"I don't think so. I've never walked out on somebody who needed me, somebody who depended on me, without an explanation."

"What *are* you talking about?"

"You! I *needed* you, you left me. No warning, no discussion. Nothing. I'm casually informed, in my own house, by a *fucking* letter. A letter! For fuck's sake Elle. I didn't know where you'd gone, if you were okay. You told me *nothing*. *That's* evil!"

"I was scared of you, Adam. I thought you were really going to hurt me. Of course I didn't want you to know where I was, I'm not an idiot."

"Hurt you?"

"Yes," she said. "Either me…" She hesitated. "Either me or the baby."

"Baby?"

"Yes," she said, a barely noticeable quiver in her voice.

Chapter 8: Violence

"Granddad?" Adam quivered with the cold.

"What is it?"

"I want to go to the toilet," Adam said. He looked up at his grandfather with large, round scared eyes, clutching at the front of his trousers.

"Can you wait?"

"No, Granddad. I want one now."

His granddad looked around furtively; the bowed heads of the other mourners formed a staccato of grief behind him.

"Come on then," he whispered. "But be quiet."

They shuffled off the end of the pew and left the church quickly. The wind cut through them, whipping their hair roughly about their faces. Granddad hurried Adam around to the side of the church in search of a sheltered corner. They darted into a small alcove where a drain squatted subversively.

"I can do it myself, Granddad," said Adam. The indignation in his voice rose as the old man tried to help him with his zip.

"Sorry, I forgot."

Granddad looked out over the moss enshrouded gravestones. It pleased him to see so much life thriving in a place of grief and pain and death.

"Granddad?" Adam said, trying not to splash his nice shiny shoes.

"Yes?"

"Where's Mummy really gone?"

The old man retrieved the already half-smoked cigar from his jacket pocket and lit it. "What do you mean?"

"Well, that's not really Mummy in that box and it wasn't really Mummy in bed last week. So where has she gone?"

"Good question." Granddad ran his fingertips across a smooth, freshly shaved, cheek. "You're right, of course, that wasn't *really* your mother, it was just her body. Some people think we have souls and it's our souls who make us who we are. When we die the soul leaves our bodies. Like when a snake sheds its skin…"

"What's a soul?"

"It's what makes us alive."

"What do they look like?" Adam said as he zipped himself up.

The old man frowned. "It looks like a pigeon. But invisible."

Adam nodded in quiet satisfaction. "So, where do they go when they leave?"

Adam's granddad looked at the sky in disbelief, sighed, and crouched down before the boy. He stubbed his cigar out on the damp concrete and looked Adam right in the eye. "I don't know," he said. "Nobody knows and I don't suppose anybody ever really will. Different people believe different things: some people think that when we die, if we've been good, we go to Heaven to live with God; others think we are reborn as a new person and we can live all over again; some people think we are reborn as animals. Some people believe that there's nothing when we die, that we're just dead. Do you understand?"

"I think so. What do you think?"

"I like to think that when we die we go to a better place; somewhere full of light and love and warmth. Somewhere where we can just be happy. If somebody wants to call that Heaven, that's fine by me." His lip trembled slightly as he touched Adam lightly on the head.

"Me too," said Adam. He clutched his granddad's hand tightly and they returned to the service inside.

Elle was furious. She had never felt rage like it before. It burned her from within, incandescent fury boiled from her. She had lost all control. She had no idea how she had reached this point, no idea of the steps she must have taken to get here, the path she must have been forced down but it had begun with Adam's confession. This moment in time was all that mattered now. This was all that had ever existed.

Shards of shattered crockery crunched underfoot. Her lips were white, all colour drained from her as adrenaline washed through her body like a tsunami. She reached over and hoisted the cast-iron sauce-pan. Each moment seemed lost in eternity; a sequence of events rushing past her in a red-shift blur, hurtling towards inevitable oblivion. The crack of plates; the scream of pain; food on walls, boiling water and scalding flesh.

She switched the sauce-pan into her right hand and swung it at Adam's head. The trajectory was perfect. The staccato sequence of still images linked together perfectly. She could see the sauce-pan, attached to her arm like it was part of it, curving gracefully, majestically, towards him. The disjointed sequence was coming together in the final impact – the splash of red and his body crumpling to the floor. His egg-shell fragile skull caving in, shards of bone driving in to his brain; soft, grey tissue making way, parting like a flower opening its petals, for needle-sharp splinters of ivory. This was everything. This was forever. If this happened, she would kill him.

His poor soft body falling helpless before her. The weight of the metal in her hand. Standing triumphant over his still twitching corpse. He would never make her this angry ever again. Never again. Never.

She shifted her shoulder, changed the angle of her weapon marginally. Was it too late? If it made contact with his head... The dull metal glanced off his shoulder as he tried to move out of the way; it brushed against his cheek, an angel's kiss, as it swung past him. Elle was pulled off-balance by the weight of it. Adam shoved her away from him. The sauce-pan clattered uselessly to the floor.

"Fuck me! What the fuck do you think you're doing? You could have fucking killed me!"

Elle looked at her hands as they lay splayed out before her on the floor. She nodded. "If you hadn't moved..." she sobbed. She allowed him to scoop her up in his arms; she was terrified by what she had almost done.

Adam smiled. A small tear edged its way across his face. "Gone to a better place? Worm-food, plain and simple."

A tiny landslide of earth tumbled into the open grave.

Now he had no-one. Everybody he had ever loved had left him: his mother, his lover, and now his granddad.

"My life is just one long bereavement, people are always leaving in one way or another," he said.

He glanced down at his mud spattered shoes. "Shit! I'm going to have to polish them *again*."

"I wouldn't worry about them too much if I was you."

Adam's head snapped round. Who the hell would talk to him at a time like this? He had isolated himself for the whole service; stood at the back and to one side; spoken to people only when he absolutely had to; had waited until everybody had drifted away from the graveside. Now there was only him left; him and his granddad and the men with the shovels.

"Sorry," said Kath. "I didn't mean to startle you."

"What are you doing here?"

"Tom told me what had happened. I just came to, well, you know. I've been watching from back there." She pointed to a small copse on the edge of the church grounds. "I didn't want to cause any fuss."

Adam scowled at her.

"With us I mean. I didn't know how you'd feel about me turning up."

"You shouldn't have worried about that."

She shrugged.

"How are things with you?" he asked.

"Okay, I suppose. You?"

He simply looked at the grave.

There was a long awkward pause.

"Are you seeing anyone yet?" he asked. His voice was casual but his eyes betrayed his discomfort.

"No. Are you?" She was hopeful; a need for him to have moved on, to have left her behind.

"No," he said.

Kath stepped forward and dropped her carnation into the grave before them. "I still love you, you know," she said.

"I know," he said. "Are you coming back for a drink?"

She took his hand gently and looked deep into his eyes. She rubbed his fingers softly between hers and kissed him on the cheek. "I don't think that would be a good idea, do you?"

He shook his head ruefully. He watched her as she walked slowly away, her hips swinging. Only once did she look back.

"See," said Adam to his granddad. He turned homeward.

"What happened to you the other night?" asked Tom.

"When?"

"After the Hallowe'en do. I lost you when I went after that girl with the breasts."

"I hung around for a while after you disappeared but when you didn't come back I wandered off home. It wasn't a problem, was it?"

Tom shook his head. "Not at all, just wondering. Have you heard the news?" he asked.

"About what?"

"That suicide behind your place."

"Oh, that! Of course I've heard, it was behind my place. I spoke to one of the coppers the morning it happened."

"Did you manage to get anything out of him?"

"He was pretty cagey to be honest; he said it *appeared* to be a suicide."

Tom leaned forward conspiratorially. "So it might not have been…"

"That's all he said and I suppose they have to say that until after the coroner's inquest." He took a sip of his drink and looked around at the almost deserted pub.

"Well," Tom said, "*I heard that this woman actually dangled from the bridge and dropped as the train came through!*" He slapped his palm down on the table-top. "*Splatt!*" He laughed.

Adam grimaced.

"Nothing ever seems to happen around here anymore," said Tom. "In the time since we finished Uni everything has suddenly become so boring. My life has turned into *nothing*. I go to work, I go to the pub, I go to sleep, I get out of bed and repeat. It's *shit!*"

"I know what you mean, apart from the work bit."

They looked mournfully into their drinks.

"Shall we go down and have a look later? There might be something worth seeing," said Tom.

"Okay."

They sat quietly.

"God this is depressing," said Tom.

"What?"

"*This*. Life. I don't know why we bother."

"Thinking about catching a train?"

"You're a sick fuck," said Tom.

"Have you been back up to Uni lately?"

Tom shook his head.

"I was wondering if the bar up there was still open."

"Probably not, it's the summer break. If it is it'll only be full of the usual knobs!"

"A sad, sad day," Adam nodded. "Let's go somewhere else."

They downed their drinks, slammed the empty glasses down on the table and left.

Adam felt hot, flushed, like he was burning-up from the inside. He could feel his cheeks glowing. The corridor outside the classroom was bustling; bodies milled and ground against each other. He pressed himself back against the wall. His bag was heavy with books; he held it in front of him at waist height, hiding his engorged, throbbing, penis.

A cacophony of voices chattered and screeched around him, penetrating his thoughts. Hot bodies pushed against him, bodies steaming with rain-water, the smell of wet hair pervading everywhere. His eyes wandered up their legs, golden hair downy and soft; up past their scuffed knees; he lingered on the taut flex of thighs in too short skirts. A breast brushed against his arm, an unselfconscious girl not yet accustomed to the space taken up by her budding womanhood. His breath caught in his throat. Fiona was standing opposite him.

He tried to avert his eyes but he was enraptured. The curve of her calf led his eye up her leg, into the shadow behind her knee and upward; the muscles in her thighs shifted under her skin as she moved her weight from foot to foot; they disappeared under the pleats of her skirt just where they were fattening and fleshing out, tantalising. He lingered on the curvature of her buttocks as she turned. He blinked. Her pelvis beckoned to him, the high, defined points welcoming the shape of him; just perfect for his body to nestle into.

A hint of her stomach, just visible through damp fabric, teased him; the muscles there quivered. He followed the line of buttons up to her chest. The button on her blouse had popped open; she hadn't noticed it or him. Her nipple thrust against the thin fabric and when she turned sideways he could see the goose-bumps as they pimpled across the top of her breast. He swallowed. He could see the flesh there wobble slightly, an unfamiliar, enticing movement. Hypnotic. What it must be like to touch them. His penis throbbed. It hurt so much; it felt like a steel rod.

Two of the boys broke into a scuffle next to him. He turned away from them just as somebody rushed past him; his bag caught on theirs. He clutched at it desperately as it pulled away. The strap slipped from his shoulder. His bag fell, twisting him around.

"Oh my God!"

Adam dropped into a crouch, hunching over his bag, hiding his tumescence but much too late.

"He's got a massive stiffy!"

A foot hooked his bag away; it skittered away down the corridor. Rough hands grabbed him by the arms and pulled him to his feet. Adam tried to lift his legs, to twist himself, to hide it. Whoops and screams went up. There were gasps of horror from the girls as they pretended not to look.

"He's a pervert!"

"He's turned-on by the corridor!"

A ruler smacked across the bulge in his trousers. He cried out.

"Sicko!"

A second ruler; a third; a fourth, were produced from pencil cases. He struggled against his captors but they held him tight. Laughter resonated around him; mocking, chiding laughter. His penis throbbed harder. Another retort of plastic against cloth covered flesh. He cried out. Hot tears of fury burned his eyes but he was helpless. Somebody grabbed at his bulge; a squeal; hands groped at him, rulers smacked across his groin. He couldn't stop himself.

Hot semen pulsed from him, the wetness quickly seeping through his trousers. A girl screamed in feigned horror. He fought free as the grip on his arms loosened; he scrambled across the floor and hugged his bag to himself. Shame scorched him like acid. They were mocking him, humiliating him. They shouted vile, unspeakable things at him. They surrounded him, prodding and kicking him. The forest of legs jostled at him, offered him no escape.

"What the hell is going on here?" The voice snapped, cold and authoritative, through the chaos. The crowd turned and snapped to attention.

"Nothing, sir."

"Just having some fun, sir."

"Get in that class-room now!"

The figure waited while the class swarmed into the room, sniggers stifled behind hands.

Adam scrambled to his feet; he pushed through the flow of bodies, scampered down the corridor, and away.

"Where do you think you're going, boy?"

Adam ran.

They giggled in the darkness. The night was soft and warm. They shushed each other drunkenly and scrambled through the bushes at the bottom of the garden.

"Shit!" said Adam as he fell forward. His forehead bounced painfully off the top of the fencepost.

"Mind the fence!" laughed Tom.

"Very fucking funny," said Adam. "That really fucking hurt!"

They climbed the fence, staggering happily down the embankment and onto the firmness of the track. The railway line stretched away into the darkness to either side. The rails glinted like dust. In the near distance, to their right, the sternness of the line vanished into the ink blot of a tunnel. The pure darkness was impenetrable.

"Can't see a sodding thing," said Tom.

"Good job I brought me torch, then," said Adam with a snigger.

"What the fuck is that?" said Tom. He pointed at the pathetic pen torch that Adam was clutching lovingly to his chest.

"It's my torch," said Adam. He switched it on. The feeble beam struggled in to the thick obsidian tunnel.

"We'd have been better off with fire on sticks," said Tom.

"What do I care? I've got a torch."

Tom blew a raspberry. They slid their arms around each others' shoulders for support and stumbled forward. Their footsteps crunched eerily, each step a hollow echo. Their voices were dampened and tinny.

"What's that?" Tom pointed excitedly at the ground a short way ahead. He scrambled forward and crouched down.

"Move the bloody torch round, then."

Adam stepped round to Tom's side and shone light at his friend's feet. He reached down and retrieved the circular piece of silver that glinted in the weak light. "It's a ring-pull," he said, raising his eyebrows in disbelief. "This must have been down here for decades!"

He stepped back, laughing. His heel caught the rail and he fell. There was a loud crack as his head hit the ground. He giggled through the pain. The torch scurried away. Their laughter echoed and resounded down their hollow world. Adam put his hands down and tried to push himself upright. Something wet gave slightly under the heel of his right hand.

He snatched his hand away and wiped it on his leg. He scrambled for his torch and shone it at his hand. He frowned at the brown smear across his palm. He wiped it on his leg again and shone his torch at the ground. He searched the gravel and let out a sigh of relief as a small clump of decaying leaves was illuminated.

"What is it?" Tom crawled closer.

"Just some leaves." Adam reached down and picked them up. He wondered at the unusual thickness of this decomposing wad.

"Are you sure?"

Adam turned it over in his hand, the unfamiliar texture was making his skin crawl. "No," he said. "I don't think it is!"

The ridges, the curves, the conch-like character of the object gradually revealed itself to him. His eyes widened in horror. He dropped it and scrabbled away. He wiped his fingers frantically on his trousers.

"What?" said Tom, barely able to control his laughter at Adam's reaction.

"It's an *ear*. It's a fucking *ear*!"

"That's pretty disgusting," said Tom.

"Let's get the fuck out of here," said Adam.

"Why? Scared she might come back for the bits she left behind?" He laughed at Adam; his own nervousness hidden by his bravado.

"Shut the fuck up," said Adam. "I'm getting out of here, are you coming or not?"

Tom nodded.

They left the tunnel and headed straight back to the house.

"You dirty, filthy, little bastard," said Joseph Clare.

Adam stood in the empty bath, sobbing

"Take your trousers off. Now," said his father.

Adam shook his head.

"Take them off now or your beating will be twice as bad; do you understand?"

Adam tugged at the waistband of his trousers and pulled them down. The smell of faeces swept up over him. He didn't understand why he had done it. He had known that he needed to go to the toilet but he had held it and held it until it hurt. He had considered, briefly, asking his teacher if he could go to the toilet but then everybody would know. He had lifted his bottom off his seat, reached across the group table for some coloured pencils, as he filled his pants. When he sat down again, he felt it squash around his buttocks. He had stood against the radiator in the rain-shelter at play-time. Claire had asked him to play but he had silently shook his head.

His daddy pulled his pants down, lips curled back in disgust. He flushed the pat down the toilet.

"Adam must be feeling very traumatised by recent events, Mr. Clare."

Joseph Clare grunted. He sat opposite Adam's teacher, his arms crossed.

"Children react to these kind of life-changing events in very different ways. We must treat him kindly, with understanding. We must all try to help him, and his brother, of course, through this difficult time."

Joseph Clare curled his lip at her; he made no attempt to conceal his contempt.

"I'm sure it must be very difficult for you too; being a single father of two young boys can't be easy but I know..."

"You know nothing," he interrupted. "Are we done here?"

"Well, yes, but..." Adam's teacher was flustered, embarrassed.

"Good. Then I'll be taking my son home."

"Mr. Clare," she said as he stood to leave.

He glared at her.

She sighed. "Please," she said, "he's just a little boy."

"This is what happens to little boys who shit their pants and embarrass me." Joseph Clare grabbed Adam by the back of the head and rubbed his face in his own soiled underwear.

Adam shrieked and struggled against his father's grip. He gagged; bile and saliva ran down his chin. He screamed; his face purple with the effort. It felt like his vocal chords were shredding.

Joseph Clare threw the underwear in to the bin. He turned the bath taps on and slapped a bar of soap in to his son's hand. Adam dropped it in the bath; his screeches pierced like needles; he stamped his feet in the shallow water.

"Michael! Come and see that your disgusting brother cleans himself properly. If I find you helping him, you'll get a beating too."

Michael stepped meekly in to the bathroom, his eyes on the floor, as their father stomped downstairs. He closed the door behind him. "Come on, Adam," he said. "Let's get you cleaned-up and ready for bed. He sat on the edge of the bath and held his little brother's hand.

Adam stepped into the silent house. He frowned as he hung his coat; he tilted his head and strained to listen. Nothing. He sniffed. He inhaled deeply. Nothing. He strolled through the lounge and into the kitchen – everything was in its place. He sniffed. He opened the oven carefully, holding his face away from the expected wave of heat. Nothing.

"Elle?"

Silence.

He went to the foot of the stairs and called again, louder. Silence.

He shouted her name as he stormed from room to room. He burst into the bathroom where he found Elle frantically drying herself. The bath was full and steaming.

"Oh God Adam, I'm sorry. I'm *so* sorry. I don't know what to say. I lost track of the time, I was *so* tired and I felt like a bath and I didn't realise it was so late and…"

The slap stopped her dead.

"Why didn't you answer when I called?"

She hesitated.

"*Why?*" He took her by the shoulders, his fingers digging into her flesh.

"Jesus, Adam, I don't know. Because I was frightened…"

"*Frightened?*" His eyes bored into her. His expression was icy cold. "I'll give you something to be frightened of."

He shook her roughly then shoved her backwards. The backs of her knees caught the side of the bath and she toppled in with a scream. Hot, soapy water sloshed up the wall and tsunamied onto the bathroom floor. Elle's mouth was awash with hot water; she spluttered and choked for breath. Her arms and legs flailed helplessly.

"And dinner?" said Adam.

Elle began to stammer a reply but he was not interested in her excuses. He sneered at her. "You're pathetic." He grabbed a handful of hair.

Elle looked up at him, begging, pleading. "Don't. Please."

He pushed her head under the water. Her fingers scrabbled uselessly at his arms, searching for a grip. He pulled her back above the water line. She gasped for air. She had barely regained her breath when he forced her back under the water. The bath foamed as she writhed in the water; her legs thrashed violently. He pulled her up. Elle coughed, soap and saliva oozing down her chin. Adam towered over her. She fought him as hard as she could as he forced her back under, her fists and clawed fingers striking and scratching at him. He grinned down at her until, eventually, her movements began to slow, until she was finally giving up, then he pulled her free and released her. She coughed water, her face tinged blue as she struggled to breathe.

"Don't do it again," he said, cradling the hardness in his trousers. "I'm going back out."

Elle sat in the bath, tears and spittle and soap and snot running out of her. "Bastard," she whispered. She cradled her stomach in concern, the life within her not yet fully realised. "Fucking bastard," she said as she got out of the bath and slumped to the floor. She began to sob.

Dark tendrils swirled around Adam; sparks of light flashed like gunfire; whiplash voices; thump of engines in the darkness. His body was swept uncontrollably along like flotsam; total loss of control. He screamed into the darkness. His voice was sucked away into nothingness.

Heat pressed down on him, oppressive, suppressive. Sweat broke out of his pores, prickling across his body. Ebony tentacles reached for him, wrapped themselves around him, caressed him. They fondled him, running themselves up and around his body. They cradled him like a baby and slowly began to squeeze. His eyes bulged, the darkness fading to grey. His tongue lolled from his mouth like a rain swollen slug as the grey slowly faded to white. He felt someone wipe the saliva from his chin as he stirred into wakefulness.

"Hey, Adam; how are you feeling?"

A light blue curtain surrounding his bed swirled in the breeze. Stark white light thrust itself like needles into his eyes. The strong hospital aroma burned his sinuses.

"What?" Pain ripped like barbs of bone through his vocal chords.

"Don't try to say anything," said Tom. "You've done enough stupid things for one day."

Adam scowled at him.

"What a way to spend Christmas Day!" said Tom. "You've had your stomach pumped, dickhead!"

Adam glared at him.

"For fuck's sake, Adam, why? Nothing's worth this shit, nothing is ever this bad! You're a self-indulgent, attention-seeking, self-destructive little prick, you know that? Christ! This doesn't just affect you; you think the nurses want to have to deal with this self-inflicted bullshit? I only came round to drag you over to ours for dinner; that's my Christmas fucked and Connie's too! Thanks mate! You're such a dickhead!"

Adam reached forward and clasped Tom's hand. He pulled Tom closer. He squeezed Adam's hand as he leaned in.

"I love you too," he said and kissed Tom on the ear.

Chapter 9: Anniversary

"I love you," said Elle softly.

The candle light chided the room to the edge of perception. The coals on the fire glowed with satisfaction. Elle smiled at Adam's slightly bemused expression. The comfortable familiar old room had been transformed; a small table, intimately set for two, sat coyly in the centre of the room. The aroma of fresh flowers hung lightly in the air.

"I thought we were going out?" he said.

Elle shook her head seductively. "I thought it would be much more intimate here; spend our first anniversary alone." She raised her eyebrows suggestively.

"Nice idea," he said.

Elle hummed enticingly. Her earrings glittered in the twilight, accentuating the graceful sweep of her neck. Her body swelled against the restraint of her suggestive black dress; not too much left to the imagination but nothing too revealing. Adam stood close to her. Their lips brushed. Elle pulled away.

"Later," she whispered. She touched his lips with a single finger, gently scolding him for his forwardness. "Go and freshen up." She squeezed his buttocks as he backed reluctantly out of the room. As he ran upstairs she dashed into the kitchen. She hurriedly applied the final touches to the meal she had been preparing all day. Everything had to be perfect.

She could hear Adam lumbering around upstairs, the heaviness of his footsteps rolling across the ceiling like thunder. The shower swished into life. She could hear him singing to himself. As things came together in the kitchen she found herself humming along with him, muttering half-remembered lyrics. She drifted back into the living room, selected something ambient and pressed 'play'.

"Perfect," said Adam coming back downstairs.

Elle kissed him slowly. She breathed in the freshness of his face before bringing the meal through. They sat together and ate in silence, gazing longingly across the vast expanse of the small table. Their hunger unsated by the food. They savoured each other. Light wafted gently across their faces, shifting shadows dancing erotically. Coal settled in the fireplace. Cutlery scraped on crockery.

"Beautiful," said Adam as he sat back in his chair.

"You liked it?"

"Yes," he said, "but I meant you. You're beautiful."

The music ended. Elle stood and slinked across to him. She took him by the hand, blew out the candles through moist lips, and led him upstairs. He kissed her but once again she pulled away. She chided him. Slowly, she unbuttoned his shirt, kissing him as each button exposed a fresh part of his chest. She slipped his shirt off his shoulders and let it fall to the floor. Gently, she bit his nipples and ran her tongue down to his navel. He ran his fingers through her hair.

Tentatively, she unzipped his trousers, unhooked the button, and slid them down his muscular legs; his wispy leg hairs soft like gossamer. She nudged him out of his trousers and deftly removed each sock as he took a step. She caressed him through his pants; she kissed his stomach all along the elastic top, teasing his stomach muscles into tensing then she pulled them down too.

She cradled his testicles as she kissed them; she ran her tongue the length of his erectness; took him gently into her mouth, her tongue teasing, darting. He groaned. She pulled away, licking the strands of seminal fluid away. She shifted her weight and kissed the base of his penis and licked his scrotum, she teased him as he moaned in pleasure. He cried aloud as she hooked a testicle with her tongue and took it gently into her mouth; his breathing came in short, sharp gasps. As she played with him, teased him, rolled him around her tongue, she could feel her own wetness mounting, her yearning for him to be inside her, to feel him pushing into her. She released him.

She stood, shrugged her shoulders out of her dress and slid it off, revealing her nakedness. She led him by the penis to the bed. She knelt away from him on all fours. He approached her from behind and, with a guiding hand from her, penetrated her. She pushed back against him, her buttocks pressing sensually into his pelvis. He cradled her breasts lovingly, resisting the urge to push into her rhythmically – too soon, too soon.

Elle hung her head, her hair fell about her sweat flushed face; she could feel him pulsating inside her, the slight pain overwhelmed by her sexuality. She gasped, over and over, tears rolled from her eyes as he began to pound into her. She felt his muscular contractions as he released a spurt of heat into her. She cried aloud. His arms encircled her waist, pulling her hard to him, his fingers clawed her sides. He bit her back and shoulders as his head rested between her shoulder blades.

They rolled clumsily onto their sides, he still deep inside her, and slowly regained their breath. Adam kissed her back, tiny whispered kisses, Elle clutched his hand to her breast.

"I want to move," she said eventually.

He nibbled at her skin.

"I want to hold you properly," she said. She shuffled forward a little and he slid wetly from her. She rolled over and embraced him.

"Happy Anniversary, Mr Clare," she said and kissed him.

"Happy Anniversary to you too Mrs E-Clare, my chocolaty lovely," he said.

"Bugger off!" she said. "It's not my fault you've got a stupid surname."

Adam hugged her close. "I love you."

She grinned.

He laughed a little laugh.

"What?"

"Nothing. I was just thinking."

"What?"

"You'll be really disappointed. Honestly, it's nothing."

"Try me."

He shrugged and held her closer. "You know when we were eating and the fire settled down?"

She nodded into his chest.

"It reminded me of something when I was little. Granddad used to put a big sheet of paper over the opening to try and draw the fire up. I think I must have been about 6 years old and I used to love sitting in front of the fire looking for pictures of the future."

Elle raised her eyes to look at him.

"What? It's not my fault! That's what Granddad told me – he said you could see pictures of the future in the blue flames. I never did."

Elle laughed gently at him. "Never mind."

"Anyway, Mum brought me around one day and the fire wasn't lit and I was really disappointed, probably sulked, I don't remember, so Granddad tried to light it for me." He smiled fondly. "The silly old sod only managed to set fire to the sheet of newspaper didn't he? And his cardigan, and he burned a big hole in the carpet. That's the only time I can remember him ever telling me off. I thought it was really funny – the way he was jumping around trying to put the fire out and trying to get his cardi off at the same time. I suppose he was scared and angry with himself. I hated him for shouting at me, for all of fifteen minutes."

Elle kissed him. "I bet you were a naughty little boy. Cheeky and beautiful."

"I was an angel. My mum told me so."

"I don't believe you."

Adam sighed in feigned disappointment.

They lay together in silence.

"I want children," said Adam quietly.

Elle sighed into the darkness.

"Please don't spoil this Adam. We've had this conversation before."

"That was ages ago. Things are different now."

"How?"

"They just are," he said. "We're more established now, we've been together longer. Things are more certain now than they have ever been."

"Yes," she agreed, "but I'm still not ready to have children, Adam. We agreed. I've still got so many things I want to do before I even start to think about something like that. I still want to get established as an artist. I want to sell my work for a living and I can't do that with children."

"You can't do it without them," he said spitefully.

"What's that supposed to mean?" She drew away from him.

"How many paintings have you sold?"

Her lips tightened, whitened, with anger.

"How many?"
"None," she said. "But that's not the point."

"I think it's *exactly* the point."

"A couple of galleries have shown interest."

"Interest doesn't pay the bills, Elle."

She glowered at him. "This is my dream," she said. "This is the one thing that I've always wanted to do with my life and I'm not going to give it up for anything until I absolutely have to. Trudi reckons…"

Adam scoffed. "You know what I think of *her*."

"Yes I do. And you know what I think of you for it. She's my best friend Adam. Why can't you just accept that fact and try to get on with her for my sake."

"Because if I did that I'd be almost as two-faced as she is."

"What?" said Trudi.

"I said you're a two-faced little bitch and I want you to stay away from my wife."

Trudi was shocked into silence for the first time in her life, not quite believing what Adam had said.

"And you'd better believe that I mean it!"

Trudi smirked. "Listen to me, you sad little man," she said, brandishing a finger with renewed confidence. "I've known Elle since I was old enough to know anything and I know her better and love her more than you ever will. If you try and force me out of her life you'll destroy your marriage. Now, that's fine by me, I think it would be the best thing that could happen to her, but I know how much you need her, how much you rely on her."

"Piss off!"

Trudi winked at his frustration. "Perhaps," she said, "but only if Elle asks me to." She smiled sarcastically.

"I'll see what I can do," he said. And shut the door in her face.

"I wish you wouldn't talk about her like that," said Elle turning her back to him. "You've spoilt the whole evening now."

"I haven't done anything of the sort. I just said I wanted children. I didn't say when, did I? There's no hurry is there."

"That's not what you were implying, Adam."

"What do you mean? What am I supposed to be *implying*?"

"You just held me close in your arms on one of the most romantic nights we've ever spent together and, straight after we've had sex, you tell me that you want children. The implication is that you want them now; that children are what we need to make our marriage whole, otherwise why say it now?"

"That's not what I said."

"Yes it was, Adam, now please just drop it. I don't want to discuss it anymore, we're not having children."

"Isn't a marriage supposed to be a union between two people? Isn't there supposed to be some element of discussion? Some small amount of compromise?"

"There is no compromise when it comes to having children. I get pregnant. I carry the child. I get the sickness and the aches and the pains and the swelling and stretch marks. I give birth. As far as I can tell, there is no compromise. You do your bit then sit back and wait. Having a baby is something that I have to do when I'm ready to do it."

Adam scowled at his wife's back. Her voice trembled with emotion and her shoulders shook a little. She was upset, he had upset her, he had pushed the conversation too far. He hated the way that she always made him feel guilty when he had done nothing wrong.

Adam looked nervously around the union bar. The floor heaved with people, their ebb and flow like that of a storm-thrashed lake. Voices raised themselves skyward, an incomprehensible babble between too loud music. Heavy bass throbbed in his chest cavity and heavy white smoke choked the back of his throat. His eyes stung.

"I can't see her," Adam shouted.

"I don't know what she looks like!" Tom yelled back.

Adam nodded.

Tom made a drinking gesture as he made his way to the bar and Adam nodded enthusiastically. Adam grabbed a couple of seats as Tom began the scramble to the front of the queue. He scanned the room; scrutinising the dance floor; peering into the dark corners. He stared at the door to the ladies' every time it snapped open.

"I can't see her anywhere," he said as Tom returned with drinks, beer running freely down his forearms from where he had been jostled.

"Does she look like that?" he asked, pointing over Adam's shoulder.

Adam turned as he drank and nearly choked as he was confronted by Elle. She was as beautiful as he remembered – absolute perfection.

She waved nervously.

A small dribble of beer escaped from the corner of his mouth. He wiped it away, hoping against hope that she hadn't noticed.

"This is Trudi," she shouted. "I brought her along."

"Me too! I mean: this is Tom, I brought him."

"I love this song," shouted Trudi to Tom. "Let's dance!"

Tom took the hint, downed his pint, and they left their two best friends alone.

"She's such a flirt!" said Elle.

They spent most of that evening wrapped up in a bubble together, sharing stories, jokes and kisses – gentle, nervous ones at first that steadily grew more passionate. They gazed at each other through the romantic haze of alcohol and Adam felt himself falling deep into her eyes.

They lay back to back, conjoined twins, in angry silence.

"Why do you have to spoil everything?" she said eventually.

"I haven't spoilt anything."

"Not much. I spent the whole day preparing tonight; planning it to perfection."

"All I said was that I wanted children. Am I not allowed to want a family now?"

"Don't be an idiot. Just don't try and force me into something that I don't want *yet*. I don't feel old enough, responsible enough, *yet*. They're not part of my dreams…*yet*. Do you understand?" She turned over and kissed him on the shoulder. "I'm sorry Adam."

"Me too," he said.

He rolled away from her in the darkness and lay in silence until sleep took them both.

Chapter 10: Falling

Silence took him. His heart thundered. A knot formed in his throat. A bubble formed in his chest and forced itself upwards and out. "Baby?" he said.

Elle nodded.

He took a step towards her. A thousand emotions jostled inside him. He took her by the hand.

"Really?"

She snatched her hand back. "Yes."

"Where? Where is he? She? Fuck!"

She sneered at him. "Christ, Adam, I don't believe you. It's dead, Adam. It died."

His face fell.

"Ironic really. The baby was the reason that I finally left you. I didn't want it, you know that, but I left you to protect it. After years of being abused by you and I finally run away to protect somebody else. And then I lost it anyway."

"Dead?"

"Miscarriage. A little boy." She fumbled guiltily with her fingers. She scowled. "You remember that time you nearly drowned me in the bath, you bastard."

Adam looked puzzled.

"No, I don't suppose you do. All those memories blurred together now, one act of violence piled upon another, mental torture and physical abuse upon sarcasm and hate. The day before I left you: that time!"

He collapsed to the sofa, a stunned look on his face. The day before; the last day that his life had any meaning. The last time that he had had a reason for coming home. The warmth of her face; the softness of her body. Her smooth skin in his too rough hands. The white thrash of bath water and half-choked cries. The gentle swell of taut skin on belly, barely noticeable. She had been pregnant.

"I remember," he said.

"That was the day I found out; the day I was going to tell you; the day that everything was going to change. You never gave me the chance."

"If you'd only said…"

"What the fuck is that supposed to mean? That you didn't give a shit about *me*? That you wouldn't have nearly killed me if you'd known I was pregnant. Fuck, Adam! What do you think I am? Did you *really* think it was okay to treat me like shit? Like I was your own personal punch-bag? And as soon as I started producing babies you could wrap me up in cotton wool and pretend everything was fine?"

"No!"

"Did you think that I'd stop being scared of you just because you'd temporarily stop hitting me?"

"It wasn't that bad," he said.

Elle raised her eyebrows, a dry laugh on her lips. "Not that bad?"

"There was nothing to be scared of. I wouldn't have hurt you if you'd told me."

"That doesn't make it all right. It wouldn't have just gone away because you'd said so. I was *more* scared of you when I found out because I wasn't just scared for myself. Odd isn't it: I never wanted the damn thing but as soon as I found out it was in me all I wanted to do was protect it. More than anything I wanted to protect him from you. To stop him becoming another you."

"It wasn't that bad," he repeated.

"How would you know what it was like? I was scared all of the time, Adam. I lived in absolute fear of upsetting you, of doing or saying something wrong, just in case you decided to take it out on me. I was always trying to do the *right* thing; trying to read your mind, trying to anticipate what it was that you wanted me to do and all the time terrified that I would do it wrong. I figured that the violence and the jealousy were because you loved me, that you only hit me because you cared. I can't believe how deluded I was. People like you only do it for the power. I don't know what it was that made you the way you are and I don't really care anymore. You were so different when we first got together. What happened to you, Adam, why did you change?"

Hatred and scorn emanated from Adam. "I don't know what you're talking about."

Elle looked deep into him, her eyes unwavering. "You really don't do you?"

"I really don't," he said. His voice was reduced, small and pathetic, under her scrutiny.

Elle sighed. "I said I wouldn't be long; I'd better be going."

"Where?"

"Back to where I'm living," she said. She smiled. "Just because I'm not scared of you anymore doesn't mean I'm stupid enough to tell you where I live."

Adam stood and peered angrily through the curtains, desperately trying to see who was waiting for his wife in the car parked outside.

"I'm leaving," said Elle standing next to him.

"I still love you," he said.

"I don't think so, Adam," she said.

Adam clenched his jaw. He struggled against his bonds. The cords bit in to his wrists and ankles; the more he struggled, the tighter they became. His fingers tingled; his feet were beginning to go numb. He thrashed his head from side to side, trying to dislodge the violet silk covering his eyes. There was a sharp sting of leather across his thigh. He groaned. There were shadowy movements visible through his blindfold. He moaned around his gag.

"Shut up," said Catherine. She paced around the bed.

Adam trembled. He could feel his erection, throbbing and exposed; vulnerable. He was completely helpless and totally at her mercy. She could do anything to him and there was nothing that he could do to stop her. He could sense her as she prowled towards where he lay. He felt the warm leather of the riding-crop as it traced the lines of his body. He shuddered involuntarily.

The leather moved down his outer-thigh, his calf, and around his feet. He held his breath as it moved inexorably upwards. It paused at his inner-thigh. He whispered to himself.

"I said *shut up*," said Catherine. She smacked him on the thigh and took the crop away.

Adam held his breath. He couldn't see her. He turned his head. Her breasts touched his face, her nipples like fingertips following the line of his nose and lips. He lifted his head and she pulled away. Leather slapped across his stomach.

"No," she said. Her fingers hooked the material from his mouth and pulled it down around his neck. He licked his cracked lips and swallowed. The bed moved under Catherine's weight as she straddled Adam's chest. "This gag is no good," she said. "I can still hear you. I have something better to smother your noise with. She shuffled up and lowered herself on to his face. He jerked and struggled. She moved against him; slow and rhythmically. He extended his tongue and matched her, pleasuring her and struggling for breath. She came quickly and wetly.

"You're a bad person," she whispered. "A very bad person."

She lifted herself off him. He could feel her presence, but where was she? A swish. A sharp pain in his penis. The smack of leather on flesh. He cried out. Memories flashed like lightening.

She took him in her mouth: hot and wet. Needle-sharp teeth threatened to clamp down. He sighed through tightening jaw muscles. His teeth hurt. She took him to the cusp of satisfaction and stepped away.

"Please," he said.

She whipped him again.

"Don't," he said.

She whipped him, giggling.

"Please."

Catherine sat astride him. She manoeuvred him into position, the tip of his penis just penetrating her.

"Stop," he said. He could feel his chest tightening, air bubbles swirling around inside him. He struggled harder against his knotted limbs. His heart thumped louder and faster; it was going to explode.

She slapped his face. Her mouth clamped down over his as she pushed herself down on to him. He turned his face away. She ground against him. He shook his head. He fought against his bonds. She sat upright, her right hand gripped his throat. He could feel the blood pounding at his temples, his forehead throbbed. He gasped for air as she ground harder and faster against him. Darkness swam at the edges of his limited vision, spots dancing before his eyes. Sweat sprung from him, prickling across his entire body. The small of his back felt wet and cold. She reached round and, taking his testicles in her left hand, squeezed hard. She came hard as he withered inside her. Catherine took her fingers from his throat. Adam tried to breathe deeply as he struggled frantically to break free.

Catherine reached up and undid the cords at his wrists. He pulled the blindfold away. He pushed her off him and began to dress hurriedly, panic in his eyes.

"Adam?" Catherine reached out a hand to him.

"Don't," he said. "I'd better go, Elle will be wondering where I am." His words fell from him in short, tight, gasps. He didn't make eye contact. His hands were shaking. Then he left.

Elle knelt quietly at the bottom of the garden, her eyes glazed over. Heavy gardening gloves made her hands look huge, made them feel cumbersome. She shed them, letting them fall to the freshly dug dirt like sloughed skin. She relaxed back on her haunches. Pulled weeds gathered in clumps at the dirt borders. In amongst the weeds squatted a small yellow digger that she had uncovered – abandoned, lost; a childhood long abandoned. Elle looked at her hands. Her nails were bitten to the quick, fresh scabs of blood were congregating at the corners. Dirt was ingrained in her skin; no vibrant colours here, just the mundane brown of loamy soil.

      She wiped the corners of her mouth with her knuckles. To be in touch with the soil now, to feel the life in the earth around her, was all she had left; was all she had been left. She sunk her bare hands deep in to the soil and squeezed the dirt between her clawed fingers. She gripped the earth as if it was possible to hang on; as if, by never letting go, it would save her. She sobbed, rocking back and forth. Her ribs ached. How had it come to this? How had she let herself fall so far?

Adam had been bottling up this anger forever. He had nursed this hatred, caressed and succoured it into a healthy living thing. It permeated his every cell. He could feel it like a physical entity, taste it in the air. He could hear and see it every time that his father spoke. Adam loathed the way that *that man* sat there like he owned life. Adam glared at his father.

      He was slumped in his chair; a dirty threadbare old thing sagging in the corner. One man and his chair. His grubby unshaven face was vacant. Clothes hung limply from his frame.

      "What?"

      "Do you ever get out of that chair?" asked Adam.

      Joseph glared at his son. They stared hatefully at each other.

"Your brother's a real comedian," he said to Michael. His laugh was a hiss of contempt.

Michael shifted uncomfortably in his seat.

"Well? Do you?" said Adam.

"What's got into you?"

"Nothing," said Adam.

"Then shut the fuck up, I'm watching the news."

"I know why you like the news," said Adam.

"Leave it, Adam," said Michael.

Adam raised his eyebrows at his brother and tilted his head to one side.

"Just leave it," said Michael.

"Don't you know, Mikey?"

Michael shook his head despairingly. Adam was trying to goad the old man into an argument and, as always, he was going to succeed.

"He likes it because it's another programme full of sex and violence, nothing more. The vicious old bastard sees it as entertainment – how many more dead Yanks; how many raped or murdered schoolgirls; who's shagging who. You know how it goes. What's the tally this week, Dad?"

"You're asking for it, *son*," said Joseph.

"If I'd been asking for it I'd have said 'Can I have it?' but I didn't, did I?"

"If you don't shut it I'm going to give you a slap you won't forget in a hurry."

"Like the ones you use to give Mum? I never forgot those."

"*Jesus*, Adam. Drop it will you," said Michael.

"I don't think so," said Adam. "Not this time, I've had enough of this poisonous old bastard. He sits in that corner just oozing vitriol. He's ruined his own life and now he's trying to drag us down with him. No wonder Mum wanted a divorce."

Joseph Clare sprang to his feet, the ashtray on the arm of his chair falling to the carpet, the ash scattering like gas oven fall-out.

"You little bastard," he said. His lips curled back from nicotine stained teeth.

"I wish I was," said Adam, squaring up to his father. Joseph's breath was stale and rank; he smelled of mildewed clothes and stale food. "Then I wouldn't have to put up with you."

"Well *fuck off* then!"

"Is that the best you can do, you sad old tosser?" Adam laughed spitefully in his father's face.

Joseph grabbed Adam by the shoulders and threw him backwards. Adam fell to the sofa and immediately sprang back to his feet.

"Go on then! Hit me!," said Adam. A tremor of adrenaline made his voice waver; attempted aggression teetered on the edge of fear. "Give me an excuse, you prick! Just fucking once, come on!"

Joseph raised his hand. His gnarled, calloused, yellowing fingers twitched. Adam glared at him in defiance. Michael stepped between the two of them; his face was unreadable. He pushed his father back and looked impassively at Adam.

"Stop it, Adam," he said. "For fuck's sake will you stop it. What's the fucking point?"

"The point is to make him feel as bad as I possibly can; as bad as he made our Mum feel. This pathetic little shit terrorised our mother, Michael. He destroyed her and made her life a misery. The more I think about what he did the more I hate him. If we stay with him much longer, Mikey, I'm scared we're going to end up like him and that's more than I can bear."

"I think you'd better go, Adam," he said.

Adam raised his brows incredulously.

"Go. Now," said Michael.

"What?"

"I think you'd better go now before you say something you'll regret, before you say something you can't take back."

"I don't *want* to take it back anymore and I'll *never* regret telling him exactly what I think of him. Aren't you with me, Michael? Don't you remember listening to him beating her; the sense of helplessness, of powerlessness? I'm not helpless any more, Michael."

"Please don't," said Michael.

"You're taking his side? After everything we've seen him do, you're taking his side?"

"I'm not taking anybody's side; there are no sides. Dad is all we have left."

"I'd rather have nothing," said Adam.

He pushed past his brother and father and stormed angrily out of the house. He did not look back.

Adam wandered the dark cold streets for hours afterwards. His anger slowly subsided to be replaced by an overwhelming sense of sadness. His pace slowed as his melancholia gathered around him. Moonlight sharpened the edges of deepened shadows creating a chiaroscuro landscape. Night sounds were deadened, hollowed out like husks; the knife edge of streetlights sliced downwards.

Adam's breath billowed in front of him, air whistling in his frost burned throat. His eyes watered in the chill air. All of his bottled-up resentment and hatred and anger had finally been released but he felt no better for it. He had been expecting euphoria, lightness, relief of some sort but it was not so. All he felt was disappointment; a sense of anti-climax. The release had felt good, empowering, like he could move mountains, but now he was just Adam Clare again. Nothing had changed; the world would carry on just the same. He shrugged his shoulders against the cold, buried his hands deeper into his pockets and headed for his grandfather's.

"Why don't you come back home, Adam?"

"Why are you so fixated on this, Michael?"

"I'm not fixated, I just want what's left of our family to be whole."

"I can't do it, Michael, I just can't." Adam sighed. "It's taken me this long to break free of that man, I can't willingly submit to it again. You can't imagine what it's like to not have him in your life. Don't you see, Michael? I'm free."

"He's our father."

"That's not enough."

Michael could hear their granddad pottering around in the kitchen, trying to keep himself busy while the boys talked. Michael leaned forward in his seat. "Listen, Adam. He'll never tell you this himself, he can't tell you this, but he loves you. You've broken his heart, leaving like you did."

"He doesn't have a heart," said Adam. "I don't believe he's ever had a heart. I don't believe he's capable of feeling anything except hatred."

"You don't know him, Adam. You didn't see what he was like when you were born. He used to dote on you. He had a hard time showing it but that doesn't mean he didn't feel it. He grew up in a very different world to us; men weren't supposed to show their feelings."

"How can you sit there and spout this shit? Don't you understand, Michael? It doesn't matter how he used to feel about me when I was a baby. What counts, is how he brought us up, *both* of us, the household he created. Don't you have any sympathy for Mum?"

"Mum loved him."

"More fool her."

"She stayed with him."

"She didn't want to. Don't you remember her asking him for a divorce? That's one of my earliest memories. Surely you remember listening to the beatings he used to give her?"

Michael hung his head. "She changed her mind; she chose to stay."

"He changed her mind for her. He beat her, physically and emotionally, until she couldn't leave. You're not stupid, Michael, why do you persist in this belief that he's worth staying for?"

"Because I have to. Because if I don't forgive him for the things he's done then I'm just as bad as he is." Michael looked at Adam. "He's a weak old man now, Adam. He'd have nothing if I left."

"He deserves to be left with nothing."

"I refuse to be the one to take the last of what he has away from him. I have to show him the compassion that he never showed us. You were too young to realise what Mum dying did to him. It broke him, Adam. It tore him apart. He never showed it but it ripped the heart right out of him."

"I don't care," said Adam. His voice was flat, devoid of any emotion. "We're going around in circles now. I know you want me to come back; I know you think Dad wants me to come back; I know you want me to forgive him but you need to know that I never will. He destroyed out mother's life; she was miserable and she would have taken us away and given us a better life if he'd let her. But he didn't. I'll never forgive him."

"You're not Mum's avenging angel, Adam."

"I'm the closest she's ever had to one."

"It's not your role; it's not your responsibility. Her life with him; the choices they made are none of your business."

"How can you say that? The things he did, the way he treated her, are part of our upbringing. His choices, his actions, are part of who we are now. He fucked us up, Mikey."

"Yes he did, Adam. You especially."

"I really don't give a fuck about anything you have to say about that man."

"Adam, just listen to me, will you?"

"Why the hell should I?" Adam tried to shut the door in Michael's face. Michael wedged his foot in the door. "Move your foot out of the way before I crush it," said Adam.

"Adam, just let me come in, will you?"

"Fuck off, why don't you?"

Michael pushed against the door. "Let me in!"

"Why should I?"

"Because I don't want to have to tell you that Dad's died on your fucking doorstep."

There was a sudden tension, a clenching of the air, an expectation that quickly withered and died. Adam's grip on the door loosened; he sagged. "You'd better come in then," he said.

Michael stepped in to what used to be his grandfather's home. Michael had been expecting Adam to have made a lot of changes but he had changed very little, as it turned out. The house smelled fresher; the ghost of cigar smoke, surprisingly, still lingered. The furniture was still the same; maybe Adam had splashed some paint around here and there but the house was still, essentially, their grandfather's home.

"Grab a seat," said Adam, "I'll make us a drink."

Michael sank in to the enveloping comfort of their grandfather's favourite chair. He fingered the cloth of the arms affectionately. His weight had squeezed the smell of the old man out of the material. It felt like he had slipped in to the old man's skin.

"He died in that chair, you know?" said Adam. "That's where I found him."

"Jesus!" said Michael.

"It's okay, he wasn't oozing or anything. It's okay to sit there."

Michael sat back in the chair uncertainly. Adam placed coffee on the table in front of them.

"Go on then," said Adam. "Tell me what happened."

Michael ran quickly through the details of their father's deteriorating health; of how the cancer had taken hold him, weakened and destroyed him. He skipped over some of the more gruesome, traumatising details, for his own sake more than Adam's.

Adam listened, dry-eyed. He hunched forward tensely and nodded when Michael had finished. "Did he say anything? You know, before he died?"

"He did." Michael hesitated. "He told me to look after my little brother." His eyes met Adam's. "He told me that he was sorry; that he loved us. He said he never meant to hurt you." Michael watched his own fingertips as they picked at the arm of the chair.

There was a long silence as Adam stared into his mug. He swallowed once, twice; dry swallows that held something back. "It's incredible, the things people say when they're frightened," he said. "Let me know when the funeral is, I'll do my best to avoid it."

"Adam..."

"Don't," said Adam. "You can go when you've finished your drink; let yourself out." He left Michael alone in the living-room.

Adam prowled the brightly-lit room. His house was empty. Thoughts and scenarios swarmed through his confused mind: thoughts of Elle. He loved her so much; the softness of her body, her warmth, her laughter. Now she was laughing at him. Who was she with? He did not understand. He had always treated her well. When she made him hit her, he always made up for it afterwards – always made love to her; always made her feel better. She had never complained. They always had such passionate sex; his rage always transformed in a gentle yearning to be inside her. True alchemy.

Why was she tormenting him like this? Just the thought of her naked body turned him on and that was all she had left him with. He felt a gentle stirring in his groin. His eyes felt like they had never been opened. A heaviness lay inside his head, a thick, congealing slowness that impaired his thoughts. He must not sleep.

The dream had been getting progressively worse. The same thing, over and over, only tattered shreds remaining when he awoke. It terrified him; whatever it was. It always had but it was getting worse, taking form, teasing him with images and narratives that he could not, did not, want to understand. Where once there had been only a tangle of unintelligible images and fear, there was now something almost tangible. Where once he had screamed himself awake, now he only felt the dream dragging him further and further down; sucking him in and swallowing him whole. This thing wanted him.

Time passed painfully and loudly. He splashed his face with cold water. He made more coffee. His hands felt like two balloons. He leaned his forehead against the work surface and rolled his head to look at the wall. He desperately scanned the wallpaper for patterns, for something to occupy his mind.

He stood wearily. He snapped his head up and stretched his eyes wide. He slumped into the sofa, just while the kettle boiled. The sound of boiling water was disproportionally loud; his eyes refused to focus. Slow, heavy blink. Black tendrils encircled him, caressed him, nursed him as his chin fell. The kettle clicked off…

Chapter 11: Dreaming

The light clicks on...

    The sensation of warmth on your face; the world is red through your eyelids and you shift your weight. Something hard digs into your shoulder blade. A gentle wind wafts across your face; again you shift your weight but you cannot get comfortable. You roll over onto your stomach with a grunt of relief. You open your eyes slowly; purple blind spots dance before you and as they clear you look at the expansive barren field. You frown; déjà vu nudges at you. You have been here before but not; things are familiar but different.

    woomera

    You had not noticed the sound initially: the soft rhythmic throbbing of the didgeridoo. It had started quietly, barely perceptible, but it was growing steadily louder. You wipe the sweat from your brow and look around. You can see brown cobbled earth sweeping away from you. The breeze increases, stirring up dust-devils that dervish themselves into oblivion. The noise grows into the sound of heavy industrial engines. It deafens you. You clamp your hands over your ears as the pain knifes through your brain. You look around in panic, the ground vibrates beneath you, you look down as realisation dawns. You see a scuffed-up section of earth at your knee. You smile. It looks like the scuffed-up carpet-tile in the kitchen. You reach down in curiosity and pick at the earth like it is a rancid old scab; dry flakes of earth fall away like shedding skin. You dig your fingers in and your face curls with a grimace as the earth gives way. You peel back the earth like an old piece of linoleum; insects scatter for non-existent shadows. They puff into ash and drift away.

woomera

You gaze in to the abyss. The sunlight from above illuminates the pit below: oil smeared cogs, wheels, gears, and chains grind on, oblivious to you in their obscure purpose. The blackness yawns beneath you, choked full of the machine. You feel a compulsion to enter, to climb into the works. You pull back the ground fully and descend into the darkness. The staircase falls beneath you into eternity. There is no reason to turn back.

The machine stops.

You look up in panic. What have you done? You did not touch anything. The daylight above is nothing but the glint of a small square star. You look around. The engine still rocks slightly, ticking as it cools; grease glistens and stillness blankets your surroundings. Your heart pounds heavily in your chest, your pulse beats a tattoo at your temple, then in the distance, you hear a voice. You squint into the darkness. The heat of the oil is hot in your nostrils. Black dust lightly feathers your face. A voice calls again. Something flits by in your peripheral vision; something near, something in the distance, somewhere through the machinery, somewhere in the machine.

woomera

You call out. Your voice echoes away. You begin to scramble through the tangle of machinery; pipes and wires claw at you, striving to entangle you, to hold you back. Your hands become slimy with grease, small shards of grit rasp across your palm. Your pulse increases, faster and faster, as you crawl closer to your goal - the source of the voice. Tired smear of oil replaces sweat tears on your face as you grow weary. You pause. You reach the small body. You sigh heavily. The body of the dead child lies crushed and mangled in the gears, thick arterial blood oozes leisurely from it. Its head hangs limply, rocking pendulously. Hair covers its face. You struggle to move the cogs. Your breath comes in sobs breaking like air bubbles in water. Your face reddens with effort as you strain and strain at the machine, your hands slip on the heavily oiled wheel. You grab at the body and pull as hard as you can. Flesh tears, pulls away in strands, a heavy lump of meat in your hand. Your heart breaks. You lean back against a wheel, the pain in your heart blossoming. You feel so helpless. The child lifts its head.

woomera

You look deep into your own dead eyes, the blackness in his pupils a dark reflection of the life in yours. The child winks and begins to laugh as the engines start once more. The machine spits the child out and draws you in. You are drawn inexorably towards the metal teeth. You scream. It crushes you. Your stomach bursts and spills your steaming insides into the pit below, blood and shit and meat slopping from your shell. The machine chews up your empty body. You scream soundlessly. It spews you out. You are falling through the void. A gentle hurricane hurtles past your ears. Words are whipped from your mouth as you fall on the breath of a golden lion. An orgasm of panic rips through you. You settle into the void, contentment and passivity wells up warmly inside you. You relax. The soft, so soft, sigh of a kiss from a lover and still you fall. You twist and turn and cartwheel and play in the vacuum like a child oblivious. The wind dies and the void is warm, almost humid. This is life inside the balloon.

woomera

The blackness around you is complete, absolute, you cannot even see your own hand in front of your face. Your pupils dilate and reflect the mere blackness; no aeon distant star hints at otherness or oneness; no paint spray of galaxies or slash of comet on obsidian canvas draw your eye; the universe is absent. You are alone. There is nothing, and you. You grow comfortable, accustomed to your plummet. You desperately try to remember the signs, the signs, this is not your dream: old friend; ruined giant; stone writing; the oath of a name. Then you forget. These moments of pleasure give you time, time you have always had – dream-time. Dream seconds that last forever and millennia that are over in an instant - Polaroid moments.

woomera

You sleep, you wake, you fall. All things are constant, everything is changing. You see two silver pinpricks of light: distant stars, gaseous bodies that are millennia distant, beautifully intricate and tiny at arms' length. You reach out to touch them, to grab them, to snatch their beauty for yourself in your selfishness but they are too far. They remain constant to you. Distant. Huge. Falling. Then they begin to grow. Fear grips you by the stomach; you feel a dull ache in your groin as your insides shrivel at the cold that now cuts through your body, slices through your soul. It laughs insanely on its way. The lights grow. Expand into galaxies that swirl in the continual clockwork of the universe. Expanding, dying, red shift, amoral, non-judgemental, cold, uncaring, petrified, random universe that wants to take you in its teeth and rip out your jugular just so it can feel something. You stop falling. The vacuum of space holds you in its grip, tender like a lover, like a mother, squeezing like a motherfucker. You watch the universe tick-tick-ticking away, winding down and clocking out: blue shift. The pinpricks of light are eyes and they are watching you.

A skeletal figure approaches; its skin is wan, waxy, drawn like death, puckered at the mouth, eyes as deep as dream itself. A ragged cloak swirls seductively, a thing alive, the wing of slumber. The figure speaks. A raven shuffles its feathers and flies away. The figure beckons to you, fingers like desiccated branches. You approach. It tells you all you ever wanted to know, everything that you will ever forget, all the things you could not bear to hear. The figure pulls you to its body. The cape swoops around you, smothering you, suffocating you. You fight to breathe. There is a pillow over your face. The dark redness squeezes you, pushes you away from itself; pulsing hot blood; muscle squeeze; push and you are born screaming into the world and you are walking down a tunnel.

woomera

The ground feels strangely regular through your shoes. There is a wet cockroach crunch of insect, hard floor, insect crunch, hard floor. It goes on forever and is bordered on two sides by hard raised ridges: the longest staircase of your life with the lowest handrails. Thunder rumbles all around, rolling through your head like a Saturday morning; dull, sharp, ache. You feel something heavy against your legs: large and slumberous. You step back in panic. The fear, like your gorge, rises in you once more. Your throat tightens, your heart pounds, your legs quiver with adrenaline. You feel like you are going to wet yourself. The thunder grows. You look up; the pinpricks of light are watching you again and they are growing, getting closer. The ground trembles in anticipation, moist with anxiety. The thunder grows. The lights are closer. You turn. You run. The ground is quaking, echoes of California. The thunder grows, thought is drowned. There is nowhere to run, nowhere to turn, to hide. This is the end my only friend, the end. The noise stops. There is a soft click and you are standing at the top of the stairs.

A worried wind moans unconvincingly around the timbers of the old house. The sky is pale violet, now that the clouds are gone. There is the first suggestion of mourning in the air. There is a sound downstairs. The carpet nestles into the crevices of your feet as a cold tear of sweat runs down the inside of your arm. You strain to see in the half light as you stalk down the stairs. You prowl, ancient sounds pervade; the shrill of the cicada; the howl of something primal; rushing water; creak of tectonic movement; lightening crack; crack of leather on willow; racial memory; gene pool cacophony; the hunter: Man. Before you lies a vast flowing field, undulating away to the horizon, disappearing at the feet of the purple-wash mountains. The smell of flowers is suddenly strong. Vases of violets: full, blooming, alive, blueing in the green, blossoming proudly from the infinite plinths on which they stand. Long cool strands of grass jostle around your legs, whipping themselves into a frenzy as you run, run, run, dancing nimbly between the children of February; amethyst flowers of the strain long extinct. A presence stalks you now. Teeth; blood; jaw; saliva; tearing; tearing; tearing. Flesh rips, blood spills, juices ooze from every orifice, bones shine wet in moonlight becomes you it goes with your hair spat from mouth, tasteless and course. Dry elastic stretch of torn skin; snap of ligament; chewing, gnawing, licking, sucking, fucking.

woomera

Sexual rush of the kill; attention seeking throb; the ache, the lust, the power, the ultimate passivity of death. You leer over your kill; rub yourself against the still warm carcass; thrust yourself against it, squirm in pleasure, in ecstasy. A low moan escapes from you as your passion intensifies; tension builds; muscles tighten; faster, faster. You violate the body. You chew on the meat and gristle of the corpse, merciful release, total control; sex and death. What a rush. Then you see the other. It warily circles your perversity. You scrabble to your feet, life blood dripping from your mouth, life force running down your leg. It giggles. You stagger away from it. You too giggle. It paces slowly after you, taking its time, savouring this moment, feeling pleasure in the fear manifest in you. The liquid running down your leg steams in the cold mourning air. You know that you are finished but you run in hope, in fear, in desperation - fight or flight. You fly. It matches your speed, shouldering aside jars of flowers. They cascade to the ground like snowflakes. You wish you could kiss them as they wake up. It is tiring you; running you into the ground. Your chest is tight. Your breath rasps in your throat. Needle pain jabs at the back of your windpipe. There is a cloud sleeping on your tongue. You swallow. It runs down your oesophagus like mucus. You shudder. You cannot focus. You fall to the dry desert sand with a fatalistic relief. The creature, muscular, salivating power, approaches cautiously. It sniffs at your feet then licks you; its tongue is warm, its breath hot. You look into its face. It smirks.

It growls at the first taste of you. It begins to feed, slowly at first, savouring the taste of you, then faster, hungrier, greedier. Waves of pain roll over you, crashing on the rocks, drowning you in violence. You cry with shame, the pain, your insides out. Hot, hungry, breath; eaten alive; screaming silence. The blood, the smell, oh God the smell. The warm burst of released pressure.

"Jesus!"

Adam sat bolt upright in sweat-soaked fear, his clothes clinging to him like rejected lovers.

Chapter 12: Dissection

Adam sat bolt upright. "That's charming," he said.

"Truth hurts. Mate, you are *so* fucked up inside it hurts me."

They met nightly in that strange and solemn interval, the twilight of the evening, in the violet dusk and, being Tuesday the pub was pleasantly sleepy; almost comatose. A few regulars, old men and couples who lived just over the road drifted in and out like the tide, casually, like habitual insects. The bar staff leaned back under the optics, their voices low, discussing superfluous transitory thoughts as they drifted through their minds. Warm air cradled their bodies, snaking through their nostrils and down inside them.

They served Tom and Adam, genial conversation passing between them. Professional flirtation, dead-eyed smiles, anything to keep the customers happy. Tom's eyes sparkled, confident sexual predator, certain of his success. Adam supped from his pint and wandered aimlessly away from the bar to one of the many seats. Tom eventually joined him.

"Well?"

"She wants me *so* much!" said Tom.

They laughed, the undulating noise rippled outwards in concentric circles. The few people there looked in their direction, curiosity writ large, the cosiness of their conversations interrupted by this rowdiness.

"So, what do you think it means?"

"It means you're seriously fucked up," said Tom.

"That's charming."

"Truth hurts. Mate, you are so fucked up inside it hurts me. I think you might be clinically depressed."

"I'm not depressed, I'm just fucking *bored*."

"Bored of what?" said Tom.

"I don't know; everything I suppose. I'm overcome with a general sense of ennui. Nothing seems to happen anymore."

"How's Elle?"

"You're not *seriously* going out tonight, are you?"

"I think you'll find that I probably am."

"Please, Adam, I won't let you. Please stay in with me tonight, just this one night. For me."

"I'm going out and I shall see you later." He closed the front door behind him emphatically.

Elle watched him through the window. She saw the sternness implicit in his face; the hardness that never used to be there. She still loved him, more than anything she still loved him, but things had changed so much since they had been together. He no longer looked at her in silent admiration, with quiet adoration; now there was something else. Something cold and unforgiving, like he resented who she was, who she had become, who she had made *him* become.

"Elle's fine," said Adam. "Nothing happening there either."

"Has she gone out? You haven't left her at home again have you?"

"Of course I have."

Tom frowned, puzzled. "Didn't you say it was your anniversary tonight?"

Adam nodded as he took a drink.

"Why didn't you take her out for a meal?"

"She didn't want to come out; she wanted to stay in." He shrugged.

"You could have stayed in with her. I wouldn't have minded."

"Nah! We don't bother anymore. After this long it just doesn't seem important. It's been too many years." He shook his head sadly.

"Did you at least get her a present?"

"She'll get her present later." Adam smirked.

"Ha! Whether she likes it or not!"

"Oh she'll like it!" Adam raised his eyebrows.

Their peals of laughter dissolved like leaden circles. The beer fuzzed the edges of their conversation; they rambled aimlessly in their conversation. They talked lazily, freely, knowing they could tell the other almost anything. They knew everything about one another – almost.

"Remember that woman at work I told you about?" said Tom. "The one with the long, long legs and low cut tops. Proper tart she is! She has been coming on to me so strong this week, honestly, she virtually dry humped me squeezing past me at the photocopier! I swear, if I thought I could get away with it!"

"You're such a lucky bastard. I don't know how you do it."

"Do what? I haven't done anything."

"Oh come on! You were exactly the same at Uni: beautiful, sexy women falling at your feet, begging you to sleep with them. Shocking behaviour!"

Tom laughed. "It was never *quite* like that. More to do with stupid amounts of alcohol and semi-consciousness than anything else. You can't create an urban sex legend out of that juvenile fucked-up nonsense. We don't speak of those days anymore anyway, I'm a happily married man."

"Ladies and gentlemen, I would like to thank Tom, on behalf of all six bridesmaids, for not molesting them in the vestry. They all look very enticing but today is really not the day for those kind of shenanigans.

"I was slightly confused when Tom first asked me to be Best-man at his wedding but then I recalled that the only other person he knew who was a man was the one he was going to be marrying.

"So, anyway, I first met Tom when we were in a young offenders' facility together – me for shoplifting, him for corrupting the innocent – and we became firm enemies. Since then, things have grown progressively worse. We have been through many things together – most memorably, those Latvian twins, and if anyone's interested there will be a talk and a slideshow at eleven in the back-room. Book now, seats are selling fast. Then, of course, there was the incident with the college cormorant and the trombone but we're not allowed to talk about that.

"Things didn't get much better when, a number of years later, Tom managed to repeat the incident with a pygmy goat and a harpsichord – how he managed it, I'll never know; they're from completely different sections of the orchestra. And it all came to a head at the Stag-night which, I seem to recall from my vague flashbacks, ended with blue flashing lights, a fight with a hedgerow and an attempt to seduce the bride's mother.

"It wasn't that long ago that Tom met Connie, a situation that she manoeuvred him into, I'm sure. She is the best thing that's ever happened to him, if you ask her. It was lust at first sight, as is always the case with Tom, but Connie soon whipped him in to the shadow of a man you see before you today.

"I ask you all to join me in a final toast to the future happiness of the bride and groom. To Tom and Connie; may their life together bring her, I mean them, much happiness and many children."

Adam slumped down in his chair and took another swig from his champagne flute. He felt very pleased with himself; he'd said a few things he'd wanted to say in a way that he could pass-off as humour. He glanced over: Connie was clearly furious. He could see her jaw muscles clenching as she tried to smile. She avoided making eye-contact with him.

Tom leaned in to him, bleary-eyed. "Great speech, mate," he said. His voice was blurry at the edges. "A bit near-the-knuckle but very funny. I'm going to get it in the neck for what you said though." He reached round and slapped Adam firmly on the back. "I can always rely on you to dig a shit-pit for me to fall into."

Adam laughed. "You're the best friend I've ever had, Tom. The only friend I've got. If there's a shit-pit, we're in it together."

"Where's my fucking shirt?"

"Thomas!"

Tom sighed and rolled his eyes skyward. "Sorry. Have you seen my shirt? The one I sorted out for this evening."

Connie walked elegantly into the room as Tom began to scatter cushions from the sofa.

"What on earth are you doing?"

"Looking for my bloody shirt. The blue one. I sorted it out this morning. I put it over the back of the sofa. Have you seen it?"

Connie picked her way casually through the mess he was making on the floor, hooked the hanger that held his shirt off the end of the bookcase and turned to him. "This one? The one I ironed and hung because you will not be leaving this house looking like you've slept on a park bench."

Tom's face lit up and he reached for his shirt. Connie pulled it away from him and pointed at the state the room was in. He turned and sheepishly tidied the room until it was immaculate once more. She gave him his shirt from the tips of her fingers and he leaned forward to kiss her.

"No, you don't," she said. "You'll smudge my lipstick." She presented him with a cheek. He kissed her gently.

"I'll be home from the conservatoire at about 3 A.M. I'll get a taxi. The bed in the spare room is made for you; do not breathe beer on me when I get home, I will not be happy."

"Okay darling, I'll see you in the morning."

"And speaking of fucked up I did do some research on that crazy wacky dream of yours."

"Wacky? What the fuck's that supposed to mean?"

"You know what it means, crazy fool! Basically, what it seems to mean, is that you're screwed all kinds of sideways. The problem is though that all these *'meaning of your dreams'* reference things are like fucking horoscopes; they're all vague, meaningless nonsense that are open enough for you to impose something meaningful onto – a dream of a cat means you'll be a bit sad one day - *'No shit! Really?'* - and anything else is proper psychoanalytical *'You need a therapist'* stuff. I think you need a therapist."

"Fuck off!"

"Okay look, the horoscope, analysis bullshit says the tunnel is *mental conflict,* like we don't all have that, the creature, dog, panther thing was *worrying difficulties,* same bloody thing if you ask me! What flowers were they? Pansies?"

Adam flicked his middle finger in Tom's face. "Violets."

"The *violets* speak of *luurrrrrve.* Cricket is a boring social affair and falling is *fear of sexual inadequacy!*"

"Your wife never complains," said Adam.

"Only because she's been brought up to believe it's rude to laugh and point."

"How is the Ice Queen?"

"Oi! She's a very passionate woman; it's you she hates."

"'Violent antipathies betray secret affinities'," said Adam.

"You what?"

Adam shook his head dismissively. "It's all bollocks then, is what you're saying?"

"That stuff is. And Freud was off his head, obsessed with sex – flying equals sex; going into a house is sex unless it's the back door in which case it's anal sex; climbing a mountain is sex; walking through a forest is penises; walking into a cave is vaginas. The man was obsessed, very much a product of his time and he'd probably be on medication if he was alive today. The thing is, all these things mean something, on some level, to you and only you. There's no point looking this stuff up anywhere because it's all too personal, too subjective. Recurring dreams however…"

"Yes?"

"Recurring dreams mean you need a therapist. They can be traced, almost without fail, to a trauma of some sort, either physical or psychological. You are so fucked up it hurts! Your mind creates these things called engrams where it stores memories that you can't access consciously. It's where all the painful shit goes that you can't deal with; where it all gets locked away, but sometimes it leaks out."

"Now you're talking bollocks," said Adam dismissively. "All this psychobabble bullshit may have done you well at Uni but this is the real world, my friend."

"This is real-world psychobabble bullshit, my friend! There was one case where this young girl had a recurring nightmare where all she wanted was a pair of ruby slippers like Dorothy in 'The Wizard of Oz' but her mother forced her to wear a pair of red shoes like in the fairy story where they won't stop dancing, the one where they have to chop her feet off and the shoes go dancing off down the road with her feet still in them. She used to wake up terrified and the theory was that it was all about her first period – nobody had ever explained what it was or to expect it or anything so she was oblivious in her childhood and then she's suddenly forced to grow up."

"So you're saying I might be having a period?"

"No, you bell-end! I'm saying these images might not be a dream; they might be your mind trying to make sense or come to terms with a suppressed memory."

"But nothing's happened to me ever to create something like that," said Adam.

"That's the point! If something had happened you wouldn't know about it anyway. Your mind is suppressing it until your conscious mind is ready to deal with it but, at the same time, is trying to process it unconsciously – hence the recurring dream. Simply put mate: you're fucked up!"

"I'll fuck you up in a minute! I'll have a pint," he said, draining his glass.

"Suit yourself, but you'd be doing yourself a favour."

The rest of the evening passed convivially enough but Adam was worried, more worried than he looked. To all outward appearances he was just the same as usual but what Tom had said was troubling him. It was nothing he could pin down, nothing specific, but it was sitting there at the back of his mind. A semi-remembered feeling, or smell or sound; a persistent nagging doubt. Perhaps Tom was right; maybe there was something there, something taunting him from the dark recesses of his psyche, calling to him. Its teeth shining wetly in the dark, hinting at something and driving him on with the metallic scrape of skin on barbed wire, slowly revealing its body to him.

Chapter 13: Celebration

The body was soft and warm. He held it close and tucked himself into the curve of its back. The waking pain of the hangover throbbed behind his eyes and his bladder nagged at him. The body next to him muttered quietly and pushed its buttocks against his warmth with a contented murmur. He yawned. Long brown hair crowded his lips, invading his mouth, suffocating him. He pulled frantically at the strands in his mouth.

"You okay?" she said, pulling her head forward helpfully.

"Fine." He pulled her closer to him and kissed her gently on the nape of her neck.

"You beast," she groaned, nestling her bottom against his semi-erectness.

He fondled her breasts, casually stroking them and caressing them, as he desperately tried to remember her name. They had danced for most of the night, their thighs and calves echoed with the memory.

She took his hand from her breast and guided it slowly down between her legs. She moaned.

"Not so loud," he said. "You'll wake my parents."

"Parents?" Concern laced her voice.

"Yup," he said as he pushed himself into her from behind.

"Easy tiger," she said. "I thought you lived alone."

He began to move inside her. His fingertips danced around her clitoris, his other arm was under her and wrapped around her pelvis, holding her close to him.

"Nope," he said.

The sex was slow and quiet, their hangover headaches forgotten temporarily, the stale thickness of their tongues ignored. The early morning sounds from downstairs barely intruded on their gentle rutting, a dim reminder of the world outside the bedroom.

He kissed her shoulders, the few red spots there adding character to her otherwise perfect skin. He withdrew wetly from her and she clutched his hand to her breast. She kissed his knuckles and rolled over languidly to face him. She looked him in the eye.

"I can't remember your name," she said.

"Thank fuck for that! I can't remember yours either! I'm Tom."

"Trudi." She smiled awkwardly.

Tom rubbed his forehead, his eyes, sleepily. "Breakfast?"

Trudi nodded.

"My head's killing me. Wait here and I'll fetch something up."

He eased himself out of the bed as Trudi modestly pulled the sheets up to her chin. He dressed quickly and scurried downstairs. Trudi could barely remember the previous night: vague images of flashing lights. Loud music and too much beer; a passionate kiss. The trail of dried sperm on her thighs told her everything she needed to know as it was joined by that now oozing from her. She grimaced and reached for the toilet roll at the side of the bed.

Her eyes, of blue that were almost violet, had not lost their troubled look. She sat on the floor at his feet and rested her head on his knee, facing him. Adam stroked her hair. "Are you going to tell me what's going on now?" he asked.

She nodded, slowly, her eyes finally meeting his. ""I'm sorry, Adam, we can't go on like this. I can't go on like this."

His hand settled in place, stilled by her words. "Like what?"

"Like we have been: meeting in secret, snatching moments together when we can; never knowing when the next time is going to be; putting our careers at risk. Christ, some of the stupid risks we've taken."

"Aren't the risks the point?" he said.

"God, yes! It's been incredible. I've had such a good time with you, Adam. It's been truly amazing but it's got to be too much. You're getting in too deep."

His eyes narrowed, urging her to continue.

"This was only ever meant to be fun," she said. "A thrill a minute plane ride; all the excitement of the fair." She smiled. "But it's starting to hurt you, and not in the good way." She squeezed his thigh affectionately. "You're falling in love with me, Adam, and neither of us can afford to let that happen."

Adam shook his head. "This is bullshit," he said.

"What?"

"This is bullshit," he said. "This was never about falling in love; this was about sex. It was only ever about sex."

"At the beginning, maybe, but I don't believe you can keep giving yourself to me without feeling something more. The absolute trust you have in me must lead somewhere, Adam, and

I can't go down that path with you. I won't go there with you. I refuse to be responsible for your marriage."

"It's true that I trust you," he said, "but don't flatter yourself. I feel nothing for you. I only ever lusted after you. You're a decent fuck, I'll give you that, but love you? I don't think so." He pushed her head off his knee and got to his feet. "That's all you ever were to me: a quick fuck in the cupboard."

"I understand you're upset, Adam, but there's no need for this."

He shrugged dismissively. "I'll see you at work in the morning."

Tom laughed boisterously as he downed the last of his drink. His face was smeared with mud and blood and his shirt half hung off his shoulder, the huge tear exposing most of his muscular back. The small gash beneath his hairline tingled. Steam danced around him and his friends as they began to dry in the warmth of the bar.

Two figures threaded their way towards the table; the crowd was jovial, their behaviour joyful yet threatening if you weren't one of them. One of the two figures was part of this group, dressed as they were, but the other was dry, clean, and short. They reached Tom's table.

"Good man," said Tom supping from his fresh pint.

"This is Adam," said John.

"Hi!" He gripped Adam's hand manfully. "Did you enjoy the game?"

"There was a game?"

"The rugger man!"

"Sorry, I was busy with something else."

"Something else? Don't be bloody daft, there isn't 'something else'! We mullered the buggers!"

John laughed. He and Tom raised their glasses and downed them in one, the rest of the crowd chanting encouragement. They slammed their glasses down on the table and belched loudly in unison. The crowd clapped and cheered.

"Progress report please, sir!" said John.

Tom wiped his hand across his mouth. "On the little blonde I've been chit-chatting to? Irish. Gorgeous accent, fabulous body. She's a good Catholic girl."

"There's no such thing as a *good* Catholic girl," said John.

"You've obviously never had one," said Tom with a wink.

Adam shook his head. "Do you have to practice?"

"Practice what?"

"Being a misogynistic stereotype."

Tom laughed at him. "No, sir, it's a natural talent."

Adam picked up his drink as he stood to leave. "I thought you said he was all right?" he said to John. "Maybe he will be when he grows up."

John tutted. "Come on, Adam, we're just having some fun."

"Fuck him," said Tom. "Let him go. We'll have more fun without the prissy little prick anyway. He can come back when he lightens up."

Adam pushed his way through the crowd, not even acknowledged by the majority there, and out of the bar.

"Little dickhead," said Tom as Adam disappeared.

A fine, mist-like rain was settling: delicate, thoughtful, wistful rain. A small group of mourners gathered at the graveside. Gentle, undeserved words were spoken. Adam stood in the shadow of the trees far from the funeral. He couldn't hear what was being said but he knew – lies, hypocrisy; anything to make those left behind feel better about themselves.

Adam thrust his hands deeper in to his coat pockets. There was a biting chill to the wind, even though the wind itself was barely noticeable; more like a whispered breath of air than wind. The tips of his ears hurt.

The final words were spoken and, one-by-one, led by Michael, the mourners stepped forward and threw a handful of earth in to the hole before them. Adam could hear someone sobbing; his auntie, that dear, frail old lady, harsh, stern and loving. She was a distant figure, forever caught in the orbit of his life, on the distant fringes of his pain. They drifted away, eventually, their babbling voices washed out to sea.

Adam stood alone for a long while under the trees, with his thoughts, before stepping out from their meagre shelter. He shuffled to the graveside and stared down at the coffin. It looked so peaceful; it was more than the man deserved. Why should he have peace when he had provided nothing but suffering? How could nobody protest at the hypocrisy of burying him here, next to the woman who had given Adam nothing but love? What peace for her now?

Adam scooped up a handful of dirt; it was thick and damp and cold. He squeezed it between his fingers; it smelled of leaf mould. It broke into lumps as he tossed it in to the grave; it rattled emptily on the lid of the coffin. Adam wiped his hand clean on a tissue and threw that in to the grave too.

"I'm going whether you like it or not."

"Over my dead body."

"That shouldn't be too difficult to organise."

"I won't have you going to that bloody University."

"You can't stop me, Dad. This is something that I want to do; it's something Mum would have wanted me to do," said Adam. "She'd have been proud to see me trying to better myself."

"And that attitude is exactly why I'm not letting you go. *Better* yourself? *Better* than who exactly? Are you saying you're *better* than your own family? Because you're not. You're one of us, boy, and you always will be."

"That's not what I mean, Dad." Adam sighed.

"Then explain it to me in words you think I might understand. This is a working-class family and it always has been; you think you can go gallivanting off and be better than that? There's nothing wrong with working hard for a living."

"I'm not saying there is and I'm not saying that there's anything wrong with manual labour either. I don't know what I want to do after Uni; I might go and work in a factory, I don't really care, but for now I'm going to Uni. I want to read, Dad. I want to learn, and there's nothing wrong with that either. I want this. I need it for myself, if nothing else. You can't stop me."

"You're a stuck-up little ponce, is your problem. You always have been. It's your mother's fault; she mollycoddled you, made you think you're something special. Well you're not. Go to University, have your mind corrupted by the shite they spout. I really don't give a shit."

"Thanks, Dad."

"You seemed to be getting on okay," said Trudi.

"He's just so lovely," said Elle. "He was really shy at first, it was difficult getting any kind of conversation out of him but when he finally got going..."

"Love then, is it?"

"You never know," said Elle. "Stranger things have happened."

"So did you?"

"What?"

"Fuck him. You know you wanted to."

"Trudi! You have to bring everything down to groin level; that's all you ever think about."

"It's all there is! So did you?"

"No I did not! He was a perfect gentleman, sort of. We talked, we drank, smoked a little and then he walked me home. A snog and a grope on the doorstep before the folks realised what was going on and he was away. It took me ages to get to sleep."

Trudi yawned. "I had a much more exciting time."

"We did notice you and Tom dancing off together. Trollop."

"That's about as much as I can remember to be honest. This morning was interesting though. He's a fabulous fuck."

"Jesus Trudi, keep your voice down, my parents will hear."

"That's what he said this morning!"

"You are crude, rude, depraved and incorrigible."

"You love it!" said Trudi. "You wish you were me so you could take that meaty young thing from last night, wrap your thighs around him and *squeeze* every last drop out of him."

Elle blushed and giggled. "I can't believe you slept with Tom."

"I'll describe his dick for you if you like then you can go and check for yourself!"

"No need, I believe you! What's he like?"

"I told you, he's a fabulous…" she leaned forward and whispered, "…*fuck*."

Elle tutted. "No, what's *he* like?"

Trudi shrugged dismissively. "He seems okay, it's not like I'm going to marry him or anything."

"Did he say anything about Adam?"

"Of course not, we were too busy trying to get into each others' pants!" She glanced sideways at Elle. "You're not getting in too deep too soon are you, sweetie?"

Elle shook her head.

"Just take it slowly," said Trudi. "You've only known him for a few hours, just be careful. We don't want you getting hurt again, do we?" She leaned across and kissed Elle on the cheek; her lips lingered and Elle did not move away.

Trudi shifted her weight and moved slightly closer. Her hand cradled Elle's jaw line. She kissed Elle again on the cheek, then again moving slowly round towards her mouth. She kissed the corner of Elle's lips tentatively, their softness making her tingle.

"You're so beautiful," she said. She kissed Elle softly on the lips. Elle pulled away.

"Trudi! No!"

"But you said you were curious."

"That was years ago! And I couldn't, not with you, it wouldn't feel right."

Trudi looked hurt.

"That's not what I meant. I mean that I couldn't do something like that with my best friend, I wouldn't want our friendship to end over something as stupid as sex."

"I know," said Trudi. "I was only winding you up."

Elle smiled and kissed Trudi on the cheek.

"You'll always regret it though; always wonder what you missed out on."

Elle laughed.

The stench of fireworks and wood-smoke clung thickly to Adam's clothes and hair. The display had been magnificent; the bite of the wind had been staved-off by the roaring bonfire. The crowd milled and jostled around him, tightly swaddled bodies pressed against him and squeezed by, excitedly dispersing. Adam and Tom drifted towards the pub.

It had been an interesting day: Graduation, the other students chattering and racing around the campus, families in tow; so much joy and excitement. Adam swished his gown out behind him and smiled at the sheer childish joy of having a cape. He had, naturally, been uncooperative when having his graduation photo taken, blinking at the last second; looking in the wrong direction and resolutely refusing to smile. He had relented in the end though; one or two decent pictures for his granddad.

He had marched confidently on to the stage during the ceremony, his nervousness hidden behind his brash exterior, his only confidence being that they would find out that he didn't really deserve to be here. He took the blank, ribbon-tied, scroll, shook a proffered hand, and strode in to the wings.

Adam and Tom strode in to the pub. The blast of hot air crashed over them like a breaker; beads of sweat sprung to their brows. Adam unbuttoned his coat and whipped his scarf off. "See if you can find us a seat," said Adam. He fought his way to the bar as Tom went off. The room was thick with people; hot dampness rose like a fug from the tightly packed bodies.

A hand clamped down on his shoulder.

"I knew you'd come here," said his father with a grimace. "Your mate is sitting with your brother at a table over by that window. Why don't we go to the bar together, it doubles our chances of getting served?" He slipped an arm around Adam's shoulder and forced his way through the crowd.

Adam propped his elbows on the bar, desperately trying to catch the eye of one of the bar staff; he didn't take his eyes off them, anything not to have to look at his father. He placed his order and watched as the bar man poured the drinks, painfully aware that his father was watching his every move. He felt like he was being scrutinised, examined, like a bacteria under a microscope. His every movement was being logged and recorded for future reference. "I didn't expect to see you and Michael today," he said. He turned to face his father as the last of the drinks were placed in front of him.

"I know you didn't. I don't suppose you thought that we'd know it was Graduation, did you?"

Adam shook his head. "No. What do you want, Dad?"

Joseph picked his pint up and raised it to Adam. "I just wanted you to know that I'm proud of you, son," he said.

Adam blushed. He felt awkward. He didn't know what to say. He picked up his own glass and drank deeply. He didn't care if his father was proud of him or not; it changed nothing, but he couldn't help but feel pleased that he had made him feel something positive. It vindicated his achievement, legitimised it. "You never wanted me to go to Uni," he said.

"Yes I did. You were the only one of us, the first of us, that I thought might be able to do it. I didn't want you to know it is all. I didn't want you getting stuck-up like all the other pretentious little wankers."

"You still don't get it, do you, Dad?" He picked Tom's pint up and made his way through the parting crowd where his brother and his best friend sat waiting. His father followed closely behind, a satisfied smile playing across his lips.

Adam felt the pressure of a hand holding his own. His hopes swam: Elle had come to see him; she'd heard about what had happened, about how desperately he missed her. She had finally heard about the depths he had plumbed in her absence and she had come to see if he was okay. His eyes fluttered open.

"Hello, little brother," said Michael.

Adam's chest imploded; the void inside collapsed in on itself. All the air was sucked from the room. "What the fuck do you want?" he asked.

"Oh, that's bloody charming, that is," said Michael gently. "I fight my way through floods and blizzards to be by your side and that's all the thanks I get!"

Adam swallowed thickly.

Michael squeezed his hand. "Tom let me know what happened."

"Bastard!"

"Be fair, Adam. Don't give him a hard time. He did what he thought was right. I needed to know."

"Pass me some water," said Adam. He took the beaker from Michael's hand and drank. His throat burned. "Why are you here? What do you want?"

"I'm here because I care for my little brother. I wanted to make sure you're okay."

"I'm fine; you can go now." He pulled his hand free of Michael's grip; his eyes threw a challenge at his brother.

"You're not fine though, are you? Tom told me what's been going on. What happened between you and Elle? I thought you two were together for life; she adores you."

"We *are* married for life; she'll be back, she just doesn't know it yet. It's none of your concern anyway. You haven't bothered about me since..." Adam looked away.

"That's not fair, is it? This is an old argument, Adam, and I'm not going to dredge it all up again now. I heard you were in hospital and needed help; I'm here to offer it."

"I don't need your help." Adam's eyes flicked worriedly towards Michael's and away again.

"That doesn't stop me talking to you, does it? I've just come out with some friends for a Christmas drink and thought I'd pop in and see how you were doing."

"Dad loved it when you talked about me, I bet. I hate to think what he said to you after I left," said Adam.

Michael shrugged. "I never let what he thought bother me. Not that I ever told him anything; he was too sick to care in the end."

Their eyes locked briefly.

"I can't stop long, Adam, I really have come out with some friends for a drink. I'm meeting them in town in about thirty minutes."

Adam stretched out a hand and Michael took it in his once again. "You're a better person than I am," said Adam.

"Don't be ridiculous," said Michael.

"It's true. You're stronger than I am; always have been. You're not like him at all and you never will be." He clenched Michael's hand. "I love her too much, Mikey. I don't think I can live without her."

Michael took Adam's hand in both of his and kissed it. "Of course you can, Adam. It hurts now but you'll be fine. You're stronger than you know. You'll get through this; you have people who love you, who care for you, people who will always be there for you, no matter what. You're my little brother, Adam, and I will never leave you."

Adam wept.

"God Elle! Are you sure?"

"Positive, yes! It's taken me a while to actually make up my mind but yes, I'm sure."

"Marriage is such a big step though; what a massive commitment. You have to be absolutely sure of this, it's not that easy to change your mind afterwards."

"I'm going to marry him," said Elle. "I can't quite believe it's real. I feel, I don't know, like I'm stoned or like I've stood up too quickly."

Trudi hugged her; tears of happiness and fear ran down Elle's face. "Look at me," she said. "My hands are trembling. You've got to keep this quiet still Trudi, I haven't even told Adam."

"Of course not."

"No, really! You've got to promise. I mean it."

"I promise! Jesus you're such a worrier!"

"It's just that I know you and Adam don't really get on too well but I love him so much."

"And that's why I wouldn't say anything. I would never hurt you, no matter how much I dislike him. What have your parents said?"

"Don't!" said Elle. "I dread to think! Do you remember practising when we were little? You, me and little Johnny in the back garden."

Trudi laughed. "Rose petals for confetti and bullying him into walking the aisle made of pebbles and your rabbit was the vicar."

Elle nodded with a smile. "And the bridesmaids were all ladybirds. A proper fairy-tale wedding."

"Whatever happened to John?"

"No idea," said Elle. "He's probably on his fourth or fifth marriage by now; the number of times we made him marry us both he might even be in prison for bigamy."

"I need you to tell me what happened."

Joseph Clare stared coldly at the old man sitting before him. "Why? It won't change anything."

"I need to hear it from you. I need to look you in the eye while you tell me you did everything you could; I need to know that you tried everything to save my little girl."

Joseph let a small smile play across his lips. The subdued chatter bubbled around them, voices rising and falling like dust-motes in a sunbeam as Clarissa Clare's friends and family caught-up and talked about the years since they had last spoken. "She made my breakfast and came back to bed," he said. "Then she died." He heard his father-in-law's breath catch. "It was over before it even began. The coroner said there was nothing that could have been done; she'd have died even if she'd been in hospital when it happened."

"But did you try?"

"I tried my best," said Joe. "Now it's just me and my boys."

"And me. I will do everything I can to help these children; I will be here for them whenever they need me."

"I don't think that's going to be necessary anymore," said Joe. "I think we're going to manage just fine without your interfering."

"Interfering? They're my grandchildren; my own flesh and blood. You can't..."

"I can," said Joe, "and I am. You're not welcome here; I don't want you anywhere near my boys. They've already been ruined and now I'm going to do my best to put it all right again."

"But they're my daughter's boys; I have a right."

"You have a right to leave my home, now," said Joe, pointing at the door.

The old man looked at Joseph in disbelief. "I knew you were a bad one right from the start, Joseph Clare, but I had no idea how bad. I know how you treated my daughter but she told me she loved you; now she's gone. I don't believe you ever loved her. You used her and threw her away. She told me what you were like, you pathetic little man, and this just proves she was right. You're taking the boys away from me to punish her and she's not even here; all you're doing is hurting them.

I'm going to leave now. I'm not going to make a fuss or a scene and I'm doing that for the sake of my grandsons, not you. But know this: I will be waiting for them when they come looking for me, and they *will* come looking for me. And I will be the father figure that you never will be. You're a nasty, spiteful, piece of work."

"Get out of my fucking house."

Anger burned in the old man's eyes as he stormed out of the room. He was brought-up short by the sight of Adam and Michael sitting together at the foot of the stairs; they looked so small and vulnerable and helpless. They looked up at him; Adam's eyes were wide and innocent, Michael's creased with curiosity.

"Are you going home now, Granddad?" asked Michael.

Granddad nodded. "I'm afraid so," he said, crouching down before them. "It might be a little while before I can see you again." He pulled them to him in a tight embrace. "I've got to go away for a little while but when you're a bit older you can maybe come and see me again, yes?"

"Can we play now, before you go?" asked Adam.

"I'm sorry, son, but I really have to go now. We can play next time you see me, okay?"

Adam nodded. Granddad kissed them both on the forehead and gave them one last hug. "See you both soon, my beautiful boys."

Adam knocked nervously on the door. He waited, shuffling his weight from side to side. He looked over his shoulder, certain that he had been followed. He thought he could feel his father's eyes boring holes in to his back. There was no way he could know; how could he?

The sun was beating down on him; he could feel the weight of it burning his shoulders and the hair on the crown of his head. His thin, white, school-shirt clung to him; he hoisted his bag of books in to a more comfortable position. He knocked the door again, harder this time, more insistent. He looked around.

The garden was less tidy than he remembered it; the flower-border was blurred, the overgrown grass smudging the line between turf and soil. The hedges were tatty sprigs of privet springing haphazardly from once clean lines like cushions that had burst their seams. Adam bit his bottom lip. A car crawled past, its tyres tacky on the hot tarmac. Adam wondered if it was hot enough yet to fry an egg on its bonnet.

There was a rattle of chains on the other side of the door. Adam stared at it, fear and anticipation welling up inside him, threatening to burst free. He felt like he was about to burst in to tears. He had nowhere else to go. The door opened slowly, cautiously; a face peered out at him from the cool darkness within. It was older, thinner, more worried than he ever remembered it being. Rheumy eyes settled on him and lit a spark within. The face creased into a smile. Adam smiled back, his heart swelling.

"Hello, Granddad," he said. "Can I come in?"

"Your granddad wouldn't have approved."

Adam stuck his tongue out in defiance and smiled at the thought of the old man. He sat forward in the chair and pulled the coffee table close to his knee. He crouched over it, concentrating. Tom leaned forward to watch and opened a can.

Adam opened a fresh packet of cigarettes, discarded the plastic wrapper nonchalantly and selected a cigarette. Sweeping sounds eddied from the stereo and the room was bathed in the flickering light of the muted television. Adam threw the packet onto the table. He pulled a single cigarette paper from its pack and laid it flat on the table top. He held the cigarette up to the light and turned it, once he had found the join he ran the tip of his tongue the length of it then picked at the end and pulled. The glued section peeled away to the filter. Adam carefully tipped the now loose tobacco onto the open cigarette paper and broke it up. He dropped the now empty husk of the cigarette into the ashtray and smiled.

"This is where it gets interesting," he said. He picked up a tobacco tin and rattled it lovingly. He popped the lid off, lifted a small black lump out, and sniffed it. "Lovely."

He thumbed his lighter into life and held the block over the nervous flame. He broke the cooked corner off the block and crumbled it evenly amongst the waiting tobacco, then returned the block to the tin. Tenderly, like he was handling something precious, he rolled the tobacco into a loose semblance of a cigarette. He twisted one end firmly and ripped a thin strip off the cigarette paper packet; he rolled this into a tube and inserted it into the open end of the joint, tucking the loose edges of the paper in with a dead match. He held up the finished product proudly.

"Now," he said. "I know you don't smoke, so listen. Inhale, don't swallow. If you swallow, you'll be sick. Your body will *not* appreciate a stomach full of smoke!"

Tom nodded enthusiastically.

"I told you you'd be sick," said Adam later that night through thick lips. His eyes were glassy and bloodshot.

Tom slumped back on the sofa, his arms and legs splayed out. "Pah! I feel like a squashed insect."

"Well you can't have one, although I do have some dead-fly biscuits if you like?"

Tom giggled.

"I ate some Jammy Dodgers once when I was stoned, a whole packet, it was like eating a bag of flour. They sucked all of the moisture out of my face. I haven't eaten one since."

Tom's face reddened as he descended into helpless giggles.

"Oh shit, it's the countdown," said Adam scrabbling furiously for the remote controls. He muted the stereo and cranked up the sound on the TV. He poured two shots of whiskey and passed one to Tom.

"Happy New Year!" they cheered and took the shots down in one.

"Let's hope it's better than last year," said Tom.

"Fuck yes," said Adam pouring another two shots.

"You know what I'll never understand?" asked Tom scratching the tip of his nose.

"What?" said Adam passing him a shot-glass.

"Russian," said Tom. He laughed loudly, wiped a tear from his eye, and downed his shot.

"Seriously though, I'll never understand women."

"Why?"

"Because they all speak bloody Russian! No really, they might as bloody well! It's like they're making it all up as they go along. Like that girl I was seeing last year…the year before…whenever. One week I was a secretive bastard and what was I hiding for not telling her something and the next week I was an insensitive bastard for telling her something she didn't want to hear. How the fuck am I supposed to keep track of shit like that?"

"I don't get it either," said Adam.

"Don't think I ever will either."

"Me neither," said Adam.

"Don't think I even bloody want to."

"Nor me," said Adam.

"Fuck 'em!"

"Fuck 'em all!"

"I intend to," said Tom.

They collapsed into fits of giggles. An air of contentedness pervaded the room as the smoke gradually dissipated, the smell of stale beer and smoke seeping into the soft furnishing. They eventually fell asleep where they sat, succumbing to the shimmer of unconsciousness as their minds deserted them.

Chapter 14: Shame

Adam staggered noisily down the deserted high street. Shop fronts gleamed dully in their silver-grey armour, confrontational and anti-social. His footsteps echoed flatly, his thoughts echoing through his drunken confused mind. Maybe there was something tucked away in his past, buried deep down. He rummaged through all of the childhood cruelties he had ever committed: playground taunts, insects burned in the summer sun, Daddy-Long – No-Legs and petty childhood jealousies. There was nothing that could or would cause such night terror.

The rhythmic tap-tapping of his footsteps changed timbre as he moved from the metallic brightness of the shop fronts and into the dead darkness of the deserted backstreets. The weariness in his legs forced him to sit briefly on the cold hardness of a low brick wall. Shrubbery jostled at him, pulling eagerly at his clothes. He tried to shrug it away but it persisted. He turned angrily to bend the branches back, to snap them away from him, the brickwork tugged at the seat of his trousers and he tumbled into the soft dirt of the garden's border.

As he struggled to his knees he became aware of the sound of approaching voices. He crouched back into the hedge behind the wall. The voices grew louder quickly, angry and raised, as three people turned into the street; running through the darkness, pushing and shoving. Their faces were contorted, ugly and twisted in their violence. Adam peered out at them. Weak, jaundiced light was shed onto the road as the raucous cries gave way to quiet grunts of animal violence. The two larger men pounded the third to the ground, the blows raining down from their fists replaced by heavy booted feet. He found himself urging them on quietly, sucking in air as each blow made contact. This would teach that bastard a lesson he would never forget; he probably deserved it too.

The two men stood panting triumphantly over the crumpled heap, hands on their knees as they fought to catch their breath. They looked at each other, laughter dancing in their eyes, and then they ran into the night singing their song of victory. Adam watched, wincing in sympathy as the slumped youth slowly and painfully recovered enough to stand and stagger on his way.

Adam's legs were heavy with numbness as he stood, the soft ground making him more unsteady than he already was. Clumps of flowers sprouted greyly in the half-light near his feet; he reached down and pulled a bunch from the ground, earth and roots trailing desperately ground-ward.

A noise: wood sliding on wood.

"Get out of me bleeding flower beds!" a voice shouted from above; an old voice, male, a nervous tremor betraying the threat. Adam looked up at the blanched white figure as it leaned out of the window. He stepped from the bushes and onto the lawn.

"I'll call the police," said the old man. A smaller voice said something from behind him; the old man replied in a hushed whisper.

"Bollocks to you!" said Adam and left to continue his walk home.

"Do you want to come round our house and watch it there?"

"I don't know if our dad will let us."

"Course he will."

"I'd have to ask him."

"Let's go and ask him now," said Adam.

He could not quite believe it. Here he was, talking to the most beautiful girl in his class and the best line he could think of was '*Do you want to come to our house?*'

The girl thought a while then nodded. "Okay."

They walked slowly in the direction of her house. Fiona talked incessantly, telling him all of the classroom gossip, most of which he already knew. A profusion of misunderstood yearnings surged through his body and he wondered what she would look like naked. He quickly dismissed the thought as he felt the eager stirring of his loins.

"Wait here," she said.

He stood patiently on the doorstep, gently kicking his heels and swinging his school bag from side to side. He waved occasionally to the cheery jeers of his school-friends and looked around worriedly in case her parents should hear.

The door opened behind him. He turned and looked up at Fiona's father.

"Hello, sir," he said.

"Right. I'm going to let my daughter come with you to your house. You are going to look after her. You are going to make sure that she comes to no harm. You are going to bring her back home before eight o'clock. Clear?"

Adam nodded.

"I know your father. I know where you live. Got it?"

Adam nodded.

"Right."

Fiona emerged from behind her father and together they headed for Adam's. "Take no notice of him," she said. "He's a pussycat really."

Adam laughed nervously. "You'll be home by eight, don't you worry yourself." She had changed out of her school uniform and looked even more beautiful; she looked at least three years older now. She was stunning. By the time they sat in the living room Adam felt like he was going to collapse from nervous exhaustion.

"I have no idea where Dad or Michael are," he said.

"That's okay," she said. "Why don't you come and sit next to me?" She patted the cushion next to her.

Adam blushed and looked at his feet. "Don't you want a drink?"

"Come and sit down," she said. Her eyes bored into him. He felt exposed, naked and unprotected. He complied.

"Do you want to kiss me?" she said.

"Yes," he said.

"Go on then!" She nudged him with her knee.

Adam's key scratched across the lock. He closed his eyes and steadied himself. He pursed his lips and opened his eyes; the key was poised over the hole. He concentrated, frowned, and slid it easily into the lock. He opened the door and stumbled into the safety of his own home. He took a deep breath.

"Elle!"

"In here," she said from the living room.

He pointed himself in the right direction and staggered her way.

"Happy anniversary," he said thrusting the battered bunch of flowers at her. Soil scattered across the carpet.

"Oh Adam," said Elle. "They're...*lovely*." She took them from him.

"I would have given you some violets but they all withered when my grandfather snuffed it." He snorted.

Elle frowned. "I'll just get a vase for these." She retired quickly to the kitchen and returned with the stalks neatly trimmed and the flowers arranged hurriedly.

"Did you have a nice night?" she said.

"Why are you still up?"

She looked at her feet. "I thought you'd like me to be awake when you came home. It's our anniversary."

"I know it's our fucking anniversary. Answer the question."

"That is the reason," she said. A tear sprang to her eye. Her lip trembled.

"You were waiting up to check on me, weren't you?"

"Oh God, Adam, no I wasn't. I swear I wasn't." She backed away as he took a step towards her; menace emanating from him. "I swear I wasn't. Please Adam, don't," she said, palms towards him in futile defence.

He stopped. He pursed his lips. He looked at her with pity and stepped back. "Okay," he said.

She released the pressure that had built up inside her in one long breath, dropping her hands to her sides. The first blow caught her on the temple; a wave of dizziness and pain swept through her. The second caught her straight on the nose, white pain flashed behind her eyes, rushed through her sinuses. Blood blossomed wetly; her face felt sticky. She could hear something far away, see something vague through the light. She felt herself being lifted, could feel her body being shaken; could hear the noises – strange disembodied animal noises.

Her husband drifted into focus.

"Adam?"

He threw her across the room. Flowers and water scattered across the floor as she crashed through the coffee table. He kicked her twice in the ribs and leaned down to her. His face close to hers.

"Look what you've done, you stupid bitch." He grabbed her by the hair and forced her to look at the wreckage she lay in. He picked up a shard of glass in his free hand and brought it close to her face. Blood trickled thickly from her nose, the front of her pyjamas were stained crimson.

"I could take your eye out. You fell over, tripped, and went through the coffee table. No-one would ever know."

She sobbed, unable to shut out the light glinting off the glass.

He tossed it away and helped her to her feet. He slapped her sharply across the left cheek, then back-hand across the right. She cried, tears commingling with the blood and mucus on her face, strands of thick fluid were hanging from her chin. He wiped his hand on her then punched her hard in the chest. Air exploded from her. She tried to fall to her knees but Adam held her upright. He pulled her close to him, scrutinising every part of her, then shoved her as hard as he could. She struck the wall, her head cracked backwards, and she fell to the floor, a bloodied ragged heap. He watched her for a while where she lay.

Adam's lips and throat were dry.

"Not like that," Fiona said gently. She turned towards him and held his chin in her hand. "Like this." She kissed him slowly, wetly, on the lips. Unsure, he kept his eyes wide open, terrified of doing something wrong. She pulled away.

"Now, *you* kiss *me*," she said.

He licked his lips and swallowed hard. He kissed her; he could feel himself, erect and throbbing, as fear filled curiosity welled up inside him. She thrust her tongue into his mouth. He jumped back, startled and a little bit disgusted, desperately trying to hide his erection.

"It's a French Kiss," she said.

He looked at her blankly.

"Never mind," she said. She noted the bulge in his trousers. "Shall we go up to your bedroom?"

"Okay," he said. He leaped to his feet and faced away from her so he stood with his back to her, hoping against hope that she hadn't noticed.

The room was small and cramped. Two single beds guarded their territory from each end of the room. Clothes were strewn around the room and tattered posters clung hopefully to the faded wallpaper.

"That's my brother's bed," said Adam as he sat on the edge of his own.

Fiona perched next to him and kissed his earlobe.

"I want you to touch me," she said.

He looked at her, hope rising in his face. She undid her bra through her top. He lunged forward eagerly. Fiona fell back on the bed with a practised moan of pleasure. Adam felt her breasts through her clothes; the warm softness of her flesh, the peculiar erectness of her nipples. She grabbed his hand.

"What?" he asked, worried that he had done something wrong.

She shook her head, her eyes clamped firmly shut. She guided his hand down; down from the warm pertness of her chest, across the firm smooth skin of her stomach; down. He fumbled clumsily, his hand snaking into her underwear; his fingers probing through her pubic hair and into her moist pinkness. He struggled to find her, his fingers digging and probing urgently and pushing until she gave him succour. He almost ejaculated. Beads of sweat trembled on his brow as his excitement mounted.

"I want you inside me," she said.

"I am," he said. His fingers probed deeper, the elastic waistband of her knickers cutting off the blood supply to his wrist.

"No," she said. "Do it to me."

Adam pulled away from her as he realised what she meant. He wiped her off his fingers.

"My dad'll be home soon," he said.

"How soon?"

Adam shrugged.

"That's plenty of time," she said. She sat up, pulled her pants off and lifted her skirt for him. He looked away, embarrassed, but quickly removed his trousers.

"Put it in me," she said.

He felt himself gushing into her almost before he had penetrated her. He lay sweating on top of her, unsure now of what to do. Fiona was moaning and wriggling around under him but she quickly realised he was finished and descended into stillness.

"Finished?" she said with a giggle.

He nodded, his face burning with shame.

"First time was it?" There was a hint of sarcasm in her voice.

"No," he said. "I was in a hurry."

A yell erupted from downstairs.

"Oh shit! It's me dad!" said Adam. He leaped to his feet, fluids running freely down his leg. He pulled his trousers on as Fiona too got dressed.

"Quick! Out of the window," he said.

"Piss off! I'm not climbing out of a bloody window!"

Adam rushed back and forth, trying to find somewhere for her to hide. His father's footsteps approached; his breathing was audible and ominous. The door was pushed open.

"Hello, Mr Clare," said Fiona from where she sat on the edge of the bed. "Adam was just showing me his comics."

Mr Clare glared at them.

"Yeah well, Adam can get his bloody arse downstairs and you can piss off home."

Fiona looked at him aghast.

"And you needn't bother with that '*nobody's ever spoken to me that way before*' bollocks either. I know your father, he's a good man, and I know you too – you're a little slut. Now piss off home!"

"*Dad!*"

Mr Clare smacked Adam sharply around the back of his head. "Get downstairs."

Adam ran from his room, anger and shame welling up inside him. Fiona followed closely on his heels and rushed out of the house without another word or glance at him. Her sobs lingered in the air of the dead home long after she had gone.

"Why do you always do that?"

"Why do I always do what?"

"Cut the toast diagonally; you know how much it irritates me. Do you do it on purpose or are you just fucking stupid?"

"It's a force of habit. I'm sorry, my father always had his toast cut that way and it's the way I've always done it. Sometimes I forget."

"You should have learned by now. What's it going to take?"

Clarissa slid into bed next to her husband as he lathered his toast with butter and tucked in. "Would you rather I didn't cut it at all?" she asked.

"I'd rather you learned to cut it properly," he said. He pulled the pillows up behind his back and settled himself comfortably into position. "That way, we could all have a nice, peaceful Sunday morning breakfast in bed."

Clarissa sighed quietly to herself and picked up her cup of tea. The cup rattled on the saucer. She stilled it with her free hand and frowned.

"What are you doing now?" asked Joe.

"Nothing," she said. "My hand feels a little tingly, is all. I must have slept on it funny, it'll be fine in a moment."

Joseph shook his head. "There's always something to complain about with you, isn't there?"

"I'm not complaining, Joe, just telling you what you wanted to know." She sipped carefully at the hot, brown liquid. "I think the milk might have gone off," she said, her nose wrinkling at the smell.

Joseph picked up the mug from his tray and sniffed at his coffee cautiously, then took a sip. "Tastes fine to me," he said. He tapped at his boiled egg and sliced the top off. He scooped hungrily at the contents, spooning it into his mouth. Hot yolk ran down his chin.

Clarissa slumped back against her pillow. Her tea spilled on the bed. The cup and saucer fell to the floor.

"Clumsy bugger," said Joe. He smiled to himself. "You'll have to clean that up before I get out of bed."

"I don't feel very well," said Clarissa. Pain burned in her temple. She winced at the light.

"You'll cope," said Joe.

Clarissa retched. Still-hot tea steamed down her chin and on to her chest. Joseph looked at her, eyes wide. Her body began to convulse, her eyes rolled up into her skull as neurons fired randomly through her brain. She twitched spastically, her body spasmed, fighting itself. Muscles and tendons clenched and released. She writhed on the bed. Thews stood out angrily on her neck; animal noises escaped from her throat – growls and howls of primitive release. Her back arched. Then, she stilled. A thin rivulet of drool crept from the corner of her mouth.

Joseph watched her for a while then finished his breakfast. He placed his tray on the bedside cabinet and got out of bed. He wiped her clean, changed her nightclothes and arranged her neatly in the bed. He combed her hair and kissed her on the forehead. "Dirty bitch," he said, then went and got the boys out of their bedroom.

"I want you to look at her," he said. "She's beautiful, isn't she?"

Michael and Adam nodded but said nothing.

"She looked like this when I first met her – peaceful and quiet; beautiful. She's sleeping now. She'll always be sleeping now. I thought it would do you both good to see her like this. To see that death is nothing to be afraid of. We'll all be like this one day, boys, so make the most of it while you're here. You have to be strong, you have to look life in the face and tell it to fuck right off if it gives you any shit, you hear me?"

They nodded.

"Of course, the world was a better place when we met; a gentler place. Somewhere where all your neighbours knew who you were and we all looked out for one another. That's how I met her: there was a travelling fun-fair at the park and she looked so lost. Pretty little thing she was, all timid and shy. Wouldn't say 'boo' to a goose, wouldn't even look me in the eye when I tried to look after her. But she soon came round; I took her under my wing, poor little sparrow, all drab and nervous, and together we made my two strong boys.

No more molly-coddling for you now though, eh? You're both going to grow up to be big, strong men like your father." He ruffled their hair. "She's gone to a better place now. Kiss her goodbye, both of you."

They each leaned onto the bed and kissed her gently. The waxiness of her skin held remnants of warmth.

"Now go and tell your grandfather what's happened. I'll be waiting here."

The laughter came at him from all sides; girls giggled at him from the corners of the playground, boys sniped at him in the classrooms and changing rooms. The jibes stinging more than the ruler strikes or damp towels flicked at his buttocks in the changing room. Blood heated his face from within until he felt like he was about to burst into flames. He tried not to see, not to hear, but wherever he went they taunted him. Fiona scurried past him in the corridor; her laughter tormented him. He was so alone. He could see her semi-naked and wished he had told her to leave him alone. He hated her for this.

"Hey, Clare!"

Adam looked up. A lanky boy, tall with unwieldy limbs, towered over him. His hair was lank, unwashed; his skin perfect and spot free.

"That Fiona tells me you've only got a little one. That must be true." His friends chuckled around Adam, encircling him with their own inadequacies.

"No," he said. His face burned.

"He's blushing! Bless him! Just like a little girl."

Adam turned, tried to walk away. The tall boy grabbed him by the shoulder and turned him back around. He leaned in close to Adam; his breath rank with cigarette smoke.

"If I hear you've been anywhere near her again I'll kill you." He stood upright and punched Adam full in the stomach. Adam fell to the floor, winded, as the small crowd of boys dispersed, laughing at him.

Adam lay on the floor trembling. He fought to hold back his tears. His face flushed with anger and fear. His hormones raced at the memory of his fingers inside Fiona, submissive on his bed, and then suppressed the image as the repercussions of the physical violence associated with it washed through him.

Adam stood over the crumpled heap of his wife. Her sobs were beginning to subside. He looked down on her small, child-like body. The flash of anger had passed; his head was now clear, his thoughts sharp.

He knelt down to her. He reached a hand out towards her. He brushed her hair away from her forehead. She flinched; a cry rising in her throat. He shushed her, brushing her hair back gently and wiping a tear softly away with his thumb. He shuffled forward and cradled her head in his hands, dabbing at the crusting blood with an old handkerchief.

"God, baby, I am so sorry," he said. I'm so, so very sorry. I didn't mean to hurt you. I love you so much."

He held her in his arms and kissed the top of her head reassuringly. He helped her to her feet, supporting her around the waist, apologising softly all the time. He chided himself, blamed himself for all that had happened. He led her upstairs to the bathroom and cleaned her up. He dabbed at her face, wiping dried blood away and kissed every newly-cleaned piece of exposed skin. Bruises had already begun to swell around her eyes.

"Let's get you into bed," he said. "I'll clean up all that mess downstairs in the morning." He began to undress her, kissing her skin as he undid each button.

"Don't," she said.

He pushed her gently but firmly back onto the bed.

"Adam, please don't."

He pulled her top off and tossed it to one side. He kissed her on her exposed throat and breasts; he lingered briefly at her nipples then ran his tongue down her body.

"No," she said.

He undressed and threw his clothes to the floor. He staggered slightly then lowered himself on top of her. She gave herself to him as the new life inside her continued to form.

Chapter 15: Fear

The ache forming inside her was growing; a mosquito-like whine of pain. Her cheekbone hurt and she could feel the flesh around her eye sockets swelling. When she had woken up the sun was barely peering over the rooftops but her plan was fully formed. She went downstairs and carefully cleaned up the mess from last night, wrapping each large shard of glass in newspaper; wiping dirt and roots from the carpet and throwing the wilting flowers away with the remnants of the vase.

When she had tidied away the violence of the night before, she sat in silent meditation until she heard Adam stirring in the room above. She padded into the kitchen and began to prepare his breakfast.

"Fabulous," he said, the smell of frying bacon greeting him as he came downstairs. He kissed her softly on the nape of her neck as she stood at the cooker.

"Go sit down," she said. "I'll bring it through."

He complied as the toast popped up, a slight hint of burning wafting through the air – just how he liked it.

"What are you up to today?" he called through to her as he opened the morning newspaper.

"The usual: shopping and stuff. Do you need anything?"

Her question went unanswered as he submerged himself in newsprint.

She brought him a hearty breakfast. A superficial smile played across her lips. She placed the tray on his lap, a nervous twitch stinging the flesh around her eyes. She blinked salt-water away and scurried back into the kitchen as the kettle clicked off.

A voice blared from the living room. Elle flinched, nearly dropping the kettle. Adam turned the volume down. She almost sobbed with relief. She made him tea and sat with him, cradling her own mug, while he ate his breakfast. She watched him passively, mutely, stared at him dispassionately. He glanced at her fondly from time to time as if there was nothing untoward.

"What?" he said, picking up his tea.

"Nothing," she said, fascinated by the bright red dot of ketchup that lingered at the edge of his lips. "Nothing. I was just making sure your breakfast was okay."

"It was lovely," he said. "Just like you."

She smiled.

He drank his tea and left for work. Elle stood on the doorstep and waved him down the street, her nightdress pulled tightly around her fragile body. She waited until he turned the corner at the far end of the street before closing the door. She went upstairs, dressed and packed a bag. She looked at the bedroom, the crumpled sheets a ghost of their union – so many bad things had happened here, and so many good things too. A train rumbled discreetly along the bottom of the garden. She wandered slowly from room to room, saying goodbye to each and every memory. She wrote Adam a letter, propped it up in a stark white envelope on the kitchen table, and left.

"What have I bloody well told you?" Mr. Clare's hand rose once more. It fell with a resounding smack on the bare buttocks that lay across his knee. The young flesh burned red. His hand lifted and fell again; the smack echoed.

It was only a small thing but it had happened again. Four times he had told the child and it wasn't sinking in. "You will do as you are told. You will listen to me, you will listen to your mother." He pulled the child upright.

Joseph Clare's eyes swelled with anger and tears. His jaw clenched. His bottom lip trembled. He was *not* going to cry. He glared at his father. "I hate you," he said.

His father smacked him clean across the face.

Tears sprang from Joseph's eyes and rolled hotly down his cheeks. "I'm never going to be like you," he said.

"You're going to be just like me and your children will be just like you," his father said. "It's in our blood." He pushed Joseph to the ground. "Now do as you're bloody well told and we won't have to have this discussion ever again."

Adam sat at the kitchen table turning the envelope over in his hand. He tore it open. He read the letter twice; his hands trembled. He folded the letter carefully and returned it to its snug envelope. Tears ran unchecked from him, a deluge of his own making. He went to bed, leaving the house as empty and as dark as his heart.

Joseph Clare rested his hand comfortingly, expectantly, on his wife's gently swelling belly. There was comfort in this, a peacefulness that was unknown to him, but there was also impatience. Whenever he laid his hand on her, the child stilled. He could sit with his hand on her belly for minutes at a time and feel nothing. She would look at him placid and bovine and ask if he had felt *that* but all he could ever feel was his own pulse.

He looked at her as a gentle smile spread across her face. He wondered if she was imagining things when she said she felt things. Then: a flurry of movement, a muscular flutter as if he was cupping his hand over a fly. Her eyes met his and she nodded. This was his seed planted here, growing strong and proud. He looked at his calloused hand on her shining skin, every nerve-end attuned to the tiniest movement. Another delicate flutter; the shuffling of an angel's feather. Life inside. To come, to grow, to carry on his family's name and traditions.

Fear and pride swelled within him. He was responsible for this life; it belonged to him.

"Shit!"

Elle looked up at her oldest friend from behind dark glasses, tears already beginning to swell behind her lids. She had not seen Trudi for years and they had been the loneliest years of her life. All of her pent-up solitude and emptiness began to pour from her as she stood in the reception.

"I didn't know where else to go," said Elle. "You moved house, I don't know where you live."

Trudi grabbed her coat and lead Elle outside; she tried to explain that she had left Adam, that she had nowhere to go, but the words caught like barbs in her larynx. Trudi held her close.

"Where's your stuff?"

Elle pointed at a lonely suitcase. Trudi picked it up, opened the reception door and shouted "Cover for me, something important has come up." She turned back to Elle and took her by the hand. "Let's get you home," she said.

The drive to Trudi's passed in silence, neither of them knew what to say; they had missed so much, had so much time to catch up on, but Adam overshadowed everything. Elle played nervously with the ring on her finger.

Trudi's flat was as eclectically decorated as anywhere she had ever lived – a few high quality prints adorned the walls; a stark light bulb nestled in an expensive Chinese lantern; ethnic art was placed carefully in corners and the smell of incense hung heavily; crystal lay scattered around the shelves and window sills.

She sat down next to Elle. "Tell me what happened," she said.

Elle removed her sunglasses. "Did you think I was wearing them because the sun was too bright?" she asked.

"But this isn't new, Elle."

"True. I think it began on our honeymoon. I laughed at him because he was sick. It was only a slap, not even really that hard, and I didn't really think anything of it. He *was* ill. He's tormented by something; as…things…have got worse so have his dreams. He only seems to get turned on now when he's hitting me and when he does he has these terrible nightmares. I don't think he even knows he's doing it."

"Jesus, Elle! You're making excuses for him even now. Can't you see what he's done to you? But you're free now, he can't touch you, it's over."

Elle's face contorted once more as the tears began to run and she nodded in agreement. She picked at the skin of her lip, the pain and the thin trickle of blood forcing her to focus. It was over. It had ended. Adam couldn't touch her anymore. She was free of him and so was her baby.

"I'm so frightened," she said.

"I know," said Trudi, holding her tightly. "But you're safe; he can't hurt you now."

The freshly rotting corpse shuffled past Adam and Tom, its hunger drawing it forward. It groaned lifelessly and hustled its way through the crowd; something thick and viscous oozed from its mouth. There was a scream; Tom looked around. A shadowy, caped figure hunched over a girl, its mouth clamped to her neck. She struggled, beating at the creature's back, before falling limp.

Pale-faced ghouls and gimps and freaks milled around the crowded Uni bar. "Superb!" said Tom, his eyes following a girl in a tight, *tight*, PVC cat-suit. She glanced over her shoulder at him and sashayed away. "I love Hallowe'en," he said.

Adam scowled as a large, corseted breast almost knocked his pint from his hand. They were standing at the top of the stairs, near the entrance to the crowded bar. He raised his glass to the apologetic girl as she mouthed her 'Sorry' over the music. He shrugged dismissively.

"Christ, mate! Make the effort!" said Tom as the girl wandered off. "You could have offered her your other elbow for a go on her left tit. I don't think I've ever seen such heroic breasts."

Adam smiled. A nurse slinked by, ripped fish-nets held up by scarlet suspenders: her cleavage exposed, her throat ripped open, shreds of meat dangling.

"Look at all of this flesh, Adam. You need to get out there, sort yourself out or, even better, sort one of these girls out."

"I don't know how."

"There is no *how*, you just do it! Look, you just flirt with them, like they're real people." He laughed. "Really, you talk to them, if they reject you, it's nothing personal, you just move on. There was one lad, last year, he was a legend! He used to just go round the bar asking every girl there "Do you want to fuck?" Ninety-nine times out of a hundred they'd tell him to piss right off but, every now and again..."

"I'm not like that and you know it," said Adam.

"I'm not suggesting you are," said Tom. "What I'm saying is that he never took rejection personally and neither should you. It can't be personal if they don't know you yet, can it?"

"I suppose not but it still feels it." Adam shrugged and put his pint down on the ledge.

Tom nudged him. A pretty girl, short with long, wavy hair had stepped up to them. She looked nervous. She turned from Tom to Adam. He eyes sparkled as she held out her hand to him. Adam shook it.

"Hi," she said, leaning intimately in to Adam, "I'm Meg. I like your jacket." She smiled up at him.

"It belonged to a friend of mine but he got fat," said Adam.

Tom spluttered in to his beer and turned away to laugh. The girl held on to Adam's hand, unsure of what to say in response. The moment stretched into awkwardness. Adam reached down with his free hand, peeled her hand away from his, and picked up his drink. They looked at each other. The girl gave Tom an embarrassed smile, turned back to her friends, and walked quickly away.

Tom slapped Adam on the arm. "What the fuck was that? 'My friend got fat so I had his coat!' Did you not think "Thanks, I'm Adam" might have been a more appropriate response? What were you thinking?"

Adam shrugged. "I thought it was funny." He hung his head.

"It *was* funny, I blew beer out through my nose, but it was no good as an introduction!" Tom flung his arms affectionately around Adam. "What am I going to do with you?"

"She's fucking gone!"

"What?"

"I said she's fucking gone!"

"Elle?"

"Who the fuck else do you think I mean?"

"Where?"

"If I knew that do you really think I'd be here talking to you?"

"Look, Adam, whatever's happened, it's not my fucking fault alright? If you want someone to blame you can fuck right off."

Adam looked at Tom. His jaw clenched, his teeth grinding, his lips white with anger. Connie looked at them disapprovingly and left the room.

"Sorry," said Adam.

Tom leaned forward. "Where's she gone, Adam?"

"I don't know," said Adam.

"Where *could* she have gone?"

"Two places: her parents and that bitch Trudi's. I'm not going to ask her parents if she's there, I wouldn't give them the satisfaction."

"And Trudi?"

"I have no idea where she is. Elle hasn't spoken to her for years as far as I know. I don't even know her surname. I was hoping you might have an idea."

"Why would I know anymore than you?"

"*You* fucked her!"

"Fuck me, Adam! That was a long time ago!"

Adam began to cry, he covered his face in shame, trying to guard himself from these emotions. He rocked back and forth slowly.

"Why did she go?" said Tom.

Adam shrugged.

"What makes you think she might have gone to Trudi's?"

Adam shrugged again. ""She was her best friend."

"Didn't you say they had a massive falling out? Isn't that why they haven't spoken to each other for so long?"

"I don't fucking know, do I? All I know is she's gone and I have to find her. She needs to be with me."

The smell of antiseptic was sickening to him. Its thick, cloying, chemical stench was just a mask; something to disguise more natural scents. He could still smell the blood and shit of birth; the natural smells of the world; the way things *should* be.

He paced the corridor; shabby walls over-lit by fluorescent tubing, and listened to the cries of Clarissa inside. He had been encouraged to go in by the midwife, he had heard Clarissa begging for him to be there, but men had no place at a birth. Not unless it was the kind where you could tie some baling-twine round its hooves and pull it out.

He thrust his hands deep in to his trouser pockets and strolled anxiously around. Nurses bustled past him, their cheeks flushed, accusing looks thrown his way like he gave a fuck what they thought.

Clarissa screamed.

He stood at the door, struggling to understand what all the fuss was about. His mother had told him what it was like in her day; how she had given birth without all of this *nonsense* just like all of her friends. And that was without all of these modern drugs; animals don't scream and cry like this so why should women? You should just get on with it.

As he looked through the door, Joseph could see the urgency with which the nurses were moving. Their encouragement was infectious. He felt himself leaning forward, urging her on, breathing with her, pushing when she pushed. He looked nervously over his shoulder to see if anyone was watching him. He was alone. He rested his palms flat against the door, on the verge of walking in.

Silence. A gasp of relief from Clarissa. A baby's cry. Joseph Clare felt his chest swell; he thought he was going to burst. He stood on tip-toe, trying to see. A tear sprung to his eye. He wiped it away roughly with the back of his hand. A nurse beckoned him in.

He stepped in to the room; the smell was over-powering but real. It had happened. He stepped to the side of the bed. Clarissa, swollen and sweaty and exhausted, looked down at the tiny creature in her arms.

"Congratulations; it's a beautiful baby boy," said the midwife.

Joseph looked down at the mewling creature and marvelled at how weak and helpless it was. He reached out a finger and pulled Clarissa's hair from her face. "Good work," he said. "I'm going to find a pub that's still open, I need a drink."

He let the door swing shut behind him as he left.

Once she had recovered from the initial shock of leaving him, and the trauma of losing the child that she had risked so much to save, Elle had felt lost. Her days felt empty. The anxiety subsided; the constant fear that dogged her waking hours drifted away on the wind. While she had been with Adam there had always been something to anticipate, the ever present-threat hanging in the air like a storm cloud.

This had given way to the fear of being discovered. Every time there was a knock on the door, or the telephone rang, she had jumped in fright, scared that he had found her. It had been several weeks before she felt safe enough to leave Trudi's flat. Fear had followed her into the streets when she had built up the courage to go that far – every blind corner caused her anxiety to peak. She felt like she couldn't move or speak or think. This was no way to live; he wasn't going to find her.

Gradually she went farther afield, with Trudi at first and then, eventually, alone. Now she was happy to wander around the shops all day, go to the park and walk the canal. The fear still lingered.

Trudi bustled in from work, her cheeks red from exertion and excitement; her eyes sparkled. "Close your eyes," she said.

Elle closed her eyes.

Trudi placed a large orange bag carefully in Elle's hand. "Surprise!"

"I can't take this," said Elle looking into the bag. "It's too much."

Trudi tutted. "Pay me back when you sell your first masterpiece; you never should have given it up."

Elle put the bag of art supplies to one side and hugged Trudi. "Thank you so much, for everything," she said.

All of the things Adam could rely on were snatched away. Where once there had been a pulse there was now nothing. Each night his home remained dead, cold and empty. His nights blurred together, his days smearing into eternity. He looked everywhere he could think of. He spent hours wandering the streets, hoping against hope that he would catch a glimpse of her. His work suffered but not as much as he did.

Tom was often round trying to get him to go out as before, to carry on his life, to start building something new; desperate attempts to drag him away from the bottle and the solitude.

"I'm frightened," he said through the haze.

"I know it, mate, but you'll be okay."

"She's not coming back, is she?"

Tom shook his head. "I don't think so."

"Bitch ruined my life. She was all I had. I'll fucking kill her if I find her."

"Come on, you don't mean that."

"I don't mean it; I love her too much. I'm scared I'll never see her again."

He closed his eyes and lapsed into unconsciousness. Tom draped a blanket over him on the sofa, tucked a pillow under his head and locked the door behind him as he left.

Chapter 16: Loss

Elle was aware that there was a blanket being draped across her but all she could feel was the pain. Voices throbbed in waves around her; roared like blood in her ears. The cold concrete pressed to her face was her only anchor to consciousness. A hand pressed to her cheek; someone spoke to her – soft, so soft.

"Come on, why don't you come out?"

"I can't."

"Yes, you can. You've been here weeks now and haven't even set a foot outside. It'll be good for you."

"I can't."

"Come on, Elle. I know this club, Adam's *never* been there; he doesn't even know it exists and even if he did it's too far."

"But he *might* be."

"But he *won't* be."

Elle felt the excitement rising in her like fear as she was getting herself ready. Her nerves scratched at her like splinters of glass. Everyone was going to be looking at her, laughing at her; they would all know. The bruises had almost gone, just a slight discolouration, easily masked by foundation.

The music throbbed in her brain like a migraine; repetitive, swelling sounds. Alcohol flushed her cheeks. Her eyes sparkled with joy. Sweat trickled down her temple as she and Trudi danced, their hair clinging wetly to their faces. Light strobed and flashed metallic blue.

White light lanced into her brain as she felt her body rise, cold concrete taken from wet face. She swept in and out of consciousness, the pain came in waves, the ebb and flow of distress. Wet life ran down her thighs.

Elle and Trudi turned. Neon flickered with uncertainty. A cobweb of drizzle settled on their still flushed faces, the world smudged through wine and rain. A flash. A cramp of pain low in her body. Red spread, oh so red. Crimson tide in the neon blue. She crumpled to the ground. Trudi. A scream. A cry.

"Fuck!"

    "Get an ambulance."   Splash of

                               footsteps through

                                             puddles.

        She   is   alone.

                    Voices.

     A flash of   white pain   and

darkness.

                    "Sorry."

"I'm sorry."

      "So sorry."

               A hand   on

                          her cheek.

Soft   and   warm.

                A   cloud on   her tongue.

Her head on a pillow.

"I'm afraid we couldn't save the baby."

Flat words, free of emotion. The same words, over and over. The pain was still there. The fear would always be there. A sacrifice for nothing. A futile exercise in freedom. A chance given and wasted.

Elle cried.

"You did it again!"

"What?"

"You called me by that bitch ex's name. Again!"

"She wasn't a bitch," said Adam.

"That's a matter of opinion."

"You never even met her."

"I may as well be her, the amount of times you call me by her name," said Elle.

"Bollocks! Look, I'm sorry I called you by her name, it wasn't intentional. We were together for such a long time that it's the first name my brain churns up. That's all. I'm not an idiot, I'm not going to call you 'Kath' on purpose am I?"

"So when you tell me 'Kath used to do it this way' you're not telling me how you want me to do it? Bullshit, Adam!"

Adam hung his head. "I'm sorry; I wasn't aware I did that. I shall try to stop it"

Pity washed over Elle. Adam had been so hurt by that woman and here she was making it worse. She placed her arm around his shoulder. "I'm sorry, Adam, I should be the one apologising but when you say stuff like that I can't help but feel like you'd rather be with her than me. You make me feel so small and useless."

"I wouldn't want to be with anybody if I was thinking about her all the time. I couldn't do that, it would be horrible. I want to be with you, you make me feel so much better about myself. When I'm with you I'm happier than I've ever been. You're all I ever think about."

They held each other close; she buried her face deep in his neck. He wrapped his arms around her and held her tight. He kissed the top of her head. He nuzzled into her, kissing her softly. He breathed her in. Her smell was subtle, a slight musk with an acrid edge; a clean smell with a hint of something else – shampoo and sweat. Her hair reminded him of freshness, of rain-washed pavements and twilight summers. So very different to Kath.

The room smelled of chemical death; a hint of sweat and antiseptic hung uneasily in the air, permeating everything. It was an insidious smell, creeping and seeping in to all places, just like the cancer that was eating Joseph Clare alive. His bed dominated the living-room, just like he had before it.

Michael held his father's hand, cupping it gently in his own, scared by its fragility. It felt so light, tiny bird-bones visible through his father's opaque skin. He could feel the light flutter of his father's pulse, but only just. How had it come to this? Joseph was a giant of a man; he stood tall and proud and strong in Michael's memory.

The waste-ground spread itself out before them, a seemingly endless opportunity for adventure. Untidy clumps of grass burst wildly through the broken concrete; a row of terraced houses teased the horizon. Joseph hoisted Adam up on to his shoulders. Adam giggled. They were walking the path that led around the edge of the waste-ground. "Go on," he said to Michael, "I'll give you a head-start."

Michael looked at him suspiciously. "You're going to cheat," he said.

"How can I cheat? I'm going to carry Adam on my shoulders and I'll let you get half-way home before I start running. You can't lose."

Michael pondered the challenge briefly then nodded. He set-off as fast as he could. His feet pounded at the pavement, his heart thundered in his chest. He had never run so fast or so far before. He ran and ran, the wind tugging at his hair. He could feel himself being carried forward by his own momentum, his speed building and building, his body moving so fast that his legs could barely keep up. He was unbeatable. Then he heard a shout to his right. He looked over – his father was the wind. His feet weren't even touching the ground; he was being swept along by forces beyond Michael's imagination. Adam's arms were clamped tightly around their father's forehead and he was laughing wildly. Michael had never seen anything like it. He staggered to a halt; his mouth hung open. His father was a god.

Joseph lay enveloped by the bed; the sheets folded around him like a shroud. His skeletal face was heavy with shadow. His breath came in short, ragged, gasps. He beckoned Michael closer.

"I proved them wrong again, Michael," he said. His words emerged from him like gossamer threads, feeble strands of consciousness, clinging on desperately to the final beats of life.

Michael shook his head. "I don't understand, Dad."

"They said it couldn't be done but I gave up smoking *and* lost weight." His laughter leaked from him like air from broken bellows; a hiss and a sigh. Joseph struggled under his own weight, he shifted uncomfortably, his arm that lay above the sheets stretching out, pointing towards the ceiling.

Michael followed the direction of his father's pointing finger, panic rising in him. "What are you pointing at, Dad? What can you see?"

"Nothing, you daft bugger, my pyjamas are pulling down on my shoulder and it bloody well hurts. Help me to sit-up properly."

Michael jumped up and pulled his father up in the bed as gently as he could; he weighed nothing, he was a blown egg – nothing but a shell. The cancer was everywhere now. It had begun as an insistent nothing, an ache behind his ribcage – wind perhaps, or just old-age – but it had grown quickly. By the time Michael had persuaded him to go to the doctor it was too late; too late for anything other than a token attempt at treatment. What had begun as nothing more than a small tumour, nothing more substantial than a shadow, had rapidly spread throughout his chest cavity. Tendril-like roots had thrust their way through his flesh; had snaked up his shoulder and neck and into his brain. Michael had watched helplessly as his father was eaten alive by his own body.

Joseph's breath was coming faster now, shallow and rapid, like there wasn't enough time. His eyes were glazed with fear and weariness. "Tell Adam," he breathed.

Michael leaned forward, his chest tight, formless grief barely contained.

"Tell Adam that I'll never forgive him." Joseph chuckled to himself at the look on Michael's face. "What? You thought all would be forgiven because I'm dying? Bollocks to that." His breath hissed out of him.

Michael held his father's hand for a long time after, the translucent flesh quickly cooling. He'd been prepared for this moment, knew that it was inevitable, for months, but the pain was unbearable. A great chasm of grief opened-up inside him, a massive, hollowed-out, world of infinite capacity that could never hold this loss. It was uncontainable, indescribable; there were no words, there was only nothing. He laid his father's hand on the bed and arranged the blankets neatly around him. He kissed his father gently on the forehead. "I forgive you, Dad. Sleep well."

"No, Michael, don't do this, not now. You can't bring him here, not today."

The gentle susurration of muted conversation drifted from the living-room, down the hall and out of the open front door.

"We're just here to pay our respects, Adam. We're not here for a confrontation."

Adam glanced back over his own shoulder; the small mourning crowd drifted between rooms, awkwardness and sandwiches stifling conversation, the cold embers of long dead relationships floating like ashes. He blinked slowly and stepped to one side, against his better judgement, but hopeful.

Michael took their father by the elbow and led him into the house. Adam closed the door and followed them through; his father was smaller than he remembered, withered like an over-ripe peach. How had he ever felt frightened or intimidated by this little man? His father's eyes were glassy like wet marbles; he was frightened and lost.

"Food is on the dining-table, kettle is where it's always been," said Adam. "Help yourself to booze."

Familial heads bobbed closer together; conversations briefly became animated and whispered as Michael sat Joseph down at the table. Eyes flashed and tuts were tutted. Adam's auntie shuffled over. "Why have you let *him* in?" she asked.

"I couldn't not, could I, Auntie?"

"Of course you could! Especially after the way he was with your poor, dead mother, and her own dear father still fresh in his grave. He's got a right nerve, that one."

"Michael said they're not here to cause any trouble. I have to believe him, don't I?"

Adam's auntie looked him square in the eye. "You're a good boy, Adam, you know that? Too good. Always ready to believe the best of people; and that can only be a good thing but it will always bring you pain."

"He's my brother," said Adam.

"Aye, and Joseph's mine," she said. "But I'm under no illusions as to the type of man he is. Look at him now – the way he's hunched over that table, he's like an old vulture. He's here to pick over the bones, you mark my words. Your Michael's too gullible."

"He looks ill; Dad, I mean."

"He probably is; all that bitterness and spite and anger he's been bottling-up inside is finally taking its toll. He needs to be lanced." She winked at him. "But that's a job for braver folks than us, eh?"

Adam gave her a wan smile and pecked her on the cheek. She waddled off. Adam cradled his paper-plate idly, glazed over, his thoughts elsewhere.

"Penny for them," said Michael.

Adam glared at him. "Nothing," he said. "There's nothing going on in there at all; just drifting away for a while."

"Anywhere nice?"

"Just away," said Adam.

"Probably the best place to be," said Michael. He paused. "I really am sorry, Adam. I know you and Granddad were close; closer than I was to him."

Adam nodded. Michael reached out and placed a hand on Adam's arm. "Look," Michael said, "if you ever need anyone to talk to, I'm here for you. I hope you know that. Yes, we've had our differences over the years but, well, I'm your brother. If we can't get along..."

Adam's teeth were hurting. The muscles in his jaw were clenched tight; a slight throb tugged at his temple. He swilled the dregs of his drink around the bottom of his glass. "I need another drink," he said and strode into the kitchen.

He stood over the sink, his arms rigid, propping him up, supporting his hanging head. He stared down the plug-hole; its dank depths beckoned to him like a dream. The sensation of falling, of being lost in the swirling darkness, swept over him. He wanted to be swallowed by the unplumbed depths of this loss, wanted it to sweep him out to sea; he wanted to feel the undertow pulling at his legs, pulling him farther and farther from land. He wanted to feel his arms growing weak, his muscles atrophying and growing impuissant; the waves lapping at his face, his lips, his mouth, his lungs burning with spent oxygen as he sinks into the silent darkness. His head snapped up. "*I'm fine*," he said to himself, pinching the bridge of his nose. "*Just thinking.*" The sound of raised voices crashed into the kitchen from the other room.

"You know fuck all, you stupid old bitch!" His father's voice.

Adam marched back into the living-room. His father was standing now, hunched over the table, glowering at the small gathering. Prehistoric fury emanated from him.

"I'd have killed myself too if I'd been married to you," he spat. "You people know fuck all about anything." Michael slipped an arm around his father's shoulders "And you can take your hands off me, you fucking queer. You think I don't know what you get up to?"

Michael's face flushed. He met Adam's eye and mouthed an apology.

"And you, you fucker," said Joseph, his voice cracking as he turned his attention on Adam. "Best day of my life when you left. What was the fucking point of you anyway?" Adam's head dropped. The family muttered quietly to one another as Michael led Joseph away. "Haven't got an answer for that one, have you, you useless fuck?"

The front door slammed shut.

Adam's auntie took one of his hands in hers. "I only told him how well he was looking," she said. "I'm so sorry, Adam, dear. I should have known to not bother and let him be."

Adam brought her hand up to his lips and kissed her softly on the fingers. "It's not your fault, Auntie, not your fault at all."

Elle watched Adam as he got undressed. "How was work today?" she asked.

He shrugged and sat on the edge of the bed.

"Did you get all of that paperwork sorted that you'd said had built-up?"

"Mostly," he said. He reached down and removed his socks. He chucked them casually on to his washing-pile.

Elle reached over and stroked the small of his back. He stiffened slightly under her touch; it was barely discernible but she noticed it, or thought she did. She sighed.

Adam stood and removed the rest of his clothes. He was, briefly, naked before her roaming eye; he slipped quickly under the covers next to her.

She propped her head up on her pillow and gazed at him. She touched him softly on the arm. "What is it?" she asked. "What's wrong?"

He looked at her; his eyes were dead, cold, unfeeling; there was something there that she didn't know, that she didn't or couldn't understand. "Nothing," he said

"Are you sure, Adam? You've been very distant lately; it's like you're always somewhere else."

"I'm sure," he said. "I'm just very tired from work. I'm always here with you, sweetheart." He took her hand and kissed it.

His words seemed empty somehow but they were the right words. He was distant; had been for a while, there was no doubt about that in her mind but maybe it *was* just the stress of work. He had been very busy lately. Maybe it was just her; her insecurity. She was beginning to see things that weren't there. "I love you, Adam," she whispered.

"I love you too," he said.

She nestled in to his chest. "Do you want to?" she asked.

He kissed her on the top of her head. She tilted her face towards him. He kissed her briefly on the lips. His hand snaked beneath the covers and touched her between the thighs. Elle lay back and let him stimulate her; she tried but he had hardly aroused her at all before he was on top of her. Penetration was painful and it was over almost before he had begun. He grunted and rolled away from her.

She ran her fingers lovingly across his chest. She promised herself that she would try to put right whatever it was that she was doing wrong. She nuzzled in to his body's warmth and tried to sleep.

Elle was trembling.

"What is it?"

She looked at her feet.

"Are you okay?"

She nodded.

"Listen. If you want to stop, just say so, okay? We don't have to do anything until you're ready. If you want to go home, that's fine. If you want to stay, that's fine too. I don't want anything to spoil this, Elle, I don't want you to feel pressured into anything, you're too special."

"I want you so much," said Elle, "but every time I think that, feel that, I also feel guilty for betraying Adam."

"It must be very difficult."

She nodded. "I haven't seen him for so long now and all I can think about is how much I must have hurt him, leaving like that."

"He hurt you too, remember."

"But it's not the same thing at all," she said. "I gave him everything I was and he destroyed me; made me into what he wanted me to be. I don't think I'll ever trust anybody ever again. But I'll always feel responsible; like it was all my own fault, like, if I'd stayed things would have got better."

"But you know they never would have."

"I know. And now I don't want to spoil what we're building here. I don't want to let the same thing happen to me again."

"It won't. And I'll never try to push you into anything you don't want. You're in charge, Elle. You say when and how and how far. You have control and I'll follow your lead. He can't hurt you anymore and I never will."

"Take me home. Please."

"Okay."

"You have no idea how much you mean to me," said Elle.

"I have an idea! I'm going to look after you now."

They kissed.

Adam felt like his heart was going to burst. Wracking sobs swelled up from somewhere deep inside him, bubbling up from the inky black depths. It was all his fault. His face felt tight, his cheeks were sore from the contortions his grief was forcing upon him. His cheeks and mouth and eyes were on the verge of cramp. He lay face-down on his bed and forced his face into the pillow to muffle his sobs.

His day had begun as normal: up with the alarm, cereal and a cup of orange juice, dressed himself for school while Mikey made a packed lunch for them both. It had been cloudy and looked like it might rain. Adam had knelt-up on his bed and stuck a small finger through the bars at Woffley.

"Don't you get cold today, little mouse," he said.

Woffley snuffled at his finger and moved off. Adam finished getting dressed, pleased with himself that that he was now able to do everything on his own. He thought for a moment, looked at Woffley's cage and moved it carefully onto the window ledge. "There," he said. "If the sun comes out later, you'll be nice and warm." He paused. What if the sun didn't come out later? He reached down and turned the radiator up to full. "And if it doesn't, you'll still be nice and toasty." He smiled, very pleased with himself.

He jumped down off the bed and left home with Michael for the long walk to school. The day passed pleasantly enough: play-time was great, as usual, and class-time was interesting. They learned about Egypt in the morning and Roman Numerals in the afternoon and then the bell rang and Adam had to wait in the playground for Mikey to finish in the big school next door. They walked home, chatting excitedly, and when they finally got home, Adam ran into the bedroom.

Woffley lay stretched out, full length, on the floor of her cage. Adam stopped, his hand poised to scoop her up. He lifted the tiny, still body out of the cage. "Woffley?" He touched the delicate little paws that seemed to be clutching at the air. Her body was hot, so very hot. He noticed her water bottle was desert-dry. He had forgotten to fill it with fresh water that morning.

His grief burst from him. Michael came running in to the room to find out what had happened; worried that Adam had hurt himself really badly. He took the dead mouse from Adam gently and placed it back in the cage. He slid his arm comfortingly around his little brother's shoulders.

"It's all my fault," sobbed Adam.

"Don't be silly, of course it isn't your fault," said Michael.

"Yes it bloody well is," said their father as he walked in to the room. ""You put it in the window and turned the radiator on, didn't you? Cooked the poor bloody thing alive, you did." He folded his arms across his chest. "You come away now, Michael, and leave him to it. He's got to grow up and cuddling him when he's killed his own bloody pet isn't going to help him do that, is it?"

Michael reluctantly took his arm from around Adam and stood next to his father.

"I'll tell you this for nothing: he's not having another pet if this is how he's going to carry on."

They left Adam alone, deserted with his guilt.

Later that evening Adam and Michael stood alone, secretly, at the bottom of the garden. Michael had found a little box for Woffley and had padded it out with toilet paper to cushion her frail corpse.

"Just like she's asleep," said Michael as he put the lid on the box.

They dug a hole together in the flower bed at the foot of the garden, underneath the hedge. Adam placed the tiny, makeshift coffin into the hole.

"Please look after my little mouse," he said to the sky. "She has been a good mouse and can climb her own tail. I love her. *A lot*. Now she can live with my mummy." He then refilled the hole and walked quietly to the shed with Michael to replace the trowel they had used.

The woman walked slowly around the small room. Adam sat on the edge of the neat bed watching her. The room had a definite smell of sex about it. The walls bled despair. A moth fluttered around the stark light. The woman took her clothes off. Adam watched her impassively until she stood naked before him. Her skin was smooth, her ribs marked with thin charcoal smudges of shadow.

"How old are you?"

"Depends," she said pushing him back on the bed.

"On what?" He ran his hands over her body.

"On the client." She pulled his shirt open and teased his nipple with her tongue. She bit him.

"What do you mean?"

She unzipped his trousers. "I've one client who wants me to be a little girl and another who wants me to be his own grandmother. Most men don't care."

"Most men?"

"I have my regulars but most of the time I just pick up punters like you on the off-chance. A girl's got to make a living." She shuffled down and began to remove his trousers.

"No," he said. "Don't." He pulled his trousers back up and began to do his shirt up.

"What's this? You think I'm a virgin or something?"

He stood to leave.

"For fuck's sake! I don't believe this."

"Here," he said throwing some money at her. "This should cover any expenses you may have incurred. The notes fluttered to the floor.

"Fuck you!" she shouted after him as he left.

"Not likely."

"Come on, you two, get out of bed. Now!"

Michael groaned. Adam sat bolt upright. Their father swished the curtains open emphatically and pulled the blankets off their beds. "You *will* get up. You *will* go to school," he said.

Michael swung his legs off his bed and staggered to the bathroom. Adam scampered down the stairs, ready for his breakfast. He clambered into his chair at the kitchen table and looked at his father as he followed Adam in to the room.

"What?" asked Joe.

"Breakfast-time," said Adam, looking at his father with wide, innocent eyes.

"Yes, it is," said Joe. "You and Michael know where everything is."

Adam frowned. "I don't," he said. "Mummy always fetches my breakfast.

"We buried your mother yesterday, son. Remember? It's time to grow up." He turned away from Adam, filled the kettle at the sink, and switched it on.

Adam was still swinging his legs at the table when Michael came downstairs. Michael's face was crumpled with sleep, his hair askew, and he was still blinking sleepily. He hadn't slept well. "Dad?"

Joseph glared at Michael. He poured his freshly boiled water into a large mug. Burned coffee singed the air. "You know where everything is. Sort it out for yourself and get your brother something while you're at it."

Michael's shoulders sagged. He should have known that this was the way it was going to be. His father had never *cared* for them the way their mother had; the caring had been her responsibility. Why should anything change now?

Joseph sat at the kitchen table with his coffee. He watched as Michael prepared breakfast for Adam. "You could make me some toast while you're at it, son. Just don't cut it into triangles," he said. He ruffled Adam's hair and winked.

"Can I stay home from school today, Dad?" asked Michael.

"Why?"

"It's just…I don't think I'll be able to focus on my work. I won't be able to do my work; with everything that's happened, I mean."

"Don't talk nonsense. Today is the same as yesterday is the same as tomorrow," he said. "Do you think your mother would want you to stay at home? Would she want you to miss school?"

Michael shook his head.

"Of course she wouldn't. She was many things, your mother, but she knew what was good for you. She knew you should get your priorities straight."

Michael nodded. He placed a bowl of cereal in front of Adam and passed him a spoon. Adam smiled happily and tucked in eagerly.

"Staying at home isn't going to help you pass your exams, is it, son?"

Michael shook his head as he buttered his father's toast.

"And if you stay at home you'll only wallow and feel sorry for yourself. You'll sit here all day, crying and fretting and worrying, won't you?"

Michael shrugged. "Probably," he said.

"Of course you will. No, the answer is to keep yourself busy. Get yourself to school, work hard, get those grades and get yourself a decent job at the end of it."

"Yes, Dad."

"Besides, I don't need you here all day pestering me. I've got things to do around the house. I've got to pack your mother's stuff and take it all away."

Adam and Michael looked at him, horrified.

"What? You thought we'd be keeping all of her stuff? We need to clear it out. We have to move on, move forward."

Adam's lip trembled.

"Don't you bloody start," he said. There was a brief pause before his shoulders dropped. "All right, look, you can keep one thing each; only one. And you'd better pick something quickly because you'll be late for school."

They nodded. Adam's spoon rattled and he ran for their parents' bedroom. Michael followed; he knew exactly what he wanted to keep. He had bought a large, fat, green ceramic fish for her birthday last year. It was amazing. Dark, riverweed green with large, fleshy pink lips; its mouth gaped wider than anything he had ever seen before. Balanced on that lower lip, fear splashed across its little face, lay a smaller, flatter fish, about to be eaten, its tail flapping desperately. It had taken him two months to save enough of his pocket money to afford it.

"I'm going to keep this," said Adam as Michael stepped into the room. In his hand: the fat green fish. Michael's heart dropped.

"But..." he said. Adam looked up at him. He looked so pleased with himself, so happy, and Michael knew that feeling wasn't going to last. "You make sure you put that somewhere safe," he said to Adam, "and we'll find a proper place to keep it when we get home from school. Go and get dressed now, we have to hurry."

Adam trotted happily out of the room leaving Michael with the tattered remnants of their mother's life.

It was late. Late enough that Adam was able to stagger down the middle of the road and not worry about getting run over. He placed one foot in front of the other carefully as he walked; the high-pitched whine in his ears ruining the peacefulness that enveloped him.

"Hey!"

Adam stopped and looked around. He frowned as he concentrated, trying to focus through the alcohol haze.

"Hey!" A small figure stepped out of the shadows by the bus-stop.

"Hello," said Adam.

"I think I might have missed the last bus," said the girl. She stepped in to the road and smiled.

"Do I know you?" asked Adam.

The girl stretched out her hand. "Not really," she said. "I'm Meg. I spoke to you earlier tonight."

Adam squinted at her. He took her hand and shrugged vaguely.

"I told you I liked your coat? Sorry if I made you feel awkward, I'm not usually so forward so didn't know what to do when you didn't react."

Adam nodded. He released her hand. "Yes," he said. "I'm not used to being approached like that so didn't know *how* to react. Sorry if I made you feel awkward too. My friend really did get too fat for the coat." His head was throbbing; pain pulsed at his temples. A vague urgency tugged at his loins.

"I think I've missed the bus," she repeated.

"I'd imagine so; it's stupid o'clock in the morning and the last bus comes through well before midnight. Can you catch-up with your friends?"

"*Them*. I lost *them* hours ago. 'Let's have a girls' night out' they said but at the first hint of a pretty boy they all bugger off their separate ways. I have absolutely no idea where I am or how to get home."

"My mate Tom is exactly the same."

"He chases after pretty boys?"

Adam laughed at the thought. "You know what I mean." He thrust his hands deep in to his pockets. He considered her briefly. "I live just around the corner," he said. "No funny business. You can sleep on the sofa. Try not to break anything."

Meg tilted her head to one side and smiled. "I knew you were one of the good guys," she said. "And I promise: no funny business." She slipped her arm through his and they walked home together.

"You don't have to do this you know."

"I know but it wouldn't seem right any other way. I need to tell him to his face," said Elle.

She watched out of the car window as the world swished by; the windows streaked with tears of rain, desperately trying to hold on. Grey clouds scurried across the drab sky. She was nervous. How was she going to say all of the things she was going to have to say?

"What?"

Elle smiled. "Nothing. You know I wouldn't have been able to cope without you?"

"Don't be silly."

"Nobody else would have come with me today; I wouldn't have asked anybody else."

"Are you sure you don't want me to come in with you when we get there?"

"Positive," said Elle. "It wouldn't help; it'd probably make things worse."

"You don't know what he's like any more; what if he gets violent?"

Elle shook her head. "He won't hurt me. Not anymore."

They pulled up outside Adam's house.

The house was as ordinary as ever; bland. It peered expressionless out over the street. Her heart raced at the thought of the life she used to live here. She swallowed, her throat was dry.

"Are you sure you'll be okay?"

"Wait for me here," said Elle. "If I'm not back in thirty minutes, come and get me. Are you sure you don't mind waiting?"

"Of course not. Now go, be strong."

Elle walked to the front door. Her breath was shallow, her heart pounding in her chest. She forced herself to breathe deeply and slowly as she stood on the doorstep. Everything was going to be fine. She reassured herself.

She knocked on the door.

Indignation had darkened her eyes to violet. "You contemptible little shit," she said. Tears broke from Catherine as she confronted Adam. Her lips trembled as she tried to maintain control of her emotions.

Adam shrugged. "What have I done?" He glanced over at two men sitting at another table, a half-smile playing across his lips.

Catherine threw the small stack of photos on to the table; they scattered like dead leaves. "These were ours. These were private moments that I shared with you and *only* with you. I gave you these because I trusted you."

Adam scooped-up the photos and flicked through them casually, eyebrows raised. "Impressive," he said. "You should try and get these published; you might even make a career out of them."

Catherine snatched them back. "How could you?" she asked. "How could you show anybody, let alone people we work with. You've humiliated me, Adam, you've ruined the job I love and you've, pretty much, ruined my career. I've had to hand in my resignation because of this."

Adam wetted his lips slowly. "You did this to yourself," he said. "I trusted you and you threw me away. You humiliated me first, *Cath*, and now it's come back to bite you on the arse."

She shook her head in disbelief. "I can't believe that you're the same person I was falling for. What is wrong with you? What makes you think this is okay; to do this to somebody?"

"I don't know what you mean. I didn't show anybody these pictures. Somebody must have taken them from my desk drawer. Terribly sorry." He smiled at her coldly. "I suppose I should have kept them somewhere safe. Still, you should be able to find a job somewhere else easily enough; why don't you include the photos with your C.V, that should help?"

The slap ricocheted around the canteen. Silence fell. The click of Catherine's heels tumbled away as she ran from the building. Conversation burbled back, slowly at first but building gradually to its previous level. Adam saw eyes nervously flicking his way as he finished his coffee. He smiled, pleased with himself, as the warmth spread across his cheek.

Adam picked at the edges of his meal. He couldn't be bothered any more. There had been women in his life since Elle had left: the curious, the strong, the determined sorts who wanted to rescue him and make him a better person; the ones who had tried to mould him and those he had 'employed.' They had all left. He descended in to the depths of loneliness; depths he never could have imagined. Nobody seemed to want to talk to him anymore. He was an outcast. So alone.

He pushed his food to one side and left it on the coffee table. He felt sorry for himself, even after all this time. It was pathetic. He felt old and slow and misused. Abandoned; lost and forlorn. He took his plate into the kitchen and scraped it into the bin. A stale, plastic waft of air wrinkled his nose. He ran the plate under the hot tap and left it on the draining board. He poured himself a whiskey.

He downed it and shuddered. It burned its way down to his empty stomach, the heat spreading like cancer. He left his glass behind and slumped back on the sofa. Something pricked at his consciousness, a familiarity or an itch that he couldn't quite scratch. Discontent flitted across his face like storm clouds. He scratched his chin.

There was a knock at the door.

Chapter 17: Confrontation

Adam blocked the door.

"What do you mean 'I don't think so'?" he said.

"Exactly that. I don't think you love me. I don't think you ever really loved me."

He pointed at her angrily. "Don't you ever tell me I never loved you. I always loved you, I always will. In spite of the way you've treated me."

"I treated you? What the fuck are you talking about?"

"You abandoned me. You left. I was so worried about you, you have no idea."

"You were worried about what people might think, what they might say if they found out. You were worried I'd found someone else; someone who really cared about me; someone who loved me."

"I went to the police," he said.

"So did I. That's how they knew not to tell you anything."

"Bastards!"

Elle was watching him closely; he was skirting the edges of true rage, she could see all the signs. He hadn't changed at all.

"Where did you go?"

"I'm not going to tell you that, Adam."

"It was that bitch Trudi, wasn't it? I fucking knew it. I can't believe you ran to her."

"I was angry and scared. I had to run somewhere."

"I fucking knew it! She'd been trying to break us apart from the very beginning."

"You did that all by yourself. Nobody talked me into leaving you, Adam, I left because of you." She hesitated. "I'd like to leave now, please."

"I'd like you to stay."

"Please move, Adam. I have to leave now."

Elle took a step towards him. She tried to push past him but he stood his ground. He shoved her away from him. She fell into a chair. She glared up at him, her anger and fear washing together, oil on water, a rainbow of hate.

"I'm not scared of you." She struggled to her feet. "I'm not scared of you anymore."

She slapped him viciously across the face. His cheek flushed. White finger lines lay in parallels on his skin. He brought his hand up to his cheek and touched it tenderly. His eyes narrowed. He hadn't believed that any blow could hurt him so much; it lanced straight to his heart. He felt it tingle as the blood rushed back into his cheek. She *was* scared of him, fear had driven the blow home, and that was what hurt so much. She was really terrified of him, in spite of all the love he had given her.

He had loved her with all he could give.

He slapped her.

Her head snapped to one side. Tears sprang to her eyes. She had taken this before, this and much, much worse. She felt the echo of the slap down through the years, tendrils of it seeping into her past. Her mind felt as sharp as moonlight, clean like a paper cut. She pushed past him, catching him off balance. He stumbled, caught her by the shoulder as she reached for the door handle, and spun her around. She kicked out, the point of her shoe catching him on the shin. He yelled. She scratched his face, thin furrows of blood welling up in the grooves she ploughed, his skin gathering under her nails. He punched her. Her legs betrayed her, crumpling under the weight of her breathless body. His lips were white. He wiped the blood from his cheek with the back of his hand.

"You cunt."

She tried to scrabble to her feet. Words tumbled incoherently from her: threats, pleadings, abstractions and profanities. He grabbed her by the hair and dragged her back into the living room. She screamed. Anger raged from her. Her fists flailed at him, her nails raking his bare arms. She could feel her hair tearing loose from her scalp. She broke free and glared at him.

"Sit down," he said. He casually discarded the clump of hair that had pulled free from her.

"Fuck you!" She spat in his face.

The spittle ran into his eyes.

"You are *not* going to treat me like this. Not anymore. Not ever again."

He laughed. "I'm not impressed."

He jabbed at her throat with rigid fingers. She gasped. She staggered backwards, clutching at her larynx, fear and panic in her eyes. He watched her fighting to breathe.

"You're pathetic. You think you're important, so fucking self-righteous. You're nothing. You're nobody. I can destroy you with just my finger, for fuck's sake!"

He took her chin in his left hand and lifted her face towards him. He poked her sharply in her left eye.

"See?"

Her hands came up to this fresh pain; her cry resounded through the dead house. She knelt before him, cradling the heat emanating from her eyeball. It felt like he had burst it open, blinded her, she thought she could feel thick, viscous fluid oozing from the wound. She could taste salt.

She squinted up at him. She screamed obscenities at him. He kicked her in the chest and she sprawled to the floor. The heat from the open fire seared across her face; the corner of the hearth stabbed into her kidney. She rolled away from the heat. The carpet smelled strong.

Adam watched her as she lay on the floor, satisfaction seeping warmly through the pit of his stomach. The adrenaline had kicked in, his head pounding as blood coursed through him. Every fibre of him throbbed, every tendon and ligament was taut, ready to be released. He felt alive.

Elle looked around desperately. The coals shifted on the fire. She reached out. Her small, tender hand closed tightly around the cold phallic length of the poker. She got to her feet. Adam's eyes widened in disbelief.

"I am leaving now. Don't try to stop me."

"Don't be silly."

"I mean it," she said. She took a step away from him.

He pushed her gently.

"Don't, Adam," she said. Frustration choked her voice.

He pushed her again.

"Don't." She raised the poker.

He slapped her.

She lashed out blindly. She screamed. The metal bar arced through the air and struck Adam across the temple. Blood flowered from the wound. Adam's eyes rolled up, the whites streaked with veins. White noise hissed through his brain, stuck between frequencies. He was floating in the grey. A quiet scream. Falling. A vase tumbling to the ground. Water splashing from the violence of impact. Years tumbling through his past, away into the now, plummeting into oblivion.

"What the hell was that?"

Chapter 18: Revelation

What the hell was that?

Adam's mind fluttered into consciousness; fudged with sleep, he struggled to open his eyes. Something had penetrated his sleep. A noise? The sharp sound from downstairs repeated itself in his memory; the sound of something breaking. He sat up in bed. He cocked his head to one side, straining to hear, searching for even the hint of a sound, hoping to pick up the clatter of claws on the wooden fence. There was silence.

He swung his legs out of the bed and walked quietly, unsteadily, over to the window. A yawn forced itself upon him, his mouth straining wide as he held the curtain to one side. He wiped a tired tear away. There was nothing in the garden. The almost-full moon bobbed in and out from behind hurried clouds; silver-grey light strobing across the garden.

There it was again.

A chink of noise from downstairs. Adam scowled. He crept over to the bedroom door and cracked it open. The hinges groaned softly. He peered through the door, wide awake, his mind racing. Another small noise. Adam backed away from the door and quickly pulled on a pair of jeans. He looked frantically around the room and then his mind struck upon a memory. A dimly remembered day; an empty day of violins and saxophones.

The house had been haunted by his granddad's absence. Adam had flung the windows wide that afternoon, tried to freshen the house, to wash out the musty stillness that lingered. Through tear-filled eyes he had bagged the old man's clothes, boxed old books and taken them to the charity shop. He had only kept a few special things: his Granddad's medals, some old photographs, a wedding ring and his cricket bat.

Adam glided nimbly across the landing and into the front bedroom, his eyes wide in the darkness. The dusty, bare boards creaked sadly beneath him as he reached for the wardrobe. It rattled as he tried to open the door, his breath caught in his throat at the noise. He hissed through his teeth as he turned the small key; it scraped, metal on metal, the loudest noise he had ever heard.

The door breathed open. He reached into the dry darkness and pulled the cricket bat out. It still smelled of linseed and the memories of summer evenings. He tested the weight in his hand, smiling fondly at the memories it evoked. He gripped it firmly and turned back to the landing.

The carpet nestled into the crevices of his feet as he stood at the top of the stairs. He shuddered at the cold tear of sweat that ran down his torso. He strained to see in the half-light as he stalked downstairs. He could feel himself trembling; was certain that if there *was* anyone in the house they would be able to hear the thundering of his heart. His mind raced with perfect clarity. He brandished the cricket bat.

Again: a noise. Small, indistinct: the living room. Adam paused at the foot of the stairs. He cautiously walked the length of the hall, the tiles cold on his bare feet. He pressed his ear gently to the wood of the living room door. He could hear movement, muffled and cautious but unmistakeable. Adam's breath was shallow and rapid. His head swarmed with anger.

"Little bastard," Adam said as he burst into the room.

The intruder whirled around with a loud exclamation.

"Don't you fucking move!" said Adam.

"You scared the life out of me!"

"I fucking mean it you fuck, don't fucking move."

The intruder raised her hands as if in surrender "What the hell are you doing?" she said, then rushed at Adam. They made rough contact and grappled furiously. Adam's anger exploded. They struggled, straining for superiority. Adam could feel himself being forced backwards, being overpowered, being beaten. Then he was released. "If this is your idea of 'funny business' I'm off," she said.

The intruder was trying to make a break for it, to run for freedom, he was sure of it. Adam sprung after her, cricket bat in hand. He swept it around and struck the intruder full on the side of the head. The crack of leather on willow.

The intruder fell slowly, her body limp and twisted as it collapsed under its own weight, momentum carrying her forward. Tattered shadows shifted in her peripheral vision. The wall crashed into her, shouldered her aside. A snail smear of blood followed her down the wall. The vase of purple flowers spun silently through the air and splintered on the floor, spilling violets and water.

Adam stood panting in the middle of the room. He watched the intruder carefully, embarrassed by the adrenaline stirring of his loins. His breath slowed, became deeper and more regular. He glared at the body on the floor as water seeped into the carpet.

"Right. You can get up now," he said.

The intruder did not move.

"I said, 'Get up'."

No movement.

Adam prodded the intruder with the end of his bat.

He knelt and shook the intruder by the shoulder. The body was soft and lifeless. He rolled the body over on to its back. Glass eyes stared back at him. Adam felt like he was going to be sick.

"Shit!"

The idea came to him fully-formed, as if he had been formulating it for years. 'Make it look like an accident.' A suicide, perhaps? Place the head so that there would be so much damage the fatal blow would be impossible to detect. He looked at his watch.

He quickly got dressed. He opened the back door and walked to the bottom of the garden. When he got there he turned back to the house; he looked intently at the neighbour's – it remained in darkness and silent. Perfect.

He rushed back to the house and grabbed a black plastic bin liner. He slipped the thick plastic over the head of the dead woman and pulled it down to the knees before tying it loosely into place. He grabbed the rapidly-cooling body by the ankles and dragged it through the kitchen. He lifted it onto his shoulder and outside. He walked the length of the back lawn as if he had done this every day of his life. When he reached the bushes he lifted the body onto the top of the fence; he struggled with the dead weight of the thing. He slid it carefully to the ground on the railway embankment and hopped over the fence after it.

He paused for breath. He looked up and down the railway line, then glanced at his watch. The clouds had slowed to watch his progress, the moon sneered, a fox screeched. Adam grabbed the body by both ankles and dragged it along the embankment towards the tunnel. This was too easy. His erection had subsided but his heart and mind were still racing.

He dropped the legs and swiftly untied the string. He lifted the body into a sitting position and lifted the bag up and off. He scrunched it up and pushed it into his jacket pocket. He hoisted the body up onto his shoulders again and carried it down to the tracks; he lined himself up between the rails and gazed into the abyss of the tunnel. He took a deep breath and walked into the darkness; the shroud of obsidian embraced him. Gravel crunched underfoot like cockroaches; the metal rails glinted.

He walked for eternity, the darkness absolute. Scurrying sounds shifted his perceptions, the *chink* of stone on metal amplified beyond reason. His shoulder ached, his back twinged. He turned back to face the way he had come; this was far enough. He could see the small glow of moonlight beyond the blackness. He shifted the weight of the body and let it slide to the ground. It leaned against his legs, the lifeless heaviness of it made him shudder. He stepped away and it flopped fully to the ground with a crunch of small stones and settled.

Adam rotated the body into position, its legs across the rails just above the knee and the head pillowed on the opposite rail. When he was satisfied he walked nonchalantly out of the tunnel and home. He locked the back door behind him. He cleared up the broken vase and threw the flowers in to the bin.

He closed the kitchen window where, Adam assumed, the intruder had gained access, turned the lights off, put his jacket and shoes back, returned the cricket bat to the cupboard and went to his bedroom. He undressed slowly. He turned the light off and stood in the darkness for a while.

As the freight train thundered past he yawned. The noise was soothing, muffled by hedgerow and glass. He glanced at his watch. It was early. He stumbled into bed and pulled the sheets up to his chin. He slipped into the warm depths of sleep and dreamed.

Chapter 19: Conclusion

Adam dreamed he could hear something in the pure darkness. A small noise, far away. He turned; his body was heavy, he felt small within it. He struggled to remember where he was. He fought his way through the oily thickness surrounding him towards the sound. A rhythmic sound; apologetic; a voice.

He cocked his head to one side, his ears pricked. He knew the voice. It was a voice he yearned for. A voice he had ached to hear. A voice that he could read so much into – love; kindness; soft sexuality. A voice he wanted to be there all of the time. He remembered it with fondness.

His eyes flickered open. The black faded to grey and swam into pale yellow. The ceiling came into focus. He refocused on the face that hovered near him. Elle knelt beside him, cradling his head on her lap. She dabbed worriedly at the wound on his temple. The blood tickled as it ran down the side of his face, into his ear and onto his neck. She was apologising, gabbling, her voice cracking.

He rolled over and scrabbled away from her.

"No," he said. His voice was thick and slurred.

Elle reached a trembling hand towards him.

"Adam, I'm sorry. I didn't mean."

"You can't," he said.

Elle frowned.

"You mustn't tell." He scanned the room wildly. "Where are the flowers? My granddad's violets?"

"Adam? Are you okay?" She crawled towards him.

"You mustn't tell," he said. He shook his head groggily.

"I won't tell, Adam. What is it?"

"They'll send me away. I know you were there."

"Where?"

"I think he might be hurt." Adam stretched his jaw wide, straining to clear his head.

"I'll go and get help," said Elle. "I'll be right back."

"You can't tell."

"I won't. I promise." Elle backed towards the front door, holding her palms out to pacify him. "I think you need a doctor."

"I can't let you go."

He lunged towards her and grabbed her by the throat. He squeezed hard; her eyes bulged. She scratched frantically at his hands. Spittle freckled his face. She gasped as he flung her back to the floor, air rushing into her lungs. She sprawled, pain shooting up her legs as her knees jarred against the tiles. She cried out.

Elle looked for the poker; she darted towards it. He pushed his foot on the cool rod of metal as she scooped her fingers under it. She gritted her teeth, her fingers trapped. She head-butted him in the knee and snatched her fingers free as his weight shifted from it. She got back to her feet.

She charged at him as hard as she could, forcing him to retreat. Her nails raked at his neck and face, her feet kicking out at his legs. She backed him up against the door; his arms were raised, defending himself from her onslaught. He bowed his head as if in defeat, hiding his face. She clenched her clawing hands into small bony fists and pummelled him about the head. As each blow made contact she released a sob, each strike taking something away from her. The violence in her trickled away.

He looked up as the blows subsided. Elle's eyes were screwed shut, thick tears rolled down her angry face. He struck out. The heel of his hand struck her hard under the nose. Her head snapped back as blood blossomed from her. A small, wet noise escaped her as she fell, her eyes wide with surprise.

He squeezed his eyes shut.

When he opened them again, Elle was lying still on the floor; her face was glassy and cold.

"Elle?"

He crouched down next to the body. His head throbbed.

"You're safe now."

The knock at the door startled him.

Acknowledgements

The author would like to thank:

Rachel Webley for being the best editor a boy could ever ask for.

Steve George for being my drinking buddy, fellow adventurer and partner in writerly angst for these many a year.

Sam Holland for reading many different versions of the manuscript in various stages of un-readiness, and for her continuing support.

Tracey Blundell four her proof-reeding skillz.

Diana Read for kicking the blurb in the right direction when I was on the verge of throwing it out of the window, and for openly admitting how traumatised she felt on finishing the novel.

Nicole Murphy for her always open and honest feedback, and for the phrase "I think that's the most disturbing thing I've ever read." From that point on I knew that I was doing something right.

Reanne, Fliss, Kayla, Callum, and **Heather** for being the rest of the 'family' that helped me to dispose of the bodies. The first rule of Creative Writing...

Mark **'Blam'** Blamire for the bloody amazing cover design.

But, most of all, I would like to express my undying gratitude to **Michael Carroll** for taking the time out of his own busy writing schedule to read an early draft. Your feedback gave me the confidence to see this crazy, mixed-up thing through to the end.

Made in the USA
Charleston, SC
19 June 2016